Also available from A
and Carina

Better No

Status Up
Beta T
Connection Error

Off Base
At Attention
On Point
Wheels Up
Squared Away
Tight Quarters
Rough Terrain

Arctic Sun
Arctic Wild
Arctic Heat

Burn Zone
High Heat
Feel the Fire
Up in Smoke

Sailor Proof

Also available from Annabeth Albert

Trust with a Chaser
Tender with a Twist
Lumber Jacked
Treble Maker
Love Me Tenor
All Note Long
Served Hot
Baked Fresh
Delivered Fast
Knit Tight
Wrapped Together
Danced Close
Resilient Heart
Winning Bracket
Save the Date
Level Up
Mr. Right Now
Sergeant Delicious
Cup of Joe
Conventionally Yours
Out of Character
Featherbed

Also available from Annabeth Albert

[illegible] Press

[illegible] Pout

[illegible]pdate

[illegible]test

[illegible]

SINK OR SWIM

ANNABETH ALBERT

ISBN-13: 978-1-335-45486-7

Sink or Swim

This edition published by arrangement with Harlequin Books S.A.

For questions and comments about the quality of this book, please contact us at CustomerService@Harlequin.com.

Carina Press
22 Adelaide St. West, 41st Floor
Toronto, Ontario M5H 4E3, Canada
www.CarinaPress.com

Printed in U.S.A.

For my amazing readers,
especially now in this brave new post-COVID world.
Your resilience and perseverance inspire me,
and your support keeps me going.

SINK OR SWIM

Chapter One

Calder

"You seriously won a whole house? Man, you are the luckiest fucker I know." Max's voice crackled over my car speaker. My signal kept fading in and out the farther outside Seattle I drove, but his skepticism came through loud and clear.

"Cabin. And yeah, it's probably my biggest score yet." I couldn't help doing a little bragging as I navigated a curve on the country highway that kept advising travelers of their elevation and the distance to Mount Rainier. "I lucked into the invite for this high-stakes poker party, and this one jackass kept going all-in. Totally out of his league. But he wasn't drunk or otherwise impaired, so his loss is totally my gain."

"Hell, yeah. So when do we get to come for a ski weekend?" Max sounded predictably eager to get away from base. "Cards and ski bunnies sound pretty damn good right now. Not that you have anything left to play for."

"There's always something to play for." I had to slow for an RV plodding along. I was relying on some sketchy directions and my GPS to get me to this place. Now that I'd left the suburbs behind, the terrain had turned decidedly mountainous, little towns with folksy names fewer and farther between long stretches of evergreen trees marching up and down scenic vistas. "You can come soon, but I need to check the place out first. For all I know it's a shack inhabited by a family of elk. This guy wasn't especially high on the place, but I figured what the hell. Even if it turns out that calling the place a ski chalet is pushing it, property is property."

"Yup. And knowing you, you weren't about to walk away from the table with a winning hand either." Max snorted.

"Too true." I wouldn't take bets I couldn't win, but I also wasn't one to back down from a challenge either. A passing lane finally opened up, and I seized the chance to pass the RV. "If the cabin is too much of a dump, I'll unload it in a quick sale as soon as I get the paperwork straightened out. But in the meantime, having my own getaway sounds pretty sweet."

"Sure does. And hell, the way Seattle real estate prices are going, some sucker's gonna be willing to buy it to attempt the long-ass commute."

"Exactly." Those same ridiculous prices were a big reason why I kept living in the barracks. As a chief I had options, but in the Seattle area all those options required more bread than I was willing to part with. For all that I loved the thrill of winning a bet, I was also notoriously tight with my money. My brothers liked to joke that getting a loan out of me required three signatures and collateral, and they weren't that far from the truth. Saving cash by staying in the barracks made sense, but all the regulations, cramped spaces, and constant drama of other sailors got damn old. Having a place to escape to and bring my buddies was going to be awesome.

As long as the place wasn't falling down. Even I wasn't enough of a risk-taker to bring the crew to a cabin that wasn't structurally sound. I'd take this weekend, inspect everything, make it as clean as possible, and draft some to-do and to-buy lists. Then I could set a date for the weekend away I'd been promising my crew. Traveling alone wasn't usually my style and my car had felt too quiet until I'd dialed Max, but I didn't want anyone around to laugh if it turned out I'd been had and the key didn't even work.

"So, how's the new duty assignment going?" Max asked, voice too careful to pass off as totally casual. *Fuck*. Maybe calling him hadn't been so smart after all.

"Awesome," I lied. "Shouldn't be too much longer before I'm out from behind a desk."

"Good to hear it. Couldn't pay me to get chained to an office." Max was a crane operator at the pier and possibly even more outdoorsy than me. Another reason to not have him along. If there were things I had to figure out, like lighting a tricky woodstove or something, I preferred to get it right before I had an audience eager to swoop in and help.

"Quit reminding me how much I wanna be back out there," I grumbled right as the phone crackled again. "Damn it. Signal's dropping again."

"No worries. I should probably run anyway. I've got a date tonight. Maybe you're not the only one with some recent luck." Max's warm laugh made me a little less grumbly. "This hottie swiped right and slid into my DMs with some killer pics."

"Have a good time. Hope they're not actually some pimple-faced kid." I kept my tone light, the sort of ribbing we gave each other all day.

"Hey, that only happened one time." The static increased, garbling whatever else he was trying to say until the call dropped completely. For once though I wasn't cursing the trees and lack of cell towers. Max had been wandering into territory I didn't want to think about, so I cranked the stereo rather than attempt a call back.

Without passengers I could indulge the musical tastes my brother the composer called hopelessly basic. Whatever. I liked what I liked, but I'd barely gotten two songs in before the GPS bleated that it was time to turn onto an even smaller side road and then another, each road more narrow and less maintained than the last. They'd been plowed at least, but not well. My sports car had all-wheel drive and was rated decent for winter, but I was still glad the forecast called for only a light dusting this weekend.

A rogue flake danced across my windshield. Probably an escapee from a nearby snowbank and not an omen. *Here's hoping.* Finally, the GPS led me up a gravel drive to a red mailbox beside a large carved wooden bear holding a cheery sign that read Dutch Bear's Hideaway. Hmm. Hideaway could be anything from a shed to a tree house, and a weird Christmas-morning-level excitement gathered in my gut as I made the turn. The house wasn't immediately visible from the road, and when the driveway turned to reveal a red Swiss-style cottage with white trim hidden among the trees, I couldn't help grinning.

This I could work with. It was older, sure, probably fifty years at least, and humble, but it looked sound, no saggy roof or missing windows. Its footprint was a basic rectangle with deep eaves, and a little white balcony indicated there was a second story tucked under the sloping roof. I followed the drive around back to where it ended at a little outbuilding painted the same red as the house. Tim, the guy at the poker party, had made it sound way shabbier than this.

True, it was remote, with no neighbors that I could see, but as long as that chimney worked and we had something resembling electricity, this could be a nice bro hangout. Like the little clubhouse we'd had in the backyard at one of Dad's duty stations. Man, I'd loved that place. Maybe I'd change the sign to something more me. Keep the bear. He was cute and homey, kind of like the place itself.

After I parked, I started exploring on foot. A little fire

circle with carved wooden benches and an ancient hot tub on a deck lurked behind the house. The hot tub might have to be replaced, but there was plenty of firewood in the little outbuilding, and lo and behold, one of my keys opened the white door to reveal snow shovels and other winter supplies. Not a bad start.

When I ducked back out of the outbuilding, a few more snowflakes fluttered over my face. Luckily I wasn't planning on going anywhere before morning, and I'd have wood and the food and supplies I'd brought if nothing else. The rear patio door next to the hot tub didn't take the first key I tried or the second or the same one as the outbuilding either. But then I went back to the first key, jiggled the knob a little, and the lock turned.

"Who's got the magic touch?" I crowed to the empty woods before opening the door. It let out a loud creak but would be an easy fix to put on my list. The door opened into a hallway with a neat row of hooks for coats and a mat for shoes and boots. Taking the hint, I took a second to take off my boots so I wouldn't track mud and snow all over the house. I left my coat on until I could assess the heat situation. The hallway led me past a modest bedroom with what looked to be a queen and bedding already on. Score.

A breaker box hung on the wall between the bedroom and bathroom. The electric was already on, so I tested the light in the bathroom. Worked. The bath was cramped with a cracked vanity, but I'd done multiple submarine tours. The tub/shower combo was practically palatial compared with the head on a sub. And after a brief pause with a gasp and sputter, the sink turned on. A little hard to turn and the water was rusty. However, I could let it run later, and I'd brought bottled for drinking, anyway.

"Running water! We're in business now." Happy, I hummed

to myself as I continued down the hall, which opened into a U-shaped kitchen. Old appliances, but neat and tidy. Like the bath, it was cramped, but it opened to a living area, making it appear bigger. I could already picture games of cards at the built-in eating nook. It'd be a tight fit for my build, but I could always pull up a chair.

The living area was dominated by a stone fireplace and woodstove. I'd come back to that in a moment, but first the stairs beckoned me. I felt like some storybook character exploring a fairy-tale cottage. So far, everything was just right.

"Come on, Goldilocks. Let's see what's upstairs." Talking to myself was helping me feel less alone, especially when the third stair creaked like in a horror movie. I'd brought a portable speaker for my phone. Maybe I could play some music while I messed with the woodstove.

The upstairs had a sleeping loft with three twin beds all in a row made up with identical quilts. "Wow. This really is some fairy-tale shit."

My nieces and nephews would go nuts for this space. My adult-sized pals were gonna be a tight fit in those beds, but it beat making them bunk down on the floor, and there was also a small room with crowded bookshelves, a rocking chair, and a small desk next to a teeny half bath tucked into the eaves.

"Nice." Giving the space one last look, I turned to head back downstairs. For a second, I thought I heard the echo of children's voices. Damn. All this aloneness really was getting to me. *Click.* I heard another sound, but the noise didn't repeat. Still, I hastened my trek down the stairs.

Whoosh. A rush of cold air made my whole body tense, every sense on red alert as the front door burst open.

"What the—" Whatever curse I'd been about to bellow was cut off by an ear-piercing shriek as a young girl appeared in the door. If I'd tried to conjure up an actual Goldilocks,

I couldn't have done much better than her pale blond curls, pink cheeks, old-fashioned wool coat, and startled expression.

"There's someone here!" Her alarmed shout echoed off the wood walls.

"Wait," I called out right as my sock slid against the stair step. "Whoa!"

I thrust an arm out, but it was already too late and I was tumbling down the last three steps, landing on my ass in a heap at the bottom. *Ouch.* Trying to figure out what I'd injured, I was still catching my breath when another form appeared in the front doorway, this one adult, male, and mad as a grizzly.

"Who the hell are you and what are you doing in my cabin?"

Chapter Two

Felix

Two hours in the car with two little girls with endless questions, and I was *done* by the time we reached the cabin. The paint was a little more faded than last time, but the same silly bear that had been there most of my life greeted us, which made my shoulders that much lighter. I pulled up even with the front door for easy unloading.

"I still don't know why we had to come," Madeline complained for the thousandth time as we exited my SUV. She'd made it abundantly clear that she was not a fan of the cabin. The snow was coming down more now, making me glad I'd had my winter tires checked before we'd headed to the mountains.

"Here." I thrust my keys at Madeline rather than argue the point yet again. Charlotte was typically slow, stretching and collecting all the things she'd strewn over the back seat, but I knew better than to hurry her. Instead, I waved Madeline toward the porch. "You go ahead. You can have first pick of the beds."

That might make her happy for five minutes as the girls always enjoyed the novelty of the loft area. The maintenance company had cleaned after the last renters left, and they'd sent someone around earlier to flip on the electric and make sure no snowdrifts were blocking the driveway. Thus, I was reasonably confident in letting Madeline go first. The place would be cold, but she could explore a few minutes. It had been a while since I'd managed to bring the girls here, and maybe getting reacquainted with the cabin would improve her attitude while I gathered up the luggage and groceries.

Dutifully, she trotted away from the car and worked the lock. She was excellent at mechanical things like that, and I grinned at her triumphant expression.

And then she screamed.

Blood running colder than the snowy landscape, I was already racing up the short path when she yelled again. "There's someone here!"

"Coming. Don't go in," I ordered as I moved faster. Hopefully it was only someone from the maintenance company, but the woman on the phone had made it sound like they'd already been by. My jaw clenched, dread battling frustration. Last thing I needed was a freaked-out Madeline, but I also couldn't rule out some sort of squatter situation. Or worse.

"Wait!" A male voice sounded right before an alarmed noise and terrible clatter occurred.

I rushed across the porch to bound ahead of Madeline only to come to an abrupt halt. A sandy-haired giant of a man lay sprawled at the base of the stairs. His rugged features were twisted, likely in pain from the fall, and he certainly didn't look anything like either of the two middle-aged women who ran the vacation home maintenance company.

"Who the hell are you and what are you doing in my cabin?" I demanded.

"Yours?" The guy struggled to sit up. At least the fall had ensured he was less of a threat to our safety. "This is my new place. I won it. I've got papers in the car and keys to prove it."

"Liar!" Charlotte came up behind me in full indignant

glory, not one bit scared of this stranger. "This is Uncle Felix's cabin. His grandpa built it and everything. You're a burglar!"

"No, I'm not." The man tried to stand, then abruptly sat back down before digging in his coat pocket. "I swear. I've got keys. I didn't break in."

He held up a ring with three keys on it. And a familiar fob, a garish cat made out of glittery beads.

"F—" I caught myself. The girls were still wide-eyed and listening intently to every word of this exchange. "Is this Tim's idea of a joke? He can't handle that he didn't win—"

"No, *I* won," the man corrected me. Infuriatingly, he had a nice voice, deep and patient, not angry or mean. Honestly, his tone was a lot calmer than mine. "At a private poker party last week. This Tim dude had paperwork and keys for me and everything."

"He was supposed to drop off the keys for me weeks ago. Tim's my ex-husband, and he tried to get this place in the divorce settlement, but the court awarded it to *me*. It's been in my family decades now."

"You don't say." He groaned as he shifted on the floor. "F—*fudge*. I knew there was a chance this might be a hoax because who the h—*heck* bets an entire piece of property, but he had paperwork that looked pretty damn legal."

I appreciated the effort he was making to not curse in front of the girls. And his calm demeanor didn't hurt either. "Tim's a former paralegal turned personal chef. I don't doubt that he handed you *something*, but this place is legally mine, not his to give away."

"He didn't give it away. I won it." The guy might be calm, but he was also stubborn. "And I can show you the papers if I can figure out how to put weight on my ankle here."

"You're hurt!" Charlotte's eyes went even wider. "Uncle Felix, you have to fix him."

Oh no, I don't. Strange guy claiming ownership of my cabin? I wasn't feeling particularly sympathetic.

"How badly are you hurt?" I asked, pulling out my phone. If I could make this someone else's problem, so much the better. "Should I call an ambulance?"

"Not that bad." Grimacing, he tried again to stand and this time succeeded by leaning heavily on the banister. "Definitely not ambulance bad. Twisted my ankle. Doubt it's broken. Been there, done that, and this isn't as sharp a pain."

"He's bleeding." Madeline wrinkled her nose and pointed at the guy's temple, which had a thin line of blood dripping toward his ear.

"Am I?" He touched his head and frowned as his fingers came away red.

"I'll get the kit," Charlotte announced, all self-important, turning back to the porch. "Don't worry. Even if you are a burglar, Uncle Felix will fix you up. He's a doctor."

Thank you, Charlotte, for sharing that little tidbit. I sighed as she headed back to the car. She was obsessed with all things medical, and it was easier to let her fetch my first-aid kit than waste time trying to talk her out of it.

"Is he gonna die?" Madeline's voice wavered.

"No one is dying." I kept my voice stern, like that could prevent this mess of a situation from getting any worse. Charlotte returned with my kit in short order, shaking the snow from her curly hair. "Thank you, Charlotte. Now let's have a look at your head, Mister..."

"I'm Calder. Calder Euler. And I'm a chief in the navy. ID is in the car too, but I'm not a criminal."

"No, that would be Tim," I muttered under my breath, then said louder, "What is a naval chief doing playing high-stakes poker? Surely there's some regulations about that."

He shrugged, his eyes taking on a sheepish cast. "There's

some guidelines. No gambling in uniform, no gambling on base, no gaming with subordinates, that sort of thing. And it's a hobby, not a sideline for me. I was there to have fun, ran into a bit of luck, and wasn't about to turn down a major score."

"Of course not." I truly did not care for this Calder one bit, but I also couldn't exactly leave him over there bleeding with both girls watching on. Opening the kit, I took out a pair of disposable gloves and approached him. "Let me see how deep the wound is. Do you feel foggy? Light-headed at all?"

"I'm fine." He winced as I reached for his head. Of course he'd have to be tall, and I wasn't about to ask him to stoop down for me, so I tried to subtly pull myself up taller.

"I'm going to look anyway." I used my patient doctor tone even if I wasn't feeling soothing in the least.

"What I am is confused as to how the he—*heck* this is happening because I'm not a gullible guy, but my brain's not foggy. I've had a concussion recently. None of those symptoms here. Didn't even pass out."

"You had a recent head trauma severe enough to lose consciousness, and you hit your head just now?" My medical training pushed past all my anger at Tim and Calder both. "Maybe we need that ambulance after all."

"I didn't hit my head. Scraped my temple maybe. Trust me, I've had enough MRIs and other tests to know the difference."

"Scraping hard enough to draw blood is still worrisome under the circumstances. You could have taken a harder blow than you think." I examined the wound, which did seem to be largely superficial, no swelling and not deep enough to warrant stitches. "I'd advise a call to your neurologist, simply to be safe. I know it's about to be the weekend, but they might want you to come in Monday or something."

"I'll keep that in mind." Calder's tone suggested he'd do

no such thing. "I'll make that my second call after I find a lawyer to try to straighten out this ownership thing."

Excellent. All my week from hell needed was another costly legal battle. Apparently Calder wasn't simply going to take my word that this was my place, not that I could fault him on that. I'd already admitted to a contentious divorce, and for all he knew, I was the liar, not Tim.

"I'll get you my contact information." I kept my tone curt but professional. Using an alcohol wipe from the kit, I quickly cleansed the wound and applied a small bandage. "There. Now what about your foot?"

"I'm ninety percent certain it's a nasty sprain, but sure, do your worst, Doc." He settled himself on the second step and stuck out his sock-covered foot.

I gently peeled off his sock so I could get a closer look at his foot and ankle. Unlike his head, there was definite swelling here. No bruising yet, but his level of grimace when I touched it said it wasn't some minor injury either.

"Even if nothing's broken, you're going to want to stay off it, rest, elevate, and ice it for a few days. If you want, I can try to remember how to wrap a sprain before you go." I didn't even try to disguise my emphasis on the word *go.* Having to hear from his lawyer was going to be bad enough. I didn't need to spend any more time in the company of this gambling sailor than strictly necessary.

"Remember?" Calder made a pained face. "What's your specialty anyway?"

"Geriatric psychiatry. We don't get a lot of sprains, but if you want to improve your cognition, I'm your guy." I liked what I did, was damn good at it, and I wasn't going to feel guilty that I wasn't a GP or orthopedist, even if one of those might have been more helpful.

"My guy, huh?" A smile danced around the edges of

Calder's mouth, and I realized too late how that statement might be taken.

I made a sputtering noise befitting my profession. "I didn't mean…"

"I know." Calder made a dismissive gesture before he again attempted to stand. "I'm only joking to avoid cursing again in front of the little ears, because this really does hurt like a b—*biscuit.* Driving my stick is gonna suck."

"Your car is a stick?" Damn it. Now I felt guilty because I was the jerk sending a guy with a possible head injury and bad ankle off down the mountain. "Truck at least? Snow tires?"

"Nah. It's a WRX. Sports car." He gave another of those way-too-endearing half smiles. Of course he'd be a car guy. Probably won the vehicle too.

"Sports car? In winter weather?"

"I've got cold-weather tires and all-wheel drive. I'll be okay." Belying his words, he let out a pained grunt as he tried to walk forward and ended up only making it as far as the couch.

"We might need to see if there's room at the lodge for you. You're not driving on that foot tonight."

He needed someplace not here, and luckily he seemed to agree, giving a sharp nod. Good. Calder wasn't in shape to drive, especially some sports car that probably wasn't as well-suited for winter driving as he thought, what with the snow coming down.

I glanced out the front window, and then it was my turn to groan. "It's really snowing heavily now."

"I can't see the road," Madeline added helpfully.

"It's probably really icy." Charlotte was gleeful as ever at the prospect of disaster.

"Let me put a call in to the lodge in Nisqually. They're the closest hotel. We'll drive you there." I hated snow driving, but I still felt better with a firm plan. This wasn't the light dusting the forecast had predicted at all.

"Ooh, maybe we'll spin like in the movies." Giggling wildly, Charlotte spun herself in a circle for emphasis.

"We will *not.* We will drive slowly and carefully and… *Darn it.*" I trailed off as I realized that I had no cell service, not even roaming. I turned back to the couch and Calder. "Do you have a signal?"

"Nope." He held his phone up, turning his hand this way and that like that might help. "Service has been spotty ever since I left the burbs behind and nonexistent once I left the main highway."

"There's one of those olden-days phones over here," Madeline called from the kitchen.

Way to make me feel like an antique, kid. But I simply smiled at her. "We call that a landline. Let me see if we've got a dial tone."

Someone, probably my grandmother, had penned the number of the lodge on a yellowed piece of paper tacked up next to the phone along with emergency services numbers. I tried it only to reach a harried clerk who told me there were no rooms.

"Are you sure? I've kind of got a situation here—"

"And we have a situation here, sir." The clerk sounded young, probably in her twenties, and was all excited to be sharing even more bad news. "They're about to close the highway because of the snow and poor visibility, so we're not taking any new reservations."

"Closing the highway?" I spared a glance for Calder on the couch. His dismal expression and slumped shoulders surely mirrored mine. "They can do that?"

"You're not from around here are you, sir? The highway patrol can put up a chains-only ordinance or close entirely if the storm's bad enough. And this one's gathering steam. Some sort of freak polar vortex."

"You don't say," I said woodenly before managing to express my thanks and end the call. I hung up and headed back into the main living area. "Well, no cell phone signal, no room at the lodge, and apparently no one's driving anywhere anyway."

"And I'm cold." Madeline gave a dramatic shiver. "We're gonna freeze. I knew it."

"We're *doomed*," Charlotte added with great relish. I couldn't readily disagree. Snowed in with an injured strange man claiming to own my cabin? *Doomed* didn't even begin to cover it.

Chapter Three

Calder

"We're not doomed," I said sternly to the younger of the two girls. I might not be what anyone would call a natural with kids, but I did know that heading them off before a meltdown was essential. Privately, I was not at all confident about our situation, but I wasn't about to project that to the kids. "Give me a second to sort out my ankle, and I'll be out of your hair before the highway closes. I'll let the lawyers figure out my rights to this place, but I'm not about to kick you all out in the middle of a storm, so I'll be the one to go."

Felix's idea about the lodge hadn't been a terrible one because I needed out of here. There was nothing I hated more than the feeling I'd been had. Either Tim had put one over on me, or Felix was a remarkably good liar, and neither prospect had me wanting to stick around. I was not, however, going to give up my claim to the place without some more investigation, but that could wait until I was back with a decent internet connection.

"How gracious." The uncle sure was a prickly one with a crap bedside manner. Typical of the doctors I'd dealt with lately, he was brisk, dismissive, and superior. Med schools must have stopped teaching empathy. He was older than me, though, but not by much. Maybe forty. And unlike my slate of doctors, he was cute. Elfin features somewhere between adorable and disconcertingly hot. Dark hair unlike the blonde nieces. And a perma-scowl just for me.

"Unfortunately, you're not going anywhere. You're injured, your car is unsuitable, and the road's about to close. I can't let you leave."

I was far more accustomed to giving the orders and wanted to tell him where he could shove his commands, but the kids were still watching us intently. And my ankle really did hurt, so working the clutch was gonna suck even if I did trust my car.

Maybe not in a blizzard though.

"Fine. Guess I'm stuck." I slumped back against the couch.

"We're doomed," Shorty repeated. This was the same kid who had been rather hyped about my injuries. Charlotte, the uncle had called her, and she was somewhere between six and nine, while the older one was a near-identical ten-or-eleven-year-old version of the same cherubic features. "Maybe we'll get frozen and have to be rescued."

"I don't want a rescue." The older girl's lower lip started to wobble. *Uh-oh.* Here came the waterworks. My back tightened, but Felix rubbed the girl's shoulder and gave her an encouraging smile before the first tear could fall.

"No one's freezing, Madeline. We'll start a fire," Felix soothed. "See the wood basket?"

"Do you remember how to light it?" Madeline was both quieter and more distrustful than her sister, who was already crouching to inspect the stack of firewood.

"Yes. It's been a while, but I haven't forgotten. You'll both be happier with some heat." Felix moved to the stove, quick, efficient movements that contradicted his stuck-up attitude.

"I can help," I offered. Doing nothing was almost as bad

as knowing I'd likely been duped, but Felix motioned for me to stay put.

"You're injured. I've got this." And apparently he did know what he was doing as he lit the fire on his second try and had a nice blaze a few minutes after that.

"See?" he narrated as he went, naturally parental like my brothers. "Now we add some bigger pieces."

"Can we roast dinner on that fork thing?" Charlotte pointed at the bucket of fireplace tools.

"No." Felix gave her an indulgent smile that transformed his face from smug to way too appealing. "I brought you nuggets."

"Darn."

"I also brought marshmallows. After we eat, we might *safely* try toasting a few."

"Oh, good. I'm holding the stick." The future pyromaniac shrugged out of her coat, leaving it in a heap for Felix to pick up and place on a chair. "You're right. It is warmer. Let's watch the blizzard take over everything!"

Bounding over to the window, she pressed her face against the glass while her older sister grudgingly let Felix take her coat as well.

"Now, I'm going to bring in the groceries. Madeline, you stand at the window with Charlotte and watch me. Stay where I can see you both." He cast a distrustful look in my direction like I might commit a felony in the five minutes it was going to take him to unload.

"I've got food too. And water. If you find me a stick or something I can lean on, I can bring them in." I'd been in a hurry leaving base, so my food choices had been rather limited at the convenience store where I'd filled my gas tank, but I could at least contribute to the whole not-starving thing.

Felix held up a hand. "You're staying put. Your car's around back? Is it unlocked?"

"Yeah." I hated the idea of a stranger poking around in my car, but I didn't have a ton of choices. No way was I making it down the hill behind the house to the car without some sort of crutch, and even then it was a dicey proposition with all the ice and snow happening. I dug out my keys because it wasn't like Mr. Overprotective Uncle was going to ditch the kids and go out for a joyride in the snow. "Food's in the trunk."

"All right. I'll gather our supplies." Felix headed for the door, and in relatively short order, he reappeared with an armful of bags and snow dusting his dark hair and the shoulders of his coat, some expensive-looking brand for the urbanites who wished to appear outdoorsy. A second trip through the back door resulted in my duffel and grocery sack being added to the collection he had going near the dining table.

"Is it dinnertime?" Charlotte asked, again eyeing that fireplace poker.

"Yes." Felix was the sort of decisive I usually admired. He'd be decent at cards, not dithering for ages like Max or Derrick, who were both too cautious for my tastes despite being my best friends. Felix, on the other hand, made quick choices, lining up food on the counter before asking, "Who wants to help me cook?"

"I can." I tried to stand, but he strode over to me and pushed me back down, a surprisingly firm grip.

"You're—"

"Injured. Yeah, I got that part." My voice came out a little too testy, but I was tired of sitting and doing nothing.

"After dinner I'll track down something to be your crutch." Felix tried the same soothing tone that worked on his nieces. "But right now you'd only be in the way."

"Well, damn, give it to me honest, Doc." I sat back down, but not happily.

"Sorry. I only meant that I can be faster without help. Madeline, you can hunt down plates and set the table. Charlotte, why don't you come tell me which vegetable you're willing to eat tonight?"

More efficiency, which was both admirable and maddening. I gritted my teeth and endured Felix poking through my bag of food.

"Jerky? Boiled eggs? What sort of dinner is this?" He frowned.

"I was planning to get more food in the morning." I hated how defensive I sounded.

"Luckily we brought more than enough to share." Felix deposited my eggs and precut vegetable cup in the fridge before turning his attention to a tray of curly fries and nuggets for the oven. I'd eaten enough meals at my brother Oliver's place to know that I wasn't a big fan of kid-friendly foods, but I'd also been raised to not complain when I was the guest somewhere, which I supposed I kind of was here. Damn it.

"Madeline prefers her broccoli raw. Can I assume you eat it cooked?" Felix called to me.

"Sure. Whatever. Just not mush." I tried to sound more agreeable. "I'd be fine with my jerky though. You don't have to make the girls share their nuggets."

"Jerky is not a balanced meal. And the sodium will only make your ankle swell more." He made a clucking noise. "And you and I are having chicken cutlets, not nuggets."

"Ah. Thanks."

"Speaking of your foot, I've got the ice packs I surrounded the frozen foods with." Abandoning his cooking, he brought a flexible blue pack over and unceremoniously deposited it on the foot I'd propped on the couch in front of me. He shoved a pillow under my heel. "There. Keep that on for about fifteen minutes."

"Aye, aye, Doc." I saluted him. Despite the brusque manner, he more than made up for the lack of charm with his competence. And I had no idea why I found watching him move around the kitchen so compelling. The ice did a good job of numbing my ankle, but it also tethered me to the spot, and with no phone signal, I had no choice but to observe Felix and the girls. They were a tight unit, and I reconsidered my judgment about his lack of charm as he supervised Charlotte whacking the broccoli into florets while deftly handing Madeline a stack of plates.

"See? This isn't so bad," he said to Madeline. The way he tried so hard with the kids was sweet, and far more than I usually managed with the nieces and nephews. "Your favorite foods, a nice toasty fire, and tomorrow when you wake up, the world will be all white and you can play in the snow."

"You're a good uncle," I told him when he brought me two over-the-counter pain relievers and a glass of water. "My two older brothers have kids, but I've never attempted a trip with them. Heck, a single night of babysitting last summer almost did me in."

"Thanks. I've had a lot of practice." He waited for me to swallow then set my glass on a coaster on the end table. More efficient care taking.

"Lots of babysitting?"

"Something like that." His mouth twisted. "I'm raising them, actually. They live with me in Seattle."

"Ah." I wasn't sure if this was something one expressed condolences over or congrats, so I tried for a sympathetic nod instead.

"The chicken's sizzling!" Madeline reported, summoning Felix back to the kitchen before I could learn more about their family arrangement, leaving me to do more observing. I wasn't sure what to make of how damn curious I was to know more about Felix. Boredom, probably, but being bored didn't usually unleash a hundred questions in my head.

"Do you want me to bring you yours?" he asked me as he placed steaming plates of food on the table, and the girls scooted into the built-in booth.

"Nah. I can come to the table." I didn't need another reason to feel ninety. Rather creakily, I managed to hobble to the table, taking the chair rather than trying to squeeze in next to one of the girls.

The chicken was basic pan-seared cutlets with simple seasoning, but it was hot and tasty, and I made sure I thanked Felix as the girls squabbled over who had more fries. Outside, darkness had fallen, an eerie stillness as the snow continued to pour from the sky, big fat flakes that occasionally smacked into the window thanks to a stiff wind.

"After dinner, I'm going to explore," Charlotte announced from her perch next to Felix as she squeezed yet more ketchup onto her plate. "I need to pick where I'm gonna sleep."

Sleep. Oh hell. We might not be doomed, but we sure were trapped, until morning at least. A prickle raced up the back of my neck. Last time I was this out of my element was my first twenty-four hours on a sub, and similarly, there was no easy escape here, only a need to endure and hope nothing else went wrong.

Chapter Four

Felix

Dinner with Calder was weird. I hadn't dated since Tim, and the number of other guests at our table had been pretty slim. This wasn't anywhere close to a date, but it was still novel having another adult human to make conversation with.

"What do you do in the navy?" I asked to break an awkward pause when the girls were silent and so were we. He'd complimented the food, and we'd remarked on the weather more than once. We were almost out of small talk topics, but also I was curious about Calder, in a way that made my legs move restlessly against the bench.

"I'm a chief on a submarine usually." He grimaced on the word *usually*. "I handle logistics."

"Usually?"

"Recently I fell during a boat maneuver. Not uncommon to lose balance on the sub, but I hit my head and rang my bell pretty good. Our sub had just deployed too, so it was a whole *thing* getting an evac because the medic on board was concerned and wanted an MRI to be safe. Powers that be have had me on light shore duty ever since." His grimace turned more sour, like light duty was a fate worse than the gallows.

"But you'd rather be back out there?" I guessed. The doctor in me wanted to know more about his injury, but he'd already made it clear earlier that it was a sore subject. I was, however, going to put him through some more concussion tests later, make sure he wasn't worsening and not saying anything.

"Yep." His lips thinned out. "Tell me about being a shrink. Your specialty is older people?"

Ah. We'd found another forbidden topic. I could take a hint, so I took the opportunity to wax poetic about my group practice and our role in caring for aging adults. It was something I was passionate about, so it wasn't a hardship to ramble on, and Calder proved to be a good audience, loosening up considerably the more I talked.

"So, no surgery?" He leaned back in his chair, way more jokey now that we weren't talking about him.

"Nope. Not my forte." I would have told him about how I liked talking to patients while they were awake, but Charlotte chose then to announce she was done.

"Now we can explore!" she announced in her carnival barker voice. "I want to see if the renters left any loot behind or changed my favorite things."

"If you find a walking stick or maybe a mop we can turn upside down for a crutch for Chief Euler, let me know." I moved so she could exit the booth.

"Calder is fine." He smiled at the girls. He hadn't paid either of them a ton of attention, and everything I'd learned thus far about the man said he was a freewheeling, gambling-loving bachelor uncle, the sort of guy who, like Tim, wore their child-free status like a badge of honor.

"Okay! We'll find you a crutch, Calder. Let's go." Even though she was younger, Charlotte was the far bossier one, and Madeline dutifully followed her down the hall, standing back as Charlotte opened doors.

Reining Charlotte in was futile, so instead I braced for every closet and drawer to be opened. I'd long since cleared out most personal effects so my management company could use the place for select rentals, and they cleaned after each renter, so I wasn't too worried about what she might find.

"Here, let me take your plate," I said to Calder, already reaching. And maybe he wasn't the most prepared because our hands brushed. An awareness that hadn't been there moments earlier sizzled up my spine. He really had won the genetic lottery as far as attractiveness went.

"Sorry." Expression surprisingly sheepish, he jerked his hand away. "I, uh..."

"You go back to the couch. I'll clean up."

"Okay." His ready acceptance of the order was another surprise. A pleasant one. If we were going to be stuck together, not arguing over every suggestion was a decent start. Again that crackle of awareness brought warmth to my skin. Hot and polite apparently did it for me.

"Ooh! Look at this!" Charlotte loudly narrated her discoveries, reports of flashlights and cleaning supplies from the hall closet filtering back to the main area, as I brought Calder some fresh ice packs before making fast work of the dishes.

"It's not fair that you have to clean when you cooked." His mouth twisted as he stretched his leg out in front of him on the couch. "I'll do breakfast."

"If your ankle is better," I said mildly. I was used to doing it all alone anyway. Up until this week, we'd had a nanny for after-school help, but she didn't stay for dinner, so I usually handled the night routine all on my own. Which was fine, and how I liked it, but I couldn't deny that it was nice to have someone to talk to as I washed up. "You're helping simply by giving me conversation."

"I'll try harder to be interesting." He laughed, but honestly, he didn't have to work hard at that. Despite my predisposition to dislike the guy, he was plenty interesting, even the things he'd rather not talk about. And he was easy on the eyes, what with his tall, broad build, rugged jaw, wide mouth, sharp eyes, and sandy hair that was like a muted strawberry blond. He'd undoubtedly been a freckled-faced kid with brighter carrot hair.

"I found a big stick." Charlotte rushed back into the living area, depositing one of Grandpa's old walking sticks next to Calder on the couch before scurrying off again.

"Thanks. This will help." He slid a hand down the polished wood. The gesture was in no way sexual, and it spoke to how long it had been since I'd touched another adult in a nonprofessional capacity that his movement made heat unfurl in my stomach. "This looks handmade."

"Yes." I forced myself to look away from his big hand caressing the wood. "My grandfather was a big outdoors person, and he kept hiking even into his later years. I'd had a feeling one of his old sticks was around here."

"This place really has been in your family a long time?" He glanced around, almost as if seeing the cabin interior for the first time.

"My grandfather built it himself, along with some friends who purchased nearby parcels. He was a professor at one of the small colleges in Seattle, and this was his escape. I spent a lot of weekends here as a kid, especially after my parents divorced." Much as I didn't like dwelling on that bit of unhappiness, my voice was fond, as it always was when I spoke about my mom's parents.

"That's neat. I was a military brat, so we moved around a ton. My family's always been big on camping and outdoors though, so I think it's cool that your family had a place to come back to like this." His face scrunched up as if he were thinking hard. "But if it's your family's legacy, why did Tim think it was his?"

I blew out a breath as I put the last clean dish in the drainer. "I inherited this place along with my grandparents' Queen Anne house early in my relationship with Tim. He hated it here, but that didn't stop him from trying to get it in the divorce."

"Divorce sucks. This is why you'll never catch me hitching up." Yup, bachelor uncle, exactly as I'd thought. And smug, the way single people seemed to get when they heard about my misfortune. "Relationships always end badly unless you catch lightning in a bottle like my folks, and the odds of getting that lucky aren't worth the gamble."

"Says the card sharp." I wiped down the counter with more force than needed.

"Hey, I don't take bets I don't expect to win."

"Well, I certainly didn't intend to get a contentious divorce, but here we are." I tossed the rag down, tempted to lob it at Calder's head, especially when he made a noise like he'd scored a point on me in some game.

"Exactly. You thought you'd won the lottery only to be one number off. Fool's gold." He shook his head with an expression that was either sympathy or pity, and I wasn't sure I liked either.

"Tim's no prize, that's for sure." Done cleaning, I checked the wood situation, channeling my frustration into poking the fire before I sank into one of the side chairs in the living area. "And back to your question, he saw the paperwork for the cabin back when I inherited and again when we were sorting out the settlement. That's probably how he managed to have paperwork that convinced you. However, we'd finally agreed on me keeping the house and cabin and essentially buying him out. I've got it in writing."

"Damn. That's cold." Calder whistled low. "If it was yours to start with, that doesn't seem fair."

To you and me both, buddy. "It's a community property state. And Tim was never the biggest on fairness, sadly."

"Assuming you're telling the truth, he's an even bigger bastard than I thought."

"Of course I'm telling the truth," I snapped as the girls returned, clattering down the stairs. Calder's skepticism was to be expected, but it still grated. I was so tired of arguing Tim's version of facts. Someone on my side would be a nice change.

"The renters didn't leave any treasure, but I picked my favorite of the little beds," Charlotte reported, oblivious to the rising tension in the room. Wearing a triumphant grin, she was holding a book with Madeline trailing behind her.

"I know." I softened my voice for her. "I always loved picking as a kid too. I'd take turns sleeping in all three."

With adult eyes now, I could see my grandmother had probably hoped for more grandkids when they'd made the sleeping loft, but they'd always made me feel treasured, and the extra beds had meant that I could bring a friend occasionally.

"I'm sleeping in the one by the teeny window." Charlotte's decisive nod dared Madeline to object. "That way I can watch the snow."

"Good idea." I glanced at the front window where sure enough it seemed to be still coming down by the bucket full and blowing around. That wasn't a great omen for plows making it through in the morning. The sooner Calder and his confounding opinions could leave the better.

"We found the closet full of games and old toys. I forgot that was here." Charlotte dropped to sit cross-legged on the rug and Madeline followed suit.

"Anything interesting?" Calder asked.

Charlotte shrugged. "Boring stuff, mainly. But then I remembered the bookcase."

Madeline made an indignant noise. "I was looking there first."

"Yeah, well, I was the one who found this." Charlotte held up the slim book. "Ghost stories! Ones from around here."

I groaned. As much as I was all about indulging the girls' interests, I was ready for Charlotte's obsession with spooky things to be over. "Why am I not surprised you found that?"

Nose in the air, she gave me an arch look. "Because I always find the best stuff."

That was debatable. "At least it's not alive."

"Or bones," Madeline added with a shudder.

"She collects live things? And bones?" Calder's expression shifted to wide-eyed horror. Oops. I forgot not everyone had a future pathologist in their family.

"Teeth aren't bones." Charlotte made a dismissive gesture, sounding far older than seven. "And I had a secret ant colony. Until someone told on me."

Her accusing look had poor Madeline squirming on the carpet.

"I'm glad *someone* did," I said sternly. "And now we have an exterminator visit. One of the reasons we came to the cabin this weekend."

"Uncle Felix had a terrible, horrible, very bad week." Madeline smiled at her own joke, a reference to one of her absolute favorite picture books when she'd been smaller.

"Oh?" Calder continued to look as if he had no idea what to make of the girls. That was okay. I frequently felt out of my depth with them too.

"The nanny quit, the school had complaints—"

"I said sorry," Charlotte interrupted. She read far above grade level, got bored by typical second-grade activities, and had a propensity to relieve her boredom in ways that made sense to her and her big brain, like the ant colony, but created a lot of mess. And at school she had a tendency to scare other kids with her dramatically gory stories, hence the complaints.

"I know you did," I soothed, trying to sound patient. "You also didn't realize that collecting that many ants would have consequences. It was a hard week for all of us, so we all needed a getaway."

There had also been an ill-timed phone call from Tim complaining about settlement terms, again, but I wasn't revealing that in front of the girls. At the time, heading to the cabin had seemed like a brilliant idea, but now that we were snowbound with a stranger I was far less certain. My back tensed. I didn't like feeling so unprepared.

"Read me one of the ghost stories," Charlotte demanded, handing me the book.

"I don't know that it's the best idea for a bedtime story." I shot a glance at Calder, hoping he might back me up, make me less of the bad guy. "And we wouldn't want to scare Calder."

"Calder doesn't scare. Read away."

Darn it. He either hadn't picked up on my hint or didn't care to be on my side. He had, however, scored a major point with Charlotte, who beamed at him.

"I scare." Madeline shot me a nervous glance.

"Me too," I said so she'd feel better.

"I'll keep you safe." Charlotte put a sturdy arm around Madeline. "Pick an extra-spooky one, Uncle Felix."

I thumbed through the table of contents, finding the shortest, least spooky story. "Here. This one looks not too scary, but I'm stopping if it gets inappropriate."

"Or bloody," Madeline added.

"That too."

As I read, I had to pretend Calder wasn't right there, listening to every word. At home, bedtime stories were one of my favorite things, and I liked to think I was good at them, doing different voices and injecting emotions. That was probably where Charlotte had found her talent for dramatic storytelling, so I couldn't be too mad that she'd been telling tales at school again. And she leaned forward intently now, hanging on each sentence, injecting commentary. She'd notice if I did less than my usual effort, so I tried not to get self-conscious about Calder listening in.

Weirdly, his expression was almost as intent as Charlotte's, and he didn't crack a single joke or roll his eyes like Tim might have. Eventually, I relaxed enough to get into the story. After I got over having another adult in the audience, Calder's attention ended up emboldening me a little, giving my words a little extra flair. Apparently, even twenty years removed, my inner theater geek appreciated the chance to perform.

"I wonder if this place is haunted," Charlotte mused as I finished.

"If so, I bet it's a friendly ghost like in the story." Calder was so not helpful with his encouragement of her imagination.

I could already predict that Charlotte would keep poor Madeline up with her own rendition of the admittedly tame ghost story. Charlotte's version would undoubtedly have more carnage.

"It's not haunted. I promise you I've slept here many times, and I've never ever seen a ghost." I smiled reassuringly for Madeline and gave Charlotte a stern look. "And it's getting close to your bedtime."

"I may never sleep again." Now it was Madeline's turn to be dramatic, complete with coming over and swooning against my chair.

"You can try. You brought Ellie, right?"

"Right. But I'm getting too big for her." Cheeks going pink, Madeline glanced at Calder, then back at me.

"Ellie?" Calder asked.

"Madeline's elephant," Charlotte explained. "Uncle Felix gave it to her when she was a baby. Ellie's been everywhere with us."

"It's not a big deal." Madeline studied the rug. At ten, she was starting to feel peer pressure about still playing with dolls and stuffed animals, but I tried to encourage her to keep the things she needed and to ignore her friends' opinions.

"I think it's cool." Calder gave her the nicest smile I'd seen from him yet. And of course he had to go and be all helpful and tender right when I'd decided he had zero good instincts for kids. "I had a stuffed dog when I was younger. He made it through several moves with us. He was a good friend."

"Neat." Madeline returned his smile with a shy one of her own before scooping up her bag, Ellie's pink head poking out the top zipper. "Okay. I'll try sleeping."

"Brush your teeth first. I'll come up and say good night," I said as Charlotte followed her up. And it was only after the girls were in their fuzzy pajamas and tucked into the beds in the sleeping loft and I was on my way back down the stairs that I realized that I was about to be all alone with Calder, no buffer of the girls and their chatter.

My stomach swooped, as dramatic as Charlotte. Which was ridiculous. Nothing was about to happen, and definitely nothing that should have my pulse skittering like this. And yet…

Calm down, Felix. Somehow I already knew my body was not about to obey.

Chapter Five

Calder

I almost called the kids back downstairs. *Help. I'm not sure I can be alone with your uncle because he doesn't seem to like me, and I don't cope well with awkward distrust.* Yeah, that would go over well. But it was true. I was used to being able to charm almost everybody. I liked being liked, but Felix appeared pretty immune to my charms.

While Felix was upstairs with the girls, I pulled out a deck of cards. I almost always had one on me, even on the sub. I'd switch them out when they got too old and bent to shuffle well, and I always kept spares too. This current deck had a maze-like pattern on the backs, and I traced it with my thumb as I listened to Felix call another good night to the girls. For all he didn't seem inclined to like me, he was an amazing uncle. I'd liked when he'd read too. Felt a little like eavesdropping on their happy family unit, but cozy too, like visiting a good memory, especially when he did voices like my mom used to.

"Think they'll actually sleep?" I asked as he came down the stairs. "If they're anything like me and my brothers on our first night in a strange place, they'll have a devil of a time drifting off."

"Likely. But then that's par for the course at home too. Endless delays of bedtime." He sighed but his smile was fond.

"How long have you had them?" I wasn't entirely sure how to phrase the inquiry, so I kept my voice carefully neutral.

"My half sister died a little under two years ago. It was sudden, but I'd already been around the girls a lot. Their father was an on-again/off-again boyfriend who didn't stay in the picture. I know not everyone does, but I loved being an uncle from the start." His tone said he likely knew I was in the *not* category. But being an uncle clearly suited him, and I could easily picture him with toddler tea parties and baby gifts like the stuffed elephant.

"They're lucky to have you." I meant the compliment too. Even though it was pretty clear he was only grudgingly tolerating my presence, he'd still fed me and brought me ice packs and meds. He was a natural caretaker and that was an admirable trait.

He checked on the fire, adding another log before turning back to me. "Thanks, but I'm the lucky one."

"They do seem like great kids. Even the bloodthirsty one."

"She is, isn't she?" Felix sat back down in the same chair as earlier with a doting sort of smile. "We're just coming off a phase where all manner of tragedies befell her dolls and animals, and we had frequent pretend funerals."

I blinked. "I might take the ants."

"I know, right?" He laughed, a nice warm sound cutting through the drafty room. "I tried to remind myself of that when I paid the exterminator."

"That probably won't be your weirdest bill. I'm sure my mom lost track of window replacements, wall repairs, vet visits, and emergency barber trips because of various stunts of the four of us boys." Simply thinking about what we'd put my mom through had me wanting to send an apology text. I shifted against the couch cushions.

Felix's eyebrows shot up. "Four boys? She sounds like a saint."

"She's pretty awesome when she's not meddling in my love life."

"Oh? She doesn't like your anti-relationship stance?" Felix's pointed tone reminded me that maybe I'd been a bit harsh earlier when we'd been talking about his divorce. He did seem like a good guy and he probably hadn't deserved my rant on the perils of relationships.

"Mom wants all of her kids happily partnered and isn't shy about making that known. It's probably why I'm so adamant about not wanting to couple up—if I seem open to it, she'll have a parade of prospects at the ready." I took a deep breath to steady my suddenly jangly nerves. I sucked at apologies, but the next part needed to be said, tight back muscles and churning stomach and all. "But I'm sorry if I sounded judgmental about your situation. I get that a lot of people *do* want the whole picket-fence life, and I'm sure you didn't know that Tim would turn out to be a jerk."

"I didn't. And we had a number of good years." Felix's sharpness was replaced by a weary resignation. "Some warning signs were there maybe, but we were happy and I ignored any alarm bells. Our main point of contention was about kids. When I decided to pursue permanent custody of the girls, he was out, and it wasn't really a choice for me."

God, what a dick. I might know myself that I wasn't dad or husband material, but abandoning someone you'd made a commitment to was weak. I should have taken him for more winnings, taught him more of a lesson.

"Of course the girls had to come first. But it still sucked for you personally." If I knew him better, I might have leaned over, patted his shoulder, but I had a strong feeling he'd flinch away.

"Yeah, it did. And now I actually agree with you. No relationships. Raising the girls is a full-time job. I don't have room for much else."

"Makes sense."

Felix's revelation made me a little sad and I had no idea why. Maybe it was that despite my pessimism about relationships, I liked seeing good people get what they wanted. Like my brothers and their relationships. I might not fully understand why they were willing to take the risk, but I still admired them in going for it.

I stretched out my tight back and tried to adjust my ankle on the pillow, which was a mistake, and I grunted to avoid cursing.

"Foot still in pain? How's your head?" Felix instantly fell back into doctor mode. The mere mention of the possibility of a concussion had me frowning.

"My foot hurts when I move it, but it's not quite as bad as earlier. And my head is fine. No headache, I swear." I nodded like a kid promising to not get in trouble, but Felix shook his head like he wasn't buying it.

"I'm still concerned. Repeat concussions are nothing to mess with."

"Yeah, I know. I certainly didn't mean to fall. Again." I groaned as Felix came to crouch next to the couch and peered deeply into my eyes. "What are you doing?"

"Checking your pupils." As he leaned in closer, I caught a whiff of an appealing scent. He smelled good. Clean, like strong soap, but not typical rich-guy pretentious aftershave. I liked it more than I had any right to, and I almost missed him sitting back on his heels to point a finger at me, drawing a line in the air. "And your tracking. Very good. Tell me if you notice any changes, even something small like suddenly feeling extra drowsy."

I was definitely noticing a change, but not one I'd share

with him. My body taking notice of his nearness had to be some sort of stress reaction, but still my insides fluttered in a way that didn't happen all that often for me.

"I'll tell you if I have any new symptoms. And I'm not even that tired yet." Not liking this impromptu medical exam, I shuffled my cards again. "If you're not going to bed yourself, would you want to play cards? Might beat watching the snow."

His mouth pursed. "I'm not playing you for the cabin."

I held up a hand. "I wasn't asking you to." *Damn.* Way to prove what a low opinion he truly had of me. Maybe I wasn't at my most charming this evening, but I still wasn't used to this level of skepticism. "I'm perfectly capable of playing a game without a bet on the line."

"Ha." Moving back to his chair, he considered me with a hard stare until I had to glance away.

"Okay, you've got me. Betting does make things more fun, but I'm not so much of a heel that I'm gonna make you wager something you clearly don't want to lose."

"Thank you." Felix's face softened. "And I'm sorry. I know you likely were taken advantage of by Tim—"

"I can usually spot a bullshit deal." I cut him off because no way was I a victim here. Bad enough that I'd likely been lied to, but Felix's sympathy was almost worse than his judgment.

"Yeah, well, he's rather convincing when he wants to be." Felix made a dismissive gesture like it was no big deal to be conned. And maybe it wasn't to him. "All I'm saying is that I'm sorry for acting like you're a bad guy simply for making a bet. That's not fair."

"No, it's not." I blew out a breath and shuffled my cards again. He didn't have to apologize, and I didn't like how the nicer he became, the more twitchy I got. Maybe distrust was easier to cope with. "But you also didn't ask to have a strange dude in your house either."

"Yeah." A silence stretched out between us. Not exactly companionable, but also not as tense as some of the earlier silences, as if we'd come to some sort of truce. Bizarrely, that unspoken agreement made my uninjured leg jiggle restlessly.

"So what do you say? Friendly game?" I made my voice brighter. "You can't be tired yet. Don't make me play solitaire."

"Oh, the horrors of making you play by yourself." Felix laughed, but I liked his ribbing far better than his sympathy or his silence.

"Hey, I have three brothers and have spent multiple deployments with a hundred sailors and no place for privacy. Playing alone is not in my skill set." That was putting it mildly. Other than sleeping and showering, I was rarely on my own, something my friends liked to give me a hard time about.

"I can think of worse fates than solo play." Felix's eyes flashed wickedly. The joke was probably not intended to be flirty, and it spoke to how on edge I was that my brain immediately skipped to R-rated thoughts. "Other than go fish, I think the last time I played cards was some overnight shift in residency. And that was likely spades or another easy game, not poker."

"I can play spades," I volunteered, totally not ready to be on my own or to sort out sleeping arrangements. Trying to encourage him into a game, I yanked a footstool closer and started dealing two hands.

"All right. But no complaining if I'm terribly rusty." He picked up the cards and proceeded to give me a great game before eking out a win with some lucky draws.

"I think you're a ringer." I immediately started reshuffling. Felix was exactly the kind of player I loved gaming with, smart and decisive with a hint of ruthlessness I hadn't expected from the mild-mannered doctor.

He shrugged like he hadn't just waxed me. "Maybe all the go fish experience with the girls helped me more than I realized."

"Admit you're having fun," I prodded.

"Oh, I can get competitive. And yes, winning was a nice bonus. We can play another round."

Crack. Right as I was dealing us fresh hands, a loud noise from outside broke through the still night like a gunshot.

"Crap. The ice must be bringing down branches. This storm isn't letting up." Felix shook his head as he went to the window. A porch light and some solar lights near the path reflected off the snow in the otherwise inky darkness. No stars tonight either, just a steady drizzle of snow and ice, and a wind that kept rattling the cabin's old bones.

"Are any trees close enough to do roof damage?" I tried to remember what I'd noticed on my way in.

"Grandpa cleared a fairly large perimeter for the cabin for much risk of that, but I suppose we should be prepared to possibly lose electricity. I'll go make sure the emergency flashlights have batteries." Efficient and take-charge as ever, he headed into the kitchen area. His willingness to take the lead on things, a sort of intrinsic independence, was really refreshing considering how much of my life was spent with others looking to me for a plan and answers.

"What can I do to help?" I stood with the help of the walking stick, happy to be his new recruit and follow orders.

"You can sit." Felix waved me back down. "The water you brought will help if we do lose electricity, as no electric means no well. But other than that, probably not a lot we can do to prepare. I'll keep the fire going while I sleep out here."

"No way." Still standing, I shook my head vigorously. "Of the two of us, I probably have more experience sleeping in weird and cramped spaces. I can sleep pretty much anywhere."

"It's not a competition, but I made it through medical school and residency. You're not the only one who can sleep in a room of bunks or upright in a chair. And you'll be more comfortable with that foot in a bed."

"Nah." I kept my voice light. My foot was going to hurt regardless of where I slept, but if I told him that, he'd simply press his case that much harder. "I'm not going to kick you out of the bedroom."

"Thanks, but I want to be closer to the girls if they wake up and need me. The couch is way more comfortable than the kid-sized beds upstairs, honestly. And you're injured." He had me with the point about the girls as it wasn't like I was a nightmare expert, but I hated the continual reminders that I was injured. As much as I liked his ability to run point on problems like preparing for a possible power outage, not being much help for anything all night was starting to grate on me. I liked being useful and hated sitting around while others worked.

"Okay, fine, I'll take the bed," I grudgingly agreed simply because it wasn't worth a big argument. Also, it wasn't like we could share the only adult bed. And damn it, now that I'd put that image in my brain—us sharing a bed, sleeping next to each other, bodies touching, everything that went along with that—I wasn't going to be able to think about anything else all night long.

Chapter Six

Felix

"Why is it still snowing?" Rubbing the sleep out of her eyes, Charlotte went to the window as soon as she and Madeline trooped down the stairs. There was no sleeping in what with worlds for Charlotte to conquer. Luckily, I'd trained myself into being a morning person in medical school, and I already had the coffee percolating when their questions started.

Leaving the kitchen, I strode over to the front window. The sky was still gray, not the crisp, clear sun that usually followed a big snowstorm, and while the icy drizzle of the night seemed to have lessened, fat flakes continued to fall lazily from the sky.

"Sometimes storms last more than one day." I tried to sound casual for the girls' sakes, but my jaw still clenched. I didn't like this. We weren't an East Coast snow state. Seattle itself didn't get much snow, and even in the mountains, multiple-day storms were still fairly rare.

"It's a weird polar vortex thing." Emerging from the bedroom, Calder held up his phone. Although like me he was fully dressed, his short hair was adorably sleep rumpled. "I got enough of a signal to check the weather before the phone fritzed out again. Weather says it may snow on and off most of the day. Darn it."

"Yeah." It was hard to muster much enthusiasm for that report.

"Maybe there will be avalanches!" Charlotte had no such problem finding the bright side as she spun in front of the window. She was still in her fuzzy pajamas, which gave her the look of a hyperactive pink poodle, all bouncing curls and endless energy. "Or there will be so much snow we can't even open the door!"

"There won't be that much snow," I reassured them before Madeline could start to fret about Charlotte's list of dire possibilities. "And we can still go out after breakfast, explore some and test out the sled."

"No big hills." Madeline shot me a wary glance. I'd probably have to talk her into bundling up, but no way were we going to spend all day cooped up in here, especially with Calder, who had bizarrely plagued my dreams. The sooner I got some distance from him the better. Maybe the snow would put a damper on some of my curiosity about the man. Playing cards with him the night before had been fun. So much fun I'd almost forgotten why he was there, and then apparently my long-frozen libido decided to put him in my dreams to torture me.

"What's for breakfast?" Charlotte bounded away from the window.

"I brought pancake mix—"

"And I can make it for you," Calder smoothly finished for me as he leaned heavily on the walking stick to make his way into the kitchen. "You did dinner, so it's only fair."

"You cook?" I asked, following Calder and leaving the girls to play in the living area. Tim had loved cooking, but he specialized in fussy gourmet dishes, not something pedestrian like pancakes for kids.

"Some. Pancakes are easy. My mom went back to college

when I was a younger teen, and I had to help with dinner occasionally. I used to make my little brother bear-shaped pancakes all the time."

"I want one shaped like a bear!" Charlotte piped up from the couch, where she was flipping through the ghost stories book again.

"Sure thing." Calder gave her a smile. Him being charming to the girls made him way more likable than when he'd taken less notice of them. "It's been a while, but I can try."

"That's nice of you, but how's the foot?" I glanced down at his sock-covered feet poking out from his jeans.

"It's fine." He deftly stepped behind the pantry door, ending my perusal of his feet, but his wince when he emerged with the pancake mix said he was lying.

"Seriously? No pain?"

"Well, yeah, it hurts." He plunked the mix on the counter, and I didn't miss the way he shifted his weight off the foot. "But I still don't think it's broken. It's just stiff and sore like other bad sprains I've had."

"You shouldn't have to cook if you're in pain," I protested even as I helped him out by retrieving a large mixing bowl from one of the cabinets.

"It's a good distraction. I'm getting tired of sitting to be honest." He took the bowl from me with a crooked grin that probably got him everything he wanted under other circumstances. "Don't worry, Doc. I'll ice it again after we eat."

"Good. I put the ice packs in the freezer for you last night." Turning to the fridge, I grabbed the eggs and milk, which he accepted and measured out while I found the largest of the skillets and the cooking spray. He had the batter all mixed and the first pancake in the skillet before I realized we'd essentially been cooking together.

"Thanks." He took the spatula I was holding for him. "You're an awesome assistant."

The compliment made my skin heat. Cooking with him felt too natural. Effortless. I had to glance over at the girls to try to get a grip on myself. We were making pancakes, not picking out china.

"And I'm good at delegating," I joked, trying to move beyond my sudden awareness of Calder. "Madeline, can you and Charlotte set the table?"

"Will they eat scrambled eggs or bacon?" Calder asked as I handed Madeline a stack of plates. "I need some protein to go along with the carbs."

"Neither of them will turn down bacon." I grabbed the package from the fridge and set up a few slices for microwaving. "Me either for that matter, although I am getting to an age where I suppose I should moderate breakfasts like this."

"Never. And you're not that old." He gave me an appraising look, one I had no idea what to do with. I'd assumed he was straight, but the appreciation in his eyes was not a look most guys would give another man.

"Thanks," I mumbled as I held out the platter for his next creation. So much for ignoring my awareness of Calder's nearness and the niceness of cooking with someone else. "The pancakes do look like bear faces."

"See? Told you I was good." He winked at me. Was this flirting or simply him being charming? I didn't know and that made my hands tighten on the plate. Not quite sure whether I wanted to continue the easy banter, I busied myself setting the food on the table and calling the girls to eat.

"I like these!" Charlotte admired the pancakes as Calder and I joined them in the eating nook. "I'm going to eat the ears first."

"That's just what Arthur always did." Smiling at her, Calder helped himself to some bacon.

"You were a good big brother to make them for him." We passed the food around as easily as if the four of us had been doing this for months. "Are you still close with your brothers?"

Calder opened his mouth, then closed it again. "Actually, I haven't always been that great. I probably teased Arthur a bit much and goaded him into more than a few stupid dares over the years. But now he's in a relationship with my best friend, and I'm trying to be a better brother."

"Your best friend?" That sounded awkward. Tim still sharing part of my social circle levels of awkward even if Calder got along with both people. "How's that working out?"

"It's sort of my fault." Calder speared his pancake. "I kinda pushed them together. Accidentally. But now they're stupidly happy together, so I guess it's working out well."

"Are you going to come play in the snow too?" Charlotte asked Calder, turning toward him. "Uncle Felix says there's a sled in the shed."

A funny expression crossed Calder's face, a softening of his rugged features. "Not sure my ankle is up to it, sadly. I better save my energy for digging out my car and driving back to base."

"There's no sense in digging out until the plow comes through." I should have been in far more of a hurry to get Calder on the road than I actually was. Maybe I was merely being realistic about the weather, but my neck prickled like more was going on. I didn't like that. I had no reason to keep Calder here. "I need to call the maintenance company about the driveway, but they may not want to send someone until it's actually done snowing."

"Better be today." Calder's firm tone was more the attitude I needed to adopt too. "No offense. I just don't want to impose on you a second night."

"I get it." Not hating the guy's presence wasn't the same as wanting him to stick around. "Maybe you should try a hot shower or bath for your ankle while we're outside? That might help with being ready to drive. The old hot tub needs replacing, but the downstairs bath is pretty serviceable."

"Thanks. That sounds great." There was nothing overtly sexy about his grin, but somehow that smile had me thinking all sorts of thoughts about Calder in the shower, thoughts I didn't need to be having.

"Maybe the weather will break by afternoon." I kept my tone even and bright, doing an awesome job of not letting my voice give away all those soapy, slippery thoughts I kept having.

"Here's hoping." Calder nabbed another pancake. I desperately needed those wishes to come true. This was the worst possible timing for my sex drive to come back online, and I needed Calder on the road ASAP before I said—or *did*—something I'd surely regret.

Chapter Seven

Calder

I very carefully did not think about Felix while I took my shower. It was one thing to enjoy cooking with the guy a surprising amount and to find him appealing on several levels, and another to perv on him, even in the privacy of my own mind. So I didn't, mainly because I had a long history of being able to tune certain desires out, but unlike ordinary stray horny thoughts, Felix kept creeping back into my brain.

After my shower, my ankle was a little looser, so I went to the window, trying to decide whether to start digging out my car. Beyond the trees, what little I could see of the main road still looked unplowed, and maddeningly, the snow continued to sprinkle down. The driveway too needed plowing. I hoped that management company of Felix's was able to get someone out because I needed to get away from here and away from pesky thoughts like how a second night wouldn't be so bad now that Felix appeared to have stopped hating me.

"Wheee!" Outside the window, Charlotte squealed as Felix pulled her on the wooden sled. Like the walking stick I'd been using, the sled looked old and likely handmade. Felix had such a history here. A clammy sensation gathered in the small of my back. I hated that Tim had likely tricked me, but I also wasn't the kind of person to try to pry Felix loose from somewhere with these kinds of roots. My own family had moved around often enough that I truly envied people like Felix who had a deep connection to a particular scrap of earth.

Wasn't ever going to be me, but it was nice to watch from a distance. Felix laughed right along with Charlotte, a rich sound that made me want to hear more of it. Leaping off the sled, Charlotte raced over to where Madeline was building a snow family. They were going to be cold when they came inside, so I checked the fire in the woodstove, stoking it hotter with some extra logs. And Charlotte looked like she'd likely been making snow angels as well with snow clinging to the back of her coat and snowpants, so I laid out a couple of towels near the door before heading to the kitchen.

We might not have had one particular place to come back to, but we'd had my mom, and I channeled her as I made two mugs of hot chocolate and one of coffee. I discovered a bag of marshmallows and was adding two to each of the hot chocolate mugs when the front door swung open and the three of them came stomping in.

"Boots off by the door," Felix ordered the girls, brushing snow off his shoulders.

"I put towels out for you." I gestured to where I'd set them. "And the fire should help you dry off too."

"Thanks." Felix darted his pink tongue out as if he wasn't entirely sure what had brought on my gesture. I didn't blame him. I wasn't sure what to make of this new side of me either. Maybe his whole natural caretaker thing was rubbing off on me.

"There's hot chocolate for the girls. Heated you up some coffee too." I held out the steaming mug for him. Our hands brushed, something that seemed to keep happening, and that my body liked way more than it needed to.

"Wow." Felix's little gasp was probably simply surprise

that I could be thoughtful, but my ego wanted to believe that the potent energy between us affected him too. "You didn't have to do that."

"I know. But I remembered getting all cold playing outside and my mom having snacks ready for us. And I figured you wouldn't want snow and mud all over the floor. Charlotte looks like she went swimming in the snow."

"That she does." Felix pointed at the stairs. "Charlotte, go get into dry clothes before you have the cocoa Calder made you."

"I'm going to change too. My socks are wet." Madeline trooped up the stairs after Charlotte, leaving me alone with a rather befuddled-looking Felix.

"Thanks," he said again. "This was sweet of you."

I couldn't remember the last time someone had called me *sweet*. Or that I'd liked it. But I did, a warm, peaceful feeling snaking up my torso. Felix was easy to do nice things for, and he made me want to do more of them. Not that I'd likely get the chance.

"How was it out there?" I grabbed my own coffee off the counter. "Think I'll be able to leave soon?"

"Both of us working together should be able to clear your car. That's not as big an issue as the fact that it's still snowing off and on, visibility isn't great, and neither the road nor the driveway has been plowed. And I'm not a car guy, but the clearance on your car isn't the best. Even if we dig you out, I'm not sure how far you'll get without plowed roads."

"F—*fudge*." I corrected my language as the girls returned to collect their hot chocolates.

"What's wrong?" Madeline asked while Charlotte snuck another marshmallow out of the bag.

"Nothing's wrong." Felix pitched his voice in that soothing tone of his that made me want to hire him to read every shipboard alert. No one would ever panic again. "Calder may have to stay a little longer, that's all. We have to wait for the plow."

"Okay." She nodded solemnly, way calmer than she probably would have been if I'd been the one to deliver the bad news. "Maybe he can show us how to play the game table. It's like the ones on old TV shows with long sticks."

"There's a game table?" I frowned because I'd missed that on my own explorations.

"Pool table," Felix corrected. "And one of those foosball games too. It's a game room of sorts located beyond the bedroom you stayed in. An addition made after the rest of the cottage was finished. It's the dickens to keep heated this time of year, but in the summer the space is a nice hangout near the grill and hot tub."

"This I have to see." I started down the hall, but quickly realized that I couldn't manage both the walking stick and my coffee. And with the way my ankle was protesting the sudden movement, the walking stick was still a necessity. Damn it. I was ready for this injury to be over.

"It'll be freezing in there." Felix trailed after me as the girls bounded ahead, opening a door I'd assumed was another closet.

"You weren't kidding." The room was a rather utilitarian space, like a lot of garage conversions I'd seen growing up. Rectangular space with a small dormant woodstove in the far corner and room for a small pool table, a foosball table, a lumpy-looking couch, and a stereo system that likely predated both Felix and me. "And no TV? No computer? This is like visiting those rec rooms from the '70s and '80s I've seen in old pictures."

"Painfully accurate." Laughing, Felix wrapped his arms around himself. "And I'll warn you right now that the pool table isn't playable. It's got this weird wobble, but figuring out how to fix it was beyond me."

"Maybe you lacked motivation." I winked at him. I wasn't sure why turning the charm on for Felix never seemed to work precisely as I expected. For instance, it was supposed to make him all fluttery, not me.

"Well, I did lack a competition-addicted sailor that trip." Felix laughed.

"Hey, I'm not that bad!"

"Tell me you're not already trying to decide how to goad me into foosball."

Guilty. Okay, he had me there. I pursed my mouth, not going to admit to it.

"You can play me and Madeline," Charlotte announced, already heading to the table.

"Calder's foot is likely too sore for lessons." Felix's tone was smug, likely because he knew he was right and because teaching kids foosball was the opposite of a competitive thrill. "I'm going to check the flue for the stove in here, see if I can get a fire going before your hands freeze onto the handles."

"I'm not that hurt. I can play." Pride wasn't going to let me back down from this challenge, but I wasn't like my brothers. Explaining games or other things to kids didn't come easily to me, mainly because I lacked their patience for endless questions, and joking around with kids always made me feel rather stiff, none of the easy teasing I had with my friends and other adults. But here the girls were looking at me all expectantly, so all I could do was remind myself I was a naval chief and I was not about to be bested by two little kids. I could do this.

"You take half and I'll take the other half." Charlotte pointed to the handles as she positioned herself and Madeline opposite me. She'd be good on a sub herself what with how take-charge she was.

Hey. There was an idea. Rather than getting hung up on how to simplify the game to the kids' level, I pretended I was explaining a complicated task for a new recruit. I still wouldn't say I was necessarily a great teacher, but the girls caught on quickly and I found way more patience than normal.

"We win!" Madeline grinned as wide as I'd seen her.

"You did it." Something weird happened to my insides, like a stubborn jar lid finally opening, a rush that was both relief and pride. And...*fun*. Yeah, that was it. I, the guy who couldn't stand losing, was having fun letting two little girls win over and over until they were a legit decent team and I wasn't faking needing to concentrate to counter their moves.

Meanwhile, Felix got the stove working and the room went from frigid to cozy, and still we played. He came to lounge against the pool table, watching us with a quizzical smile. Likely I was confounding him again. Good. I liked throwing him off whatever assumptions he'd made about me.

"Excellent job!" Felix cheered and I wasn't sure whether he meant me or the girls, but I liked the praise nonetheless.

"I'm bored. Let's see what else there is." Charlotte scampered away from the table.

"Play me?" I asked Felix. "And don't give me that 'it's been years' line. I'm onto you now."

He shrugged as he moved to where the girls had been standing, but his sly smile gave him away. "I did used to be pretty good at this a zillion years ago."

"Show me." I could be as demanding as Charlotte when I wanted to be, and like the kid, I added a coaxing smile.

"Fine." Felix gave a long-suffering sigh as he twirled the handles experimentally. "Have mercy on my rusty skills."

I'd intended to let him win the first round, similar to what I'd done with the girls, going at half speed so that he'd give me more than a single game, but he was too good for a lazy effort.

"I'm beginning to think we have differing definitions of rusty." I shook my head as he won the round both because I'd started too slow and because he was that good.

"You're flattering me so you can wax me next round." Felix chuckled. Was it possible to get addicted to making someone laugh? I'd never found laughing a particular turn-on before, but each time I made him relax enough to chuckle that freely felt like a major victory. And the sound, rich and warm, lit me up in a way that was decidedly erotic.

"Maybe." I waggled my eyebrows at him, the line between flirty and friendly blurring further.

"Oh, now it's on." The determination in Felix's eyes was every bit as sexy as his chortle. "Stop going easy on me."

"I'm not." But I was highly distracted. Maybe I should have taken advantage of the alone time in the shower because this level of awareness of Felix couldn't be healthy. And I couldn't chalk it all up to a long dry spell either as I'd had plenty of those in the past without getting obsessed with a laugh or the nuances of someone's expressions.

"Damn." Felix made a triumphant noise that rasped over my already raw nerves. "Okay, maybe that was fun."

"Says the guy who won." I was breathing hard and the game was only part of the reason. Our gazes met across the table, potent energy crackling between us. The girls had abandoned the game room, leaving only Felix and me and this almost unbearable tension.

If I leaned across the table, I could kiss him and I had a feeling he wouldn't stop me. Maybe—

Ring. Felix's phone rang from his pocket, killing whatever moment had passed there. Probably for the best, but my muscles sagged nonetheless.

"Surprised I got a signal." Fishing his phone out, he paced away from the table. "And it's my maintenance company."

He answered the call, and judging by his ever-deepening frown, he didn't like what he was hearing.

"Bad news?" I asked after he'd ended the call.

"Plow is likely tomorrow." He didn't drag out the update with a lot of preamble, which I appreciated. "Weather is finally expected to break overnight."

"Crap." My frown likely matched his. Somehow in the midst of all this playing I'd forgotten I was supposed to be leaving. I'd even forgotten about my sore ankle, which had started throbbing again the second Felix's phone had rung.

"I guess you're stuck with us." Despite his grim expression, Felix didn't sound too terribly put out, not like he had the day before.

"More rematch chances for me." I couldn't help my smile. I definitely should not be enjoying being trapped with Felix this much. And I absolutely should not be hoping for more of that delicious awareness that kept surging between us. But judging by my prickly neck, I totally was and that was a huge problem.

Chapter Eight

Felix

Another night snowed in with Calder had seemed inevitable from the moment I'd seen the extent of the snow that morning, but the confirmation that tomorrow was the soonest we could expect a plow still had me on edge. And not because I was miserable, but because I wasn't. I wasn't sure what this was—a genuine attraction or a sign of how hungry I was for adult conversation. My non-work social circle was a rather small dot at the present, but somehow I doubted that any reasonably pleasant person would be having the same effect on me.

And maybe it would be nice having any sort of helper to make lunch for the girls, but the fact that it was Calder, specifically, had me talking faster and moving more lightly, like I'd accidentally had a quad shot espresso. Something about him both lit me up and made me jittery.

"I like your grilled cheese." Charlotte grinned over at Calder as we finished our lunch of sandwiches and tomato soup from a carton. "They're more cheese-tastic than Uncle Felix's."

"Hey!" I faked outrage to make her giggle.

"Guess I'm good with things that require flipping." Calder likely meant things like pancakes and sandwiches and burgers. But my suddenly rejuvenated libido helpfully supplied an image of Calder and all his ripped muscles flipping *me* around.

Gulp. I accidentally made a soft noise as I tried to get my brain to move on, and Calder shot me a questioning look.

"Don't get too impressed. You're getting my greatest hits cooking playlist here. My skills top out somewhere around spaghetti."

"I eat spaghetti." Charlotte gave a regal nod, the queen who might allow Calder the privilege of making her more food.

"Excellent. I'll remember that." Calder had another easy smile, like there might actually be spaghetti dinners in our future. However, the opportunity would likely not present itself, and that was a much-needed reminder of why I was selective about who I brought around the girls. Them ending up disappointed was way worse of a prospect than my own disappointment and loneliness.

"There was too much cheese." Madeline scowled, far less impressed with Calder than Charlotte. I sympathized with her wariness, but I still couldn't let her completely forget her manners.

"Madeline. Don't be rude."

"Sorry." She didn't sound particularly convincing, but it was better than nothing. "Can I be done?"

Nodding, I gestured toward the kitchen. "Put your plate in the sink, then yes."

"I'm going to look at the bookshelf again." Her expression remained a surly contrast to her earlier glee playing the game with Calder and Charlotte.

"You okay?" I asked. She was always moodier than her younger sister, but my shoulders still tightened.

"I'm fine. But bored. I miss TV. Snow is so boring." She groaned like boredom might literally do her in. "Come on, Charlotte. Let's see if there's any good books."

"They never read this much at home," I remarked to Calder as they headed up the stairs. "We should go without Wi-Fi more often."

"Maybe without the several feet of snow?" He pointed out the dining nook window at the snow-covered drive and yard. As much as I was conflicted about our unexpected guest, I couldn't deny how compelling the white landscape was, the way the snow and ice brightened everything, including the gray skies.

"At least it's pretty."

"Yeah. It is." Calder was looking at me, not the window, and my skin heated.

"Here. I'll get the plates," I mumbled as I collected our dishes and headed for the sink, but Calder was right behind me.

"I have an idea." He was much too close, the already cramped kitchen seeming much more so with him near enough behind me to feel the warmth rolling off him. He smelled like a hazy memory—some basic soap or shampoo that I associated with my younger years.

"What?" My voice came out husky, my thoughts already turning inappropriately sexy.

"Let's fix the pool table."

"Oh. That." *Fool.* Of course he didn't share my problem of a wandering brain. But doing something, anything sounded better than more chances for my mind to get me in trouble. "Let's do that."

"I found a toolbox earlier. It has a level in it, so we should be able to fix the table by tightening the legs and adding a shim if necessary."

"You're a man of many talents." I followed him back to the game room, stopping to collect the toolbox from the hall closet.

"I try." Calder shrugged as he started examining the pool table this way and that. "With my dad at sea so much, Mom made sure that we all had basic fix-it skills."

"Smart mom. I need to remember to show the girls things like screwdrivers and drills." I wandered over to check the woodstove.

"Good idea. On the sub, I'm the guy who handles all the requests—everything from what brand of tea to toilet paper to broken facilities—and I've learned that a lot of the time it's easier to fix something myself than try to delegate it out." Opening the toolbox, Calder took out the level and a screw-driver, moving with the sort of competence I'd always found extremely sexy. Give me a person who knew what they were doing in some area over practiced flirting and buff muscles any day, but Calder *also* had the muscles and the charm.

Damn it. Why did he have to be so attractive? I paced back over to the pool table.

"See, I'm much more of a call-the-plumber sort of guy." I had to work to keep my voice joking, not let on how distracting the flex of his arm and back muscles was. "I outsourced most of the renovation I've done on my grandparents' place."

"I've lived in the barracks so long, I'd probably end up calling for help too, but there's something satisfying about doing it yourself."

"Agreed. And you'd likely be excellent at DIY." It made me strangely wistful that Calder didn't have a home or a dream of getting one. For all he put on the freewheeling bachelor persona, he was surprisingly good at domestic tasks, and I wished he had more of an outlet for that side of himself. "I'm not entirely sure how I'm supposed to be helping here."

Watching him work was a pleasure, but I shuffled my feet against the worn carpeting, needing something to do besides ogling him and thinking fanciful thoughts.

"Here, hold this." Calder handed me the level, stepping closer than I expected. And then he dropped to his knees, an awkward movement thanks to his injury, but him kneeling in front of me still made my pulse gallop.

I sucked in a breath. "What are you doing?"

"Checking this leg." He gave me a quizzical look, like there was no other possible explanation. And there wasn't. My overheated imagination was not his problem.

"Barracks, huh? That must make a…social life challenging." Perhaps hearing about a parade of girlfriends would cool off some of my obsession and make his nearness less intoxicating.

"Yes and no. It does get old, but I like being around people. I wouldn't want to live alone. And I've always been able to find a good time when I wanted one."

"I'm sure." The answer told me exactly nothing. "Pretty woman in every port? Isn't that the stereotypical sailor lifestyle?"

He snorted at that. "I think you've seen too many bad movies. And come on, Felix. If you want to ask whether I'm straight, you can do better than some silly fishing expedition."

Oh. I hadn't expected his directness. My grip on the level slipped and I caught it right before it could hit Calder's head. "Sorry. It's none of my business."

"Ha. I'm bi, but honestly, the number of people of any gender in any port is probably far smaller than people assume. Even my friends like to give me crap about the number of contacts in my phone, but I'm way more about hanging out than sleeping around."

"Ah. Poker's more captivating than sex?" I teased rather than let on how his being bisexual complicated everything that much more because maybe he *did* know what his looks and nearness and little quips were doing to me. My hand tightened around the level.

"Sometimes." Calder shrugged.

Huh. I rubbed the back of my neck with my free hand. I'd had a fair bit of mediocre sex in my life, but I couldn't say as I'd ever had a card game better than an orgasm. "I think that says more about the quality of sex you've had than your skill at the poker table."

"Maybe." His sly grin made me want to offer to show him that cards and truly transcendent sex weren't even on the same plane of existence. He patted the pool table leg, and damned if I didn't envy the hunk of varnished wood. "There. That should do it."

"Thanks." My breath caught again as he straightened, again too close. I could have stepped back. I didn't. And neither did he, occupying my personal space with a dizzying level of confidence. He peered deeply into my eyes, like he could see every single sexy thought I'd had that day, and maybe he could.

Reaching out, he stroked his broad thumb down my jaw. I hadn't shaved that morning, and I had the ridiculous urge to apologize for that fact. Anything to break this rising tension. But no words came, only a shiver at how damn good the contact felt. He ghosted his thumb across my lips, callus rasping against my lower lip, as electric as a kiss.

But he didn't.

Didn't kiss me.

Didn't move away either and didn't break eye contact. The intensity in his eyes unnerved me, rattled me on some cellular level. I worked all day with people struggling to remember various details, but I knew with a staggering amount of certainty that I was never forgetting his expression in that instant. His rugged features were soft yet startled, like he wanted me and was more than a little surprised at that turn of events, and like kissing me might be the answer he'd been looking for.

God, I wanted that, wanted to be what he was looking for.

"What are we doing?" I whispered, hoping he knew more than me.

"Hell if I know." The gentleness of his touch on my skin belied his flip words. Maybe we could figure out the answer to both our questions together. I stretched, needing—

"Come back here!" A giggle echoed from another room.

Damn it. I couldn't be Calder's answer. Couldn't kiss him, not now, probably not ever. I didn't get to bumble around kissing strangers simply for the hell of it. Didn't matter how important such a thing felt, I knew my priorities. And so I did what I should have done way sooner.

I stepped back.

Chapter Nine

Calder

I wanted to kiss Felix. Even from my lazy sprawl on the couch, I wanted to kiss him every time he passed by me all damn afternoon. Naturally he'd been giving me a wide berth ever since that interrupted encounter in the game room, but that hadn't cooled off my interest at all. My taste didn't usually run to adorably devoted uncles, but I'd also never had a type precisely. Other people would talk about butts or biceps, but attraction always tended to take me more by surprise. Like "oh hey, we were just hanging out and now I really want to kiss you" surprise, and I couldn't usually predict what triggered the change. With Felix, the air around him seemed charged, a magnetic pull that increased with every conversation and every observation.

For hours, I'd had kissing on the brain. He ordered me to the couch with a fresh ice pack and I wanted to kiss him. I listened to him patiently explain to Charlotte why she couldn't go hunting for mice, and I wanted to kiss him after as he walked away with this little bemused smile. I watched the three of them playing in the snow in the fading light and I wanted to kiss him warm again. Every time he laughed, I wanted to be the one who made him chuckle.

Forget hot abs. Maybe I was a laugh guy or maybe it was

just Felix. I liked how he wasn't afraid to let me take point like with fixing the pool table, but he was also so effortlessly competent and take-charge the rest of the time, ordering me around in the name of healing my injury and meeting the endless questions from the girls all while keeping the woodstove burning and making sure everyone was fed and hydrated.

I'd never found being bossed into a glass of water with a pain-killer chaser sexy before, but here we were. I'd never admit it to my buddies, but I was enjoying being taken care of a little more than I probably should.

"At least let me help with dinner," I begged, tired of the couch and also strangely craving cooking with him again.

"As it happens, dinner might be in your wheelhouse." Felix offered me a hand up from the couch. Accepting made me feel creaky and ninety, but it was also a nice chance for another electric brush of his skin. "Cheesy noodles for the girls. More chicken for us."

"I'm good at the kind of pasta that comes from a box." I hobbled after him into the kitchen area. Standing for foosball and fixing the table had left me more sore and stiff, but no way was I going to complain. "No one boils water like me."

"Even with macaroni, you need to be a winner?" Felix teased back, matching my light tone, but my neck still heated.

"I hate to lose," I admitted as I found a pan suitable for boiling pasta. Something about Felix seemed to pull even uncomfortable truths loose from their tightly guarded hiding spots.

"I've noticed. I guess it's a good trait for a military career that you were born with that competitive gene. You probably won races while crawling."

"Yeah." I exhaled hard and could have left it at that. Everyone always assumed I'd been obsessed with winning from birth, and given my family's love of friendly games and bets, it was easy to let people have their assumptions. But somehow, I didn't like Felix having the same opinion as everyone else. "Actually… I wasn't always like this."

"Oh?" Felix plunked a box of pasta and sauce on the counter. He sounded curious, but not pushy, which made me more talky than usual.

"My two older brothers were way better athletes and natural competitors. They were the ones having races in diapers." I laughed, but it was true. Oliver and Roger even looked more alike. And after Roger had left home, Ollie had been happy enough to pal around with me, but when we were younger, they were a definite one-two punch. "Until Arthur came along, I was the little brother who seldom got a win in against them, but I didn't care. I was happy just to tag along and have a good time."

"What changed?" Felix reached around me to add a sprinkle of salt to the pasta water. Cooking with him was relaxing in a way I wasn't sure I'd ever experienced. It was like dancing, but better because I was a crap dancer and here I didn't have to try to guess Felix's next move. We worked together like we shared a brain, and maybe it was that connection which made it easier to open up.

"Seventh grade. Dad was transferred to a new base midyear." I moved so that he could add a skillet for the chicken next to the pasta pot. "We didn't know anyone there. Ollie and Roger were off to high school, and Arthur was still in elementary. So I was alone in a new middle school, and my parents talked me into trying track to meet other kids."

"Didn't go well?" Felix was likely simply a good guesser, but it felt like he *knew* in a way that had my shoulders easing. I almost never shared this story, but telling Felix was like letting go of a boulder I'd been clinging to for years.

"Nope. Went terrible. I'm strong, but speed has never been

my strong suit. I lost." Even now, decades removed from the memory, my voice lowered and I couldn't meet Felix's kind gaze. "Over and over, I lost. Practice races, track meets, I lost so much, other people started to notice. It became a joke, and this one guy, this..."

"Bully?" Felix supplied when I trailed off.

I nodded sharply. "I hate that word, but yeah, I guess that's what he was. He gave me shit every damn day that spring."

Felix made a sympathetic noise and took a break from stirring the chicken to touch my arm. "That's terrible. What did your parents do?"

"I never told." My jaw made a clicking sound from how hard I ground my teeth together. Felix's concern was like a fuzzy blanket, but I'd been out in the cold so long I didn't quite know what to make of the warmth.

"Why?" His voice was pained, a realness there that couldn't be faked, making my chest hurt. Maybe I shouldn't have cracked the lid on this memory.

"We'd just moved." I added the star-shaped noodles to the boiling water, watching them spread out. "Mom was starting college classes. Dad was deployed. The older two were busy with high school, and I didn't want to look like more of a loser by involving any of them."

"Oh, Calder." Felix touched me again, this time making me look at him. Unlike the few others I'd shared this with, he didn't make me feel stupid for not telling. Instead, there was an understanding in his eyes. "You didn't tell the school either?"

"Nope. Just tried to ignore it, best I could. His dad got transferred that summer and...*man*." I had to stop and swallow hard against the rush of relief that echoed across the decades.

"Lucky break." Felix's voice was strained.

"That's one way to put it. But even then I knew not to

trust luck. So I resolved right then that I was never going to let anyone call me loser again." My voice hardened because I wasn't sure how much more sympathy I could handle before I turned into a limp noodle, swamped by feelings I thought I'd left behind. "I went out for eighth grade football, left track behind, and suddenly I was the most competitive Euler brother. Didn't look back."

"Wow." He sounded dazed, as if his head was as murky as mine. I still wasn't entirely sure why I'd shared that old tale, only that his soft eyes and his hand on my arm felt necessary, a warm presence filling the space that boulder had left behind.

"Sorry. That got heavy fast." I moved to stir the pasta, but he didn't let me go. Damn. He could be strong when he needed to be.

"No, don't apologize. Thank you for sharing. Truly."

"I'm not usually such a buzzkill," I mumbled, having no idea what to do with the thanks.

"Trust me. As a guardian, I appreciate this story more than I can say. Charlotte has...issues with her peers sometimes. This is a good reminder to be more vigilant and not take either of their words that things at school are fine." Felix continued to hold my gaze, and the depth of emotion in his eyes made my breath catch. Maybe that was why I told him. Not only did he seem to understand, but he found value in my sharing, as if I'd done him some sort of favor, opening that old memory box.

"You're a good one. They're lucky." My voice went husky and I couldn't seem to look away. Felix stepped closer, his touch gentling on my arm, other hand soft against my jaw.

"Thanks." He stretched up, and time itself seemed to spread out, everything moving in slow motion, even my own heart rate. The first brush of his lips against the corner of my mouth was like silk slithering over my nerve endings, waking me up and soothing me in the same instant. This. This was what I'd been craving all afternoon.

Adjusting the angle of my head, I met him more than halfway, letting our lips meet in earnest.

Years. Forget all afternoon. I'd been waiting years for a kiss like this. I'd heard songs and movies joke about the earth moving, never quite getting what the big fuss was. Kissing was fine and fun but not…

This. This was all-consuming. Maybe some kisses were about on par with deciding to play another hand of cards, but kissing Felix was like a mission-critical task on the sub, deadly serious, and no real choice about it. Heat gathered low in my gut, spread out to my limbs, each pass of his lips a fresh log on the fire of my need for him.

Hell, the air itself seemed to sizzle, a hissing—

"The pot!" Panting, Felix pulled away from the kiss to point at the stove where the noodles were starting to boil over.

"Oops." I laughed nervously as Felix grabbed a pair of potholders and rescued the pot. The hot water hitting the range was an easy explanation for the noise, but there was no such answer for why Felix affected me like a damn magician. It was only a kiss.

"We shouldn't have done that." He drained the noodles with curt movements, not looking at me.

"Noodles seem to have survived. Chicken too." I stirred the pan before the chicken could go from brown to burnt. But I'd take charcoal briquettes if it meant getting another of those kisses.

Felix made a flustered noise. "That's not what I meant."

"You kissed me," I pointed out. Even frustrated by his reaction, I still passed him the milk to add to the noodles and sauce packet.

"I know." He stirred like he could erase the last five minutes with his movements. "I kissed you. But I shouldn't have."

"I didn't *ask* for a pity kiss." I'd seen the empathy in his eyes. I'd known it was something softer than lust driving him to touch me, and still I'd welcomed it. I really was a jackass.

"That wasn't sympathy." Stopping his mixing, Felix peered intently at me, forcing me to study him closer. His cheeks were pink. Eyes bright. Lips still damp. He sure as hell *looked* like he'd been into the kiss.

"Then why apologize?"

"Because it was a mistake— *Whoa.*" He abruptly shifted his tone as the girls came racing toward the kitchen. "No running in the cabin. And wash those hands!"

"You're such a *dad*," I teased, but my laughter died in my throat as the truth of my words pierced my thick skull. "Oh. Wait. That's it, huh? You've got your priorities and kissing isn't on the list. I get it."

"I'm sorry." His mouth was a tight line, so different from how soft and open he'd been a few moments earlier. Part of me wanted to slap the counter, but I couldn't argue with his logic. He had to put the girls first, and casually kissing strangers wasn't in his careful plans. Besides, it wasn't like we could continue to make out in the kitchen with hungry kids racing around.

"Don't be sorry." I patted his shoulder before scooping up the plates and silverware. I meant it too. I didn't want him regretting that kiss. It had been practically…magical, dopey as that sounded, and no one should regret something that good. If I was lucky, maybe we'd get another shot after the girls were asleep. And if I wasn't? Well, now I knew what kissing could be, and that alone was a gift worth making the effort to be an adult and not pout.

I set the table and helped him plate the food and made

small talk and tried desperately to not act like a lovesick puppy needing another belly rub. Mooning around wasn't what Felix needed. He needed someone to joke with Madeline about the vegetables Felix had left raw for her and someone to ask Charlotte what skeletal remains she'd uncovered in the eaves of the upstairs. Someone to make dinner fun, and I could be that someone.

My friends always joked about my large social circle, which had an awful lot to do with not liking to be alone, but I genuinely enjoyed gatherings of all sizes, and I'd always managed to find a good time even in unlikely circumstances. Eating mac and cheese with Felix and his nieces undoubtedly counted as unlikely, but by the time dinner ended, I had a warm, cozy feeling, like I'd pulled on an extra sweatshirt.

"I want the spookiest story you know," Charlotte demanded as we all helped Felix clean up.

"Maybe Uncle Felix will read to us again," I said lightly as I dried the pasta pot. I'd already told him one of the scariest tales I had, and rather than scare Felix off, it had earned me that kiss. I scrubbed at a nonexistent spot rather than give in to the urge to sigh dreamily.

And hell if I didn't want Felix to read the longest, most boring tale. Bedtime couldn't come soon enough.

Chapter Ten

Felix

"And they all lived happily ever after." I closed the book with a snap. As with the night before, I'd enjoyed reading aloud, maybe a little too much given the audience and the circumstances.

"That's not how it really ended! I read that one earlier. And then the wolf *ate* them. The end." Charlotte's grin made it hard to discipline her, so I merely groaned.

"Well, at least the wolf lived happily." Calder winked at her. He'd listened intently to both of the stories the girls had talked me into. If he had a better use for his Saturday night, he sure didn't act like it, the easy way he lounged on the couch all relaxed smiles and jokes. Almost like he'd totally forgotten our kitchen kiss.

Oh, to be that lucky.

I'd replayed the moment our lips had met dozens of times already. I was excellent at multitasking. I could, for instance, pass the chicken at dinner while remembering his little startled gasp at the start of the kiss and the way it had given way to a low groan. And I could rinse plates while also recalling his bristly cheek against mine. I'd been distracted by reading the stories aloud, but not enough. Every time our glances met, that kiss was right there to make me lose my place. And my head. I absolutely could not risk another kiss.

I really wanted another kiss. Damn it.

"I'm sleepy." Madeline yawned and some traitorous part of my soul hoped she fell asleep fast. And stayed that way. I *should* have been hoping for a dozen nighttime wakeups because what the heck was I supposed to do with all this temptation once Calder and I were alone?

I took a breath and reminded myself that I was forty-two, not seventeen. Still, I didn't glance at Calder as I carefully addressed the girls. "Go on up and get into your pajamas. Both of you. I'll be up in a moment to say good night. Charlotte, you let your sister sleep tonight."

"I'm gonna dream about a snow fort. Hint, hint." Charlotte gave me a kiss on the cheek on her way up the stairs after Madeline.

"Guess you've got your project for tomorrow." Calder stretched on the couch, arms over his head, emphasizing his big body and all those muscles.

"Yeah. They keep me busy. Happy but busy." I was tempted to ask Calder if he wanted to help with the snow fort idea. But he'd likely be gone as soon as the roads were safe, and getting any more involved with him was foolhardy.

Even friendship with Calder seemed unlikely, and as I tucked the girls in, I told myself that I didn't need anything else in my life. I had the two most important things in the universe counting on me. Kisses hot enough to melt my snow boots were not part of the plan.

However, as I descended the stairs, my pulse sped up, lust wanting nothing to do with all my lectures. And damn, Calder looked good leaning back on the couch, legs up, head tipped back as he smiled at something in the story book I'd left behind. Catching him unaware like this made him look more boyish, and there was vulnerability there that made my chest hurt.

Perhaps my protectiveness was sparked by his earlier story, but I'd heard plenty of sad tales over my years in practice and never been tempted to kiss the other person. Or to do battle on their behalf, go fight some decades-old dragon so they could rest easier at night.

"I had a great idea." Calder looked up when I reached the last step, usual impish grin firmly back in place.

"Oh?" My stomach quivered. Had to be dread because no way was I *hoping* for some lewd suggestion. *Liar.* Skin heating, I made my way to the chair by the woodstove, very carefully not sitting next to Calder.

"We should play pool. Test out my repair job." Pointing toward the hallway, he gave me a crooked smile, one I wasn't entirely sure I trusted.

"You want to play pool? Now?"

"Well, it's that or talk you into coming over here on the couch with me, but I figured my chances of making out would go up if you were more certain they were asleep." Moving his legs, he patted the space next to him.

Yup. I definitely didn't trust that grin. "Calder..."

"I know, I know. You didn't mean to kiss me. But you did." He shrugged like accidental kissing was something people wandered into all the time. "And the way I see it, there's no reason you can't do it again. Tomorrow I'll be out of your hair and you can go back to being Doctor Responsible Parent, but maybe tonight you can have a little fun for yourself."

"That would not be prudent." I licked my suddenly parched lips. *Fun.* He'd used that term earlier. Did I even remember what R-rated fun was like?

"Probably not, but it sure would be memorable." He waggled his eyebrows at me, all silly, and that lightness made him infinitely more appealing, that much harder to turn down.

I stood before I could let my growing temptation win. There might be something to his logic, but I wasn't quite ready to let myself agree with him. "I'm going to go make a fire in the game room."

Grabbing the walking stick, Calder hobbled after me. "So, pool first. And then..."

"Pool *only.*" I headed right for the woodstove and busied myself with starting a fire. "And no, you're not playing me for articles of clothing or something ridiculous."

"Felix. You wound me." Calder put his hand on his heart, as dramatic as one of the kids. "Strip pool is strictly an after-midnight enterprise."

"Don't make me poke you with the cue," I said as I retrieved one for each of us.

"Oh, you can poke me..."

"You don't give up easy, do you?" I peered closer at him, trying to see a shadow of that bullied kid. He'd showed amazing tenacity in his story. The navy was lucky to have someone with his sort of perseverance and resilience.

"Nope." Laughing, he grabbed the chalk. "Giving up wouldn't have gotten me through basic training and sub school and making chief."

"Why did you pick the submarine force? That's all volunteer, right?" Like with cooking, we worked together without needing a lot of negotiation. He passed me the chalk, then waited while I racked the balls, leaning against the table. I hoped his foot wasn't hurting too badly, but chances were high that he wouldn't own up to the pain if it meant missing out on a game.

"Yup. You have to volunteer and then get picked. A good percentage of the personnel who raise their hands never make it through the training. It's intense. And my dad served on submarines. I wanted to prove that I could do it too. Wasn't going to let anyone tell me I was too tall or that I'd wash out of sub school." The defiance in his voice said there was another story there, one that had likely added even more mettle to his steel-plated spine.

"You had something to prove."

"Guess so. I know my limits though." He gave a harsh laugh before I indicated that he should go first. Balls clattered across the table. "I don't have the sort of math brain you need for being a nuke. Instead, I picked logistics as my duty rate because I've always been good at making stuff happen, working out details, facilitating deals. Less math, more people skills."

"You'd be a good salesperson." I took my turn, shots less aggressive than Calder's, but still racking up some points.

"Nice job." His appreciative gaze made warmth pool low in my gut. Damn, I wanted him. "And that's what my mom's always saying. She likes to joke that I could sell ice in a blizzard. She's not wrong."

"And you're so humble." I made the joke simply for the pleasure of hearing him laugh.

"Hey, it serves me well in cards too. People who don't know me tend to think I'm a nice-but-dumb jock." He frowned as he lined up another shot, deftly sending a ball into the corner pocket. "They don't see my victory coming."

"Like Tim?" I probably shouldn't have brought my snake of an ex up, as all day we'd both avoided talking about Calder's possible claim on the cabin. And he didn't need my frustration at the whole situation.

"Like Tim. He thought he had a win in the bag, but I showed him." Pausing to stare me down, Calder pursed his mouth. Maybe I wasn't the only frustrated one.

"Good for you." My voice came out too clipped to defuse the growing tension between us.

"Look, I might be dying to kiss you again, but I'm also not going to apologize for going to the poker party." *Snap.* He sank the last two balls with a fancy move, but didn't smile at his victory.

"You didn't know he was lying." I reached out to touch his sleeve. Even if it made me shift my weight from foot to foot, I appreciated his directness. He owned his choices, and I could respect that. "Trust me, I know how convincing Tim can be. And I've already put a reminder in my phone to call the lawyer first thing Monday."

"Good." Calder nodded sharply. "And don't think I didn't notice you avoiding the kiss comment."

I quickly dropped my hand. "You said we weren't playing for that sort of thing."

"No, I said I wouldn't take your shirt. Never promised not to steal a kiss." Stepping closer, he did exactly that, a quick peck that only left me that much more hungry for this to continue.

I groaned, more at my own fickle resolve than at his audacity. "Calder…"

"How about you play me for another kiss?" With the earlier tension evaporated, his playful grin made him awfully hard to resist.

"This is a terrible idea." I racked up the balls for another round anyway.

"I know. You go ahead and break."

Calder wasn't the only one with a repertoire of trick shots. Not sure exactly what I was playing for or which outcome I wanted most, I nonetheless scored several points in succession.

"Oh, it's on." Calder whistled low. Impressing him felt better than it had any right to. "I think you have a secret competitive streak of your own, Doc."

"Maybe." I rubbed the back of my neck, still unsure whether I wanted to win or not.

"I guess you kind of have to be to make it through medical school." He easily won some points of his own before leaning against the table. "How'd you pick your specialty? I bet you would have been a great pediatrician or something like that."

"Kids are great. I always wanted to be doctor. And you're right. Originally, I'd thought pediatrics." I hesitated, not sure how much he really cared to know, but like with the story earlier, he listened with his whole body, eyes sharp, body turned toward me, and attention locked on me. He was too damn easy to talk with. "But then my grandmother spent her later years battling dementia and cognitive function loss and the accompanying depression and anxiety. I became fascinated by the research into treatments. I might not have been able to help her, but I can help others, and that means something to me."

"Yeah. I can see that." Calder tilted his head like he'd truly *heard* me, the solemn regard in his eyes more potent than a shot of bourbon. "She'd be proud. You're a good guy."

"I try." I had to look away then before I kissed him senseless. I busied myself with the game, not keeping track of my shots until Calder groaned.

"Well, heck. You win." His disappointed tone echoed through me.

"I do." My voice was as grave as his, and I held his gaze until the air became thick, the moment almost unbearable.

And then I lunged for him.

Forget meaningless games. I wanted to kiss him, so I did. And unlike that first kiss, which had been born of an urge to comfort, this kiss was all combustible lust. He met me eagerly, as if he'd known all along that this would be the outcome.

His happy noise as our lips met went straight to my cock. Being able to give him something he wanted this damn much made me light-headed, giddy with power. Not content with little nips and sips, I delved deeper into his mouth, which parted on a needy gasp. He tasted sweet, like the marshmallows we'd toasted with the girls after dinner. His tongue against mine made my cock swell further until all I could think about was the next kiss, existing simply for that next brush of contact.

When he pulled away to suck in a deep breath, I grunted at the loss, an undignified protest, but I was beyond caring about appearances. I tugged him back closer. However, he winced.

"What?"

He shifted again, leaning more heavily against the table. "Sorry. My foot. Ignore it."

"If you're in pain…" My insistent desire was replaced with concern.

"It's not that bad. But I wouldn't turn down doing more of that in a bed. My room?"

Hell. He'd broken through my lust fog, and doubts rushed in. What was I doing? I couldn't seriously be contemplating sex with Calder. Even this kiss was a serious indulgence, one I shouldn't get in the habit of.

"I should go," I mumbled, glancing back at the door. He reached for me, but before he could try to convince me with a kiss, I sidestepped him to go take care of the woodstove, bank it for the night.

"Sleepy already?" Calder followed me to the stove.

I nodded, not sure I trusted myself to speak. If he kissed me again, I'd be toast, but he didn't. In fact, instead of making a case for me giving in, he turned toward the door.

"Liar." Pausing in the doorway, he gave me a pointed look. "But you know where to find me if you find yourself… awake."

Damn it. Just like that, he'd left the ball in my court. If I wanted more, I'd have to go to him. No getting overwhelmed with persuasive kisses and telling myself afterward it was a mistake or that I'd had no choice other than to get caught up in the moment. He was making me have to own my desires, and I made a frustrated noise to the now-empty room.

The smart thing would be to head straight to the couch, attempt something resembling sleep. Even taking a long shower would be a better choice than going to Calder. He was a near-stranger and I'd never been one for one-night stands, which this would surely be.

But I wanted. Oh, how I wanted.

I checked on the woodstove. Checked on the girls too, who were sleeping soundly. And then I stood in front of the couch.

You're always so noble, I could practically hear Tim complain along with his frequent refrain, *What would it hurt?* And I was most definitely not taking life advice from my ex, but he had a point here. Whether I kissed Calder again or not, he was still gone in the morning. Why shouldn't I have…*fun*.

That was what Calder had been advocating for. A diversion. A little secret fun that didn't have to mean anything serious. My feet headed back down the hall without waiting for the go-ahead from my brain.

Calder had left the door to the bedroom cracked, as if he'd known I'd end up right here, and sure enough, he called out before I had a chance to retreat.

"Insomnia already, Doc?"

"Something like that." I took a step into the room. Calder was lounging on top of the covers, book next to him. "This is nuts."

"Says the psychiatrist. Come over here."

"I can't stay long," I hedged, hand on the doorknob, not sure whether I was about to shut it or beat a hasty retreat. "I should be on the couch before the girls wake up."

"Understood. But there's a lot of hours between now and then. Come in anyway. And lock the door."

Chapter Eleven

Calder

Snick. Felix locked the door and took a few shuffling steps forward. Smiling, I sat up in anticipation of him joining me. *Thank God.* I hadn't wanted to beg, but I desperately wanted more kisses like we'd had in the game room. Maybe I'd proposed a bed too soon. Stupid foot. I'd been motivated more by wanting to get off my ankle than by an urge to replace the kissing with other activities.

Slowly, Felix walked over to me. "I have no idea what I'm doing here."

"Me either." Grabbing his hand, I tugged until he got the hint and sat next to me on the bed. I liked his uncertainty because it made it easier for me to ask for what I wanted most. "Kiss me again."

"I can do that." He twisted around until we were sitting face-to-face. Fucking adorable, the way he tucked one foot underneath him, situating himself like he'd be here awhile and like kissing was a damn serious business he cared about getting right.

I cared too, so I waited for him to finish arranging himself before I reached for him. The way he'd kissed me after he'd won had been such a revelation. He didn't have to. He'd won. He owed me nothing. And still he'd kissed me like he'd just heard a planet-ending meteor was headed our way. Desperate. Out of control. I wasn't sure I'd ever been kissed quite like I had from Felix.

"Comfortable?" I asked as I stroked his jaw, drawing out the inevitable, letting the moment build, become that much more potent.

His nod as he leaned in was the sweetest of victories, and I let him be the one to kiss me first. The way he started so gentle and soft was addictive, like caramel sauce, smooth and endlessly sweet. The sweetness flowed over every rough edge I had, muting any urgency until I could appreciate each little detail.

The roughness of his stubble under my thumb. The surprising fullness of his lips. His clean scent. His hand on my shoulder, firm anchor in the river of sweet. The way he gasped when I used my tongue to tease his lower lip. The moan when our tongues met.

"Damn. So good." I sounded dazed. Which I was, amazed at how different this was, how much I wanted to keep kissing Felix for decades.

"It is, isn't it?" His voice held the same sense of wonder as mine.

"I could do this all night," I confessed. And probably a lot of people would be racing ahead, but I was serious. This kissing was everything and I was in no hurry for it to be over with.

"Let's." Felix blessed me with a boyish grin before tumbling me back against the pillows. I went happily, following his lead until we were both on our sides, facing either other like we were sharing secrets at a sleepover. I felt like a balloon at one of our homecoming events, high and bouncy, a level of pure happiness I wasn't sure I'd reached in years.

And when we kissed again, my chest expanded as my limbs

loosened, more of that giddy balloon-in-the-sky energy. I loved how Felix didn't seem in any more of a rush than me, trading easy kisses back and forth. We took turns exploring, and the roughness of his jaw against my lips made me shiver. I loved learning his little secrets like that nibbling his ear made him be the one to tremble.

"Calder." His hand swept up and down my side.

"Yeah." Whatever the question was, my answer was already yes. Whatever he needed, I wanted to give it.

"I want to touch you. Can I touch you?"

"Please." I figured he'd go right for my fly, but he surprised me by snaking a hand under my shirt, stroking my side and back. Continuing to kiss me, he heated up all my nerve endings with each pass of his hand. He made going slow not only good, but *necessary.* I hadn't realized how much I missed lazy making out like this, kissing with no point other than to lead to more kissing. My shirt bunched up between us, the nubbly fabric of his sweater teasing my stomach and making me want to touch too. "You too."

He nodded, and by some unspoken agreement we both shucked our shirts before returning to our sides, letting our bare chests touch.

"Oh." His sound of delight lifted me even higher, and I followed his lead, touching his back, pulling him tighter against me.

"Fuck. I can't get enough of you."

"Same. You feel so good. Warm." His smile was so playful that I couldn't help but grin back.

"That's me. Human furnace."

Laughing, he kissed my jaw. "Well, you sure light me up."

"Cheesy lines like that, you're lucky you're so damn cute." I dipped my head to nuzzle at his neck.

"I'm n— *Oh.*" Whatever protest Felix had been about to

make died as I licked at his neck. He shuddered and arched toward me.

"Like that?"

"Do it again," he demanded.

"I can do that." I liked how obvious his responses were, how easy it was to tell what he wanted, and how simple it was to give it to him. I teased his neck with little bites and kisses, finding the spots that made him moan and doubling down on the ones that made him wiggle against me. He was hard against me and his grinding felt so good that I dropped a hand to his ass, pressing him even closer against me.

Moaning softly, he stretched to offer me more of his neck. His grinding became more purposeful the more I nibbled at his neck and shoulders.

"Calder," he whispered, his voice the first sign of urgency. "I'm going to come if you keep that up."

"Please." That sounded like the best idea I'd ever heard. Making him climax simply from my kisses was the life goal I'd never known I needed. "Do it. I want to get you off."

Figuring he might not want to come in his pants, I reached for his waistband, but his hands were already there. Laughing, we both wriggled free of our pants until we were down to our boxers and kissing again.

A few more kisses and I couldn't resist going for his neck again, loving the way he groaned and bucked against me. "That. Right there."

"This does it for you?" I was still more than a little amazed at how easy he was to turn on. Before, sex always felt like a race, one that I was always two steps behind on, but with Felix, there was no sprinting, no mad dash, only kisses that tasted like victory and moans that made me feel like a winner.

"And how." He wriggled against me, hard cock unmistakable, so close I could feel it pulse when I sucked on his shoulder. "Fuck. Almost..."

Chuckling, I looked up at him. "I love it when you curse, Doc."

"Please. More." His voice was thready as his ass flexed under my hand. I used the rhythm of his grinding to guide my attention to his neck, getting more intense and deliberate in time with his motions. "Yes. Yes. Oh sweet... *There.* Calder."

My name never sounded as good as it did on his lips as his whole body tensed. Warmth bloomed between us as he came, pulses that I could *feel.* Knowing he was coming was a gratification like nothing else I'd ever experienced. What I liked best, the kissing and touching and slowness, had brought him unmistakable pleasure, and my own body vibrated with happiness.

"Damn. That was something." I was transfixed by his face, the way his eyes had fluttered shut, the high color on his cheeks, the slight swelling of his lips.

"So much. Thank you." He pressed a gentle kiss to my mouth. I wasn't quite sure what to do with the praise, so I simply gathered him closer.

"Trust me, I loved it."

"I can tell." He shifted, bumping against my own still-hard cock. "What do you need?"

He wasn't the first to ask me that question, but with him, I didn't feel any pressure or expectation. He made it so damn easy to ask for what I truly *needed*, no internal judgment and second-guessing. "Can you just kiss me again?"

Of course there was no *just* in kissing Felix. When our mouths met again it was all-consuming, and I gave myself over to it, like floating in the ocean and deciding to let the current carry me. He stroked my chest and arms, and each touch, each kiss took me someplace new and beautiful.

When I reached for my cock, it felt inevitable, but also good and right.

"Yeah, that's it," Felix encouraged in between kisses. "Get close."

"I am. Damn. I am." My wonder at how damn *easy* this whole thing was had to be showing because Felix chuckled softly.

"Good." Still kissing me, he settled a hand on top of mine, not moving mine aside or trying to take over, simply another point of connection to share. "Fuck. You're so sexy."

His kiss seemed to find my rhythm or maybe it *was* the rhythm, that current again, carrying me along, getting more urgent. My hand sped up, and my cock had never felt as good in my fist, his nearness another layer of sensation to enjoy.

"Please." I wasn't sure what I was asking for, but Felix seemed to know, nodding solemnly.

"I've got you." That was apparently the magic phrase, that and the sweep of his thumb against my fist, and my body arched, spine tighter than it had maybe ever been. The pleasure went higher and higher, an almost impossible climb, before it crested all at once.

"Oh. Fuck. Fuck. Coming." My come dribbled over my fist, a messiness level I didn't always care for, but here it felt so good and sexy that the slick slide of my hand coaxed out a few more shudders.

"Yes." Felix exhaled hard like he'd been the one to climax, like he truly had ridden that ocean wave with me. Damn. I liked sharing that with him, made the last tremors that much better.

"So. Good." My tongue was thick in my mouth, true speech more than I could manage.

"Oh, Calder, that was so hot. Thank you."

"Feels like I should be the one saying that." Still breathing hard, I found more of my words. "That was…"

"Better than cards?" he laughed wickedly.

"Fuck yes." I pulled him in for another hard kiss that said more than I could. "I don't always…"

"It's okay." He caressed my shoulder, touch gentle and understanding. For all he'd teased, his eyes were soft too, like he really did understand that sex wasn't always quite this good for me, and he wasn't judging. "I'm glad. Really glad."

"Good." I took a few more gulps of air, still feeling invincible, as giddy as I'd been since he locked that door. Sometimes an orgasm was simply a decent prelude to nap, and sometimes it was…whatever that had been. An earthquake in the well-trodden terrain of my life. I wanted it to have been as good for Felix, but I could already sense his retreat from the more cautious way he was holding himself. I wagged a finger at him, wanting one more smile. "And don't you go having regrets."

"Think you know me so well?" Yawning, Felix dropped his head to my shoulder.

"Maybe. You're easy to read." I stroked his bare back. In a moment we were going to need to clean up. In a minute he'd be gone and I wanted to enjoy this as long as I could. "And you're entitled to some adult fun without beating yourself up, Felix."

"I'll try." His conflicted sigh said he was likely already at war with his own expectations for himself. I kissed the top of his head, wishing I could chase all those doubts away. For myself, I had zero regrets other than that I probably wouldn't get a repeat of this night.

Probably. Wait. I remembered who I was. If a crew member on the sub had a need, I was the go-to guy who could make it happen. There were few problems I couldn't solve. I wanted more of Felix, and I might not be exactly sure how to get it, but I was sure as hell going to figure it out.

Chapter Twelve

Felix

"So I've been thinking about skeletons." Charlotte pounced on the couch, disturbing both my sleep and makeshift bed.

"Skeletons?" I tried to blink myself more awake. Not surprisingly, I'd slept terribly. After a hasty retreat from Calder's room, I'd showered before spending a bunch of restless hours replaying our encounter. But now the sun was peeking in the front window, and Charlotte had bones on the brain. I couldn't afford another minute to think about Calder.

"Who wants pancakes?" Except here he was, leaning on the walking stick, and looking far too chipper for the early hour.

Maybe *he* had slept soundly, a thought I didn't find the least reassuring.

"I want a skull-shaped pancake." Charlotte scampered off the couch and raced over to the kitchen area.

"Like a pirate?" Calder's eyes narrowed, but his smile didn't dip. "Skull and crossbones?"

"Not a pirate, silly! Like human bones. You could do vertebrae too. Or ribs. Do you know how many bones are in a hand?" Charlotte pranced around, sharing random facts from the kids' anatomy book I bought her some months back.

"That's amazing." I couldn't help smiling at her enthusiasm for fact sharing as I headed to the coffeemaker.

"Feel free to make it extra-strength," Calder said in a low voice as he retrieved the skillet from the dish drainer. Perhaps he hadn't slept that well after all. It was hardly that charitable of me, but I didn't like being the only one who had been tossing and turning.

"You don't have to make pancakes again," I said, trying to remind myself that I could be a nice person versus a petty one.

"I want to." Calder already had the mix out, so I retrieved the eggs and milk from the fridge rather than continue to argue. We worked together as seamlessly as we had the day before, but there was a certain caution now to our conversation. Not awkward as much as both of us trying overly hard to not bring up last night. Even without the girls flitting about, I still wasn't sure what I would or should say.

I might be over forty, but it had been the single hottest make-out session of my life, and I couldn't get enough of the way Calder kissed with this intense presence and how nothing was rushed with him. In fact, he'd seemed to crave going slow every bit as much as I had. That kind of match was rare, chemistry and compatible turn-ons combining for a brew more potent than the best Seattle coffee.

"Thanks," I said to break the silence as he turned out a stack of bear-face pancakes along with one I guessed was supposed to be a femur. Why did he have to be as sweet as he was sexy? A jerk would be so much easier to deal with on multiple levels.

"No problem." His voice was overly cheerful, and he didn't look my way. He'd moved on to scrambling some eggs, which were apparently riveting. Or maybe he too had no clue what to say.

"I meant..." I swallowed hard and lowered my voice. I was making this far harder than it needed to be. "Last night. It was amazing."

"It was good, wasn't it?" There was a bashfulness to his smile that I found utterly charming.

"Unexpectedly stellar," I said, enjoying the blush that spread across his cheeks.

"Do you think—"

"There's a plow!" Madeline interrupted whatever Calder had been about to ask. She motioned at the front window, where sure enough a pickup with a plow attachment was clearing the drive.

"Roads are probably clear too." My throat was strangely cottony, and a swig of coffee didn't help it. This was it. He'd be on his way in under an hour most likely, and chances were high I'd never see him again. My hand fumbled the plates I'd been grabbing.

"Careful." Calder's quick reflexes stopped the stack from tumbling to the floor as he rescued the plates and handed them to Madeline to set the table. "The plow helps, but we'll still need to dig out the cars."

"I'll help with yours after we eat." The words felt flat in my mouth like biting down and discovering cardboard, not pancakes. Weird to be disappointed at being rescued. The departure of one-night stands and unexpected houseguests didn't usually make my chest hurt, and I didn't like how tender I felt now, making way more of a single cataclysmic encounter than I needed to.

"Will we still get to make a snow fort?" Charlotte asked as I carried the plate of pancakes to the table.

"I think so. Tomorrow is a school day, but we should have time for some snow fun after we get Calder on the road." Turning toward him, I asked, "Do you think you'll be okay to drive?"

"Yep. My ankle's a lot less stiff this morning. Don't worry,

Doc. I'll stop if I need to." He gave me that winning grin of his.

"Good." I busied myself with serving the girls rather than give in to the urge to ask him to stay a little longer.

"So..." Calder drew the word out in a way that had me instantly on edge. "You still planning to call your lawyer?"

Oh. Of course last night hadn't changed anything. Calder still thought he might have a claim here and was worried about that, not a way to eke out another few hours together.

"Yes, certainly. First thing tomorrow. If nothing else, you may have some recourse against Tim." No way in hell was Calder getting any part of my cabin, but if he could shake a few coins loose from Tim, so much the better.

"You figure we'll need to have a meeting?" He seemed remarkably upbeat at the prospect.

"Probably. You can bring whatever papers Tim gave you." I didn't even try to match his cheery tone.

"Good. I was thinking we should get food after the meeting. Like lunch or dinner or something." His tone hadn't shifted—still casual and happy, but I had to blink. Was Calder asking me out? Or was this some weird sort of guilt? Take my cabin then take me out for a consolation dinner?

"Whoops." Charlotte sent the syrup flying and the resulting cleanup meant I had to stew on that question until later when he and I were scraping off the cars and the girls were playing in the snow away from the car.

"You think we should have dinner?" I asked as I swept the snow off the hood of his little sports car.

"Yeah, it might be fun." He shrugged, massive shoulders stretching the fabric of his sporty coat.

"Fun? Sorting through my divorce settlement is *fun*?" Even with my voice low, my disbelief came through loud and clear.

"Not the paperwork." He gave me a lopsided grin. With

his cheeks all red from cold, he had even more boyish charm than usual. "The meal. Come on. What do you like for food when it's just you choosing, no kids? Man cannot live on grilled chicken alone."

"Well, you're not wrong there," I admitted, apparently unable to come up with the quick refusal this idea warranted. Damn him and that devilish smile and easy attitude. "All the kid-friendly fare does get boring. I've yet to convince even Charlotte to share my love of spicy things like Korean barbecue."

"I'd share a hot pot with you, Doc." He winked at me.

"You're tempting. But we shouldn't mix business with..." Trailing off, I made a vague gesture.

Laughing at that, he held up a finger. "First, I'm expecting the lawyers to explain why you're right about Tim not being able to bet the place, and I'm not going to be a dick about it if I don't have a claim."

"Then why even want a meeting?" I sent more snow flying over my shoulder.

"Mainly I want to see Tim's face when he gets called on his BS. I might not be able to sue him or anything, but he needs to stop screwing you over." His voice had gone all fierce, the defender I hadn't realized I wanted until precisely that instant. God, it had been so damn long since I'd had someone unequivocally on my side.

"I know," I groaned. "My bank account and I are both more than ready for him to stop coming up with new challenges to the settlement that was supposed to be final months ago."

"And see, that's exactly it, I'm really sorry to have been another challenge, even if it is his fault. You took care of me. You fed me. You didn't kick me out into the snow. Let me take you for dinner after the lawyers light into Tim. It'll be—"

"Fun," I finished for him. Because it would. Spicy food, adult conversation, mutual dislike of Tim, and more of Calder's bottomless well of charm. There was a lot to like.

And two really good reasons not to give in. I glanced over at where the girls were mounding up snow, Charlotte energetically directing Madeline through laying out the snow fort.

"I shouldn't." I kicked at a big chunk of snow and ice on the ground.

"You never use a babysitter? Or go out while they're at school?" Calder's head tilted, clearly doing single dude math where cheap babysitters were plentiful and kid-free hours abundant.

"Obviously, they can't go to the lawyer's office." My tone came out too sharp, so I took a breath before explaining more. "I'll likely ask my stepmom to help if she's in town since we're between nannies right now. She's their grandma, and they love her."

"That's awesome," said the guy who had never been forced to deal with Gabrielle and her many whims. If I was lucky, she'd be around long enough for me to find a nice, stable nanny for all the times she had better things to do.

"Uh-huh. She travels too much for permanent custody, but she does take them occasionally. And yes, there is school too. But fun is a luxury I don't get right now."

"Even my folks did date night." Calder shrugged like my objections were minor inconveniences. "My mom always said kid-free time was a key to her being a good mom. You're already a great uncle and guardian. I think you can afford to let me buy you some food."

"Maybe." Why I still wasn't flat-out refusing, I had no clue. It was only some dinner. Perhaps I could simply let myself have a meal before we parted on amicable terms. "Let me see what I can work out."

"Excellent. It's a date." Calder grinned at me like he'd just won a game. And maybe he had. *A date.* That was exactly what I was afraid of.

Chapter Thirteen

Calder

"You're in a good mood," Max observed as we stood in line at the chow hall.

"Yeah, I guess I am." It was my lunch break and rare winter sun streamed in through the windows.

"Seeing as how grumpy you've been about desk duty, either you got word that they're shipping you out or you've got a hot date tonight." He gave me an easy grin as we both grabbed entrées of meat loaf and potatoes.

I frowned at the mention of work stuff, but in truth the week had passed surprisingly fast. Not only had I sorted out a tense situation involving inventory for a sub on the verge of deploying, using all that salesperson charm Felix had noted, but I'd also had thoughts of Felix and Saturday night to keep me company. Even now, I could still feel the buzz from the sex. It was exactly the distraction I needed. And it also gave me an out to use with Max.

"Actually, yes." I didn't have to work hard to summon back the smile I'd had most of the day. "Soon as I finish up this afternoon, I'm heading for the ferry. I'm meeting someone for...dinner."

"Nice pause, there." Max laughed and grabbed a fruit cup

and a soda. "Translation: it's a hookup and you might eat while you're there?"

"It's not like that." My neck heated as we made our way to a table. I'd paused because Max didn't need to know about the lawyer part. As to the rest, I wasn't sure sex was remotely a possibility that night. Which was okay. I wanted to kiss Felix again in the worst way, but I was also capable of biding my time. Simply hanging out together would be fun.

"Uh-huh." Max gave a knowing laugh before digging into his food. "At least you won't have to spend this weekend snowed in again."

"Snowed in wasn't so bad," I hedged. I'd told my friends precious little about the weekend. Nothing about Felix, only that I'd slipped and turned my ankle. I wasn't ready to have to confess to being screwed over by Tim. And the personal stuff…well, that could stay personal a little longer. Maybe Felix would become a friend, in which case how we met could be a funny story, not evidence of how I'd been so stupid. I didn't like the gnawing in my gut every time I thought about Tim getting the better of me. I hated feeling like a loser. However, Felix was a pretty awesome consolation prize, and when we'd kissed I'd felt like I was holding a million-dollar lottery ticket.

"So when do we get to come?" Max leaned forward, not dropping the subject like I'd hoped.

"I'm not sure. I need to work out some things regarding ownership." I wasn't going to outright lie, but I was also trying to figure out how best to save face. Maybe if nothing else Felix would let me rent it for a weekend.

"Okay, let me know before ski season ends." Agreeable as ever, Max went back to eating, but I continued to mull over how to spin the cabin mess in a way that everyone laughed and I didn't look stupid.

I was still thinking hours later when I caught the ferry heading downtown. I didn't want Felix to lose part of his family legacy, but I also hated feeling gullible. Accordingly, I was in a muddled mood when I reached the law offices located on an upper floor in a posh skyscraper in downtown Seattle, not too far of a walk from the ferry even with a nippy wind at my back. Felix hadn't been kidding about his legal troubles costing money. The building was all gleaming chrome and tasteful signage, the sort of place populated by high-end law firms where the hourly rate approached a weekly check for a new recruit. My back tightened. I hated being part of Felix's troubles.

Guilt dogged me on the elevator ride, but I spotted Felix as soon as I stepped off and my weird mood was replaced by a sudden surge of joy that loosened my muscles and made me walk faster.

"Hey!" I called out. Part of me wanted to whistle, but this was hardly the place for more than an appraising glance. Even so, I let my eyes linger on his lean frame. "Damn. Is this your usual doctor wear? Or were we supposed to dress up for the lawyer?"

After ditching my uniform, I'd pulled on nice jeans and a date-worthy shirt, but Felix was in dress pants, a blue button-down shirt, and a tie I wanted to remove with my teeth. I wanted to kiss him again, explore his neck, see if magic could happen twice. No sex had ever felt so good, like unlocking a cheat code on a video game, and I needed more.

"I came right from office hours. Sorry." Felix slowed down outside the glass doors for the law firm reception area.

"Don't apologize. You look great." I smiled at him. I wanted to greet him with a handshake or maybe even a fast, friendly hug, but Felix seemed decidedly guarded, holding himself stiffly and not smiling back.

I tried not to let it bug me and kept my tone all cheerful. "So I found a great Korean place nearby for after this."

"Calder..." he started, then sighed. "I'm still not sure dinner is a good idea."

"Did you get someone to watch the girls?" I asked, undeterred by his reluctance.

"Yes, my stepmom picked them up from school and is taking them out for dinner at their favorite burger place."

"See? They get a treat. You get a treat. It really is that simple." I gestured like I was handing out treats and managed to get a laugh out of Felix.

"You're persistent. Maybe—"

"Felix." A nasal voice cut him off. Tim. Shorter than me but taller than Felix, he was thin with a hawkish nose and hard eyes. Some would probably find his surly Hollywood star looks hot, but I wasn't one.

"I see you brought your lawyer." Felix regarded him and the younger man accompanying him coolly.

"Well, if you're going to haul me back in front of the mediator instead of settling this quietly, like adults, I had no choice," Tim said archly, as if he had the high ground here.

"We tried settling quietly. Multiple times." Felix's voice was strained. "But then you went and gambled away my property."

"Maybe we should save the complaining for the mediator?" the younger lawyer guy proposed. He wore a slick gray suit and had a sneer for Felix even as he used an agreeable tone.

"Good point," Felix said tightly.

I wanted to touch him, steer him away from these jerks. And it was my fault he had to deal with them. I'd pushed the issue in large part because I had wanted an excuse to see Felix again. That and I didn't take losing well, but the set of Felix's shoulders and tension around his eyes made my stomach cramp.

I didn't have another chance to speak to Felix before we were led to a conference room where Felix's own attorney, a pleasant if overly formal middle-aged woman in a purple suit, was waiting for us. Then the mediator, a stern-faced woman in somber black, joined us, along with a couple of assorted clerks and record keepers.

Quite a crowd. I should have simply let this go and asked Felix out like a normal person. Having miscalculated so grievously was not a comfortable feeling, and my feet itched every time I glanced at the door or at Felix next to me. I wanted to grab his hand and make a break for it. But this wasn't a heist movie, and instead I had to show my documents and present my account of what happened and watch Felix getting more and more tense.

"So the question is whether Mr. Spalding could convey the property given that the latest settlement awarded it to Mr. Sigund?" The mediator clicked around on a slim laptop, face impassive.

"Mr. Spalding contends that the bet happened prior to that settlement." Tim's attorney had an officious tone and a crafty glint in his eye. He reminded me of the guys in school who lived to make others feel dumb. I'd had more than one officer like him too, young lieutenants with puffed-up egos and a knack for one-upmanship.

But I wasn't here to play games, and my elbow dug into the padded arm of my chair as I racked my brain for how I could make this better for Felix.

"Even if so, at most Mr. Spalding could convey a half interest in the property, but all disputed assets were agreed to be frozen pending settlement." Felix's lawyer was equally good at adopting a persuasive tone, her clipped East Coast accent skewering Tim as much as her steely gaze. "Thus, regardless of the date on the deed he gave Mr. Euler, he could not convey his interest in the property."

The date? I stared down at my paperwork. Huh. That didn't make sense. "He didn't get me paperwork until last Thursday."

I was undoubtedly shooting my own case in the foot, but all the lawyer-speak was making my head hurt. I had expected a swift rebuke of Tim's actions, not this legal maneuvering. I could see a possible outcome where I had a half interest in the cabin and never got to kiss Felix again and that simply wouldn't do.

"So you're saying the paperwork is backdated?" The mediator's eyes narrowed.

"Yes." I nodded and that set off a flurry of new arguments from the attorneys. While they bickered, I chanced a glance at Felix. Eyes fixed on a bland ocean print on the wall, he looked so tired and worn down.

Fucking hell. This was what love got a person. Felix was generous and caring and Tim had not deserved an ounce of his affection. I didn't care how many good years they'd had together, no one should get to treat someone else like an ATM. Love made people so fucking entitled. And no way could I continue to add to Felix's suffering.

"I don't want a half interest." I raised my voice to be heard over the bickering attorneys. "Tim—Mr. Spalding—never should have bet the cabin deed. Tell me what to sign so Mr. Sigund gets to keep the property as they apparently originally agreed on."

I glared at Tim, letting him know exactly what I thought of people who went back on their words.

"You're sure you don't want to pursue compensation or ownership?" The mediator pursed her mouth. "You might want to consult with counsel of your own about your options in small claims court."

"Oh, Mr. Spalding owes me compensation. But this property wasn't his to gamble, and I'm not going to tie the property up in a separate lawsuit. I'll sign whatever Mr. Sigund needs to prove it's his free and clear as long as Mr. Spalding doesn't get a piece."

Felix blinked at that and sat up straighter. "You don't have to do this."

"It's the right thing to do," I insisted, speaking only to him and shutting out the rest of the room. "You deserve it. He broke his word. It's yours."

"Thank you." Felix's knuckles were white around the pen he had a death grip on.

"Your forthrightness is appreciated, Mr. Euler." The mediator nodded at me. "Now let's review the final settlement terms and what it would mean to be in contempt of those terms."

She proceeded to go over a lot of legalese, including warning Tim about failure to follow the settlement. Tim's attorney wanted to argue something about rising property tax values, the upshot of which seemed to be Felix owing him more.

"Oh and since the cabin is apparently yours, you can deal with this." Tim slid a piece of paper across the table at Felix. "It's a list of repairs the property management people want before they can rent it again. Came to my email by mistake along with a bill for driveway plowing."

"Lovely." Felix scrubbed at his hair, and I wanted to smooth it back down.

And maybe I couldn't make up for Tim being an ass, but I did have something to offer. I waited until the lawyers were arguing again to lean toward Felix and drop my voice to a whisper. "I'll help you with the repairs."

"What? Why would you do that?" He wrinkled his nose even as his eyes flashed with something that might have been hope.

"Because you're a nice guy in a crap situation." God, I wanted to touch him in the worst way. When he shook his head and frowned, I added, "I promised some buddies a ski weekend. Let me help with repairs and maybe we can trade."

I'd do it even without the trade because maybe I'd get at least one more weekend with Felix out of it, but something told me he'd accept a deal over an offer of friendship right now.

Sure enough, he nodded. "We'll see."

I could work with that, so I smiled at him. "I'm sorry for putting you through this."

"It's okay," he said but his grim eyes called him a liar.

The mediator started talking again, and there were no more chances to whisper at Felix. The guy desperately needed a friend. I could be that guy. Neither of us wanted a relationship, but that didn't mean I couldn't be what he needed short-term, make up for his asshole ex's greediness. When we'd kissed, I'd never felt so taken care of or safe sexually, and as much as I wanted to explore those feelings more, I also wanted to take care of Felix in return. Starting with dinner. As soon as we were free of this mess, I'd make it my mission to get Felix smiling again.

Chapter Fourteen

Felix

"Now on to the fun part." Calder sauntered purposefully toward the bank of elevators. I'd been planning on begging out of dinner, but Calder moved like a man determined to see a plan through. Something told me that telling him I was tired wasn't going to get me far. And honestly, I wasn't even sure I wanted to make the excuse. Calder was the only bright spot in this whole mess, and I wanted more of his sunny determination, less of my own head.

"This place I found has great reviews." He hit the button for the elevator before turning back to me. "All the kimchi you can handle and some interesting fusion dishes too. Apparently they even have some spicy Korean cocktails, and you look like you could use one of those."

"No kidding. That was…" I trailed off because Calder didn't need my complaints about Tim, so I stretched my back instead. And even without voicing my ire, Calder still gave me a sympathetic look.

"Yup, it was pretty bad. And it was my fault, insisting on a meeting. I'm sorry I put you through that." He looked so serious as the elevator arrived that I touched his jacket sleeve.

"It's not your fault. If Tim is going to go gamble my property away, we needed to have it out. It wasn't pleasant, but it was necessary."

"Yeah, still sucks though. You deserve better." Calder stepped ahead of me into the elevator and hit the close door button, not the lobby. He gave me an intense once-over, and the scrutiny made me want to loosen my tie. Suddenly, it was very warm and cramped with only him and me in there.

"We are not making out in an elevator," I said with all the sternness I could muster.

"Well, there's an idea." He laughed lightly, but still didn't hit L. "I was going to steal a fast kiss, but if you want to go all the way there, I'm more than game."

"I don't." No matter what I said, I still snaked my arms around him when he dipped his head to claim my lips. It wasn't my smartest move, but after that meeting, having someone to hold on to felt so damn good. Calder was good at being comforting too, pulling me close and kissing me gently. True to his word, he didn't try for a grope or even go for tongue, simply offering sweet solace and then releasing me to finally hit the Lobby button.

"You might be better than a cocktail as far as stress relief," I teased, liking how he preened at the praise.

"Good. If you want, we could get the food to go. I wouldn't object." He gave me another of those heated looks. I reached to loosen my tie, but he batted my hand away. "That's for me for later. Or sooner if you want the to-go option."

"You're too tempting." I groaned as we reached the lobby. "But my stepmom is bringing the girls back to my place after their burger dinner."

"Ah. Limited privacy and opportunity. I got you, Doc. It was only an idea." Calder didn't sound particularly put out. Confident as ever, he led the way out of the building. "Cocktail it is."

"Do you need directions?" I pulled out my phone.

"Memorized them." He tapped his temple before zipping his jacket. The sun was already fading, replaced by a wintery wind rolling in off the Sound. Holding out a hand, he smiled, demeanor all mischievous and his excitement contagious. "Come on. It's not far."

Holding hands was decidedly date-like. I should decline. But the memory of that sweet kiss lingered, and I took his hand before I could talk myself out of it.

"You didn't have to do that. Giving up your claim to the cabin so easily, I mean." I studied his face, but his cheerful expression never wavered.

"Yeah, I did. Tim's a jerk, looking for loopholes and trying to milk you for cash. That cabin means something to you, and maybe he couldn't see it, but I do."

Buttery warmth spread across my chest, chasing away the chill. Calder truly was a good guy. "If the lawyers said you had a half interest, I'd buy it out."

"Nah. I'm not hurting for cash, and you don't need another of Tim's messes."

"Too true." I followed him into an upscale restaurant. The smell of meat and strong spices greeted us along with a lively after-work crowd. Tastefully decorated in a black-and-gray color scheme with pops of red, the place was half-full. A young hostess led us to a table near the window and left us with an impressive drinks menu.

"I drove, so I better stick to something light," I mused as I scanned the list, considering a kimchi Bloody Mary or a Seoul Mule cocktail or another of the inventive drinks before settling on a fruity soju drink that promised more fruit than alcohol. "However, my car being close means that I can drop you at the ferry, save you the walk or bus."

"Excellent." His expression turned decidedly smug, small smile and crinkles around his eyes.

"What's that smirk for?" Flirting with him was simply too easy, my voice already that much lighter and huskier and we hadn't even gotten our drinks.

"Nothing. Only that I'm totally getting another kiss after dinner."

"We'll see." Cheeks burning, I studied the menu to avoid his cocky gaze. After we placed our drink and appetizer order, the prospect of more kissing kept dancing through my head, making my pulse thrum.

"Is that why you offered to help with cabin repairs?" I asked, trying to keep my voice light. "You're hoping for a repeat?"

"Well, I'm not going to turn it down." He winked at me as the cocktails arrived, waiting until the server departed to continue. "I'll be honest. Sex for me doesn't usually feel like it did with you. I want to explore more, see if I can figure out why."

Smile dipping, he darted his gaze around the room before taking a long sip of his soju and tonic, which was garnished with thin strips of celery.

"So, you want to sleep with me as research?" I used a stern tone even as my ego thrilled.

"That and it would be fun." He shrugged, tone carefully casual. The little bit of hesitance there in his eyes made my resolve soften. "Maybe I can't ever duplicate it, but I can enjoy a second helping or two."

"My inner science geek is rather impressed at the chance to help you test a variety of findings." Yup. We were totally kissing again later. And maybe more. But I didn't need him thinking he needed to trade me for the experience. Fiddling with my garnish, I dropped the flirty tone. "But I could still kiss you again sometime and hire a handy person to do the repairs."

"Your asshole ex already took enough of your cash. And where's the fun in hiring it out?"

"Indeed." It all came down to fun for Calder, and I needed to remember that. No matter how good he was at comfort, he wasn't the kind of guy to stick around for life's unfun parts.

The appetizer arrived right then—an assortment of meaty skewers and little bites like crispy mushrooms, and we each grabbed a skewer.

"I've got leave next weekend," Calder said between bites, more of that take-charge nature of his. Of course he'd want a firm plan. "Couple of days off as long as I'm back by Sunday evening. What do you say?"

"My stepmom is heading to Aspen. I'd have to bring the girls." As always, I couldn't seem to find my way to a firm no with him.

"I figured they'd come. You can probably use their help on easier cleaning tasks. And as for the other, if you visit me after lights out, I'll never tell." He grinned slyly.

"The work does need to get done." I was waffling my way toward yes.

And Calder knew it, grinning wide and raising his glass. "Excellent. It's a—"

"We're not dating." I held up a hand, but he simply kept right on smiling.

"Of course not. We talked about that—neither of us dates. But there's a wide territory between no relationships ever and long-term commitment. Like friendship. You need a friend." His tone was perfectly reasonable, yet it also made my stomach do this weird clench.

"A friend who kisses me silly?" I went for the joke because

no way was I letting myself get disappointed at the reminder that Calder didn't do relationships.

"Yup. Definitely that. I'm planning on it." His twinkling eyes made all sorts of promises for after we ate, and made my insides glow. He was right. I did need this, even if I didn't want to.

"I'll pack extra pancake mix." I sighed dramatically like giving in was such a hardship. "And you'll get your weekend with your friends on your next weekend off after that as a thank-you for the help."

"It's a deal." He popped one of the beef appetizer bites in his mouth. "This is good. I like all the choices here. What do you say we order a few more small plates instead of entrées? That way we can share and try more things."

"Are you sure this isn't a date?" I teased as I reached for the appetizer menu.

"Call it what you want, Doc. As long as I get a kiss at the pier."

"That easy?" I shook my head.

"Yup, I try. Now, let's see what food sounds fun..." He leaned across the small table to point to a selection on the menu, and I nearly kissed him right then.

Oh, he was trouble all right. The fun kind, for sure, but also the kind that could leave a mark if I wasn't careful.

Something about him, though, made me reckless. I let him talk me into trying new things to eat as easily as he'd convinced me to do the cabin repair weekend. Work. We were going to work, not play. But it was easy to forget that as we ate our way through an impressive selection of small plates while sharing stories of other food we liked.

"If you like spicy, there's this place near base in Hawaii that does these ginger chili wings. Man, I love visiting that base." Calder's tone was decidedly wistful.

"They sound good. Is it hard not being out on a sub right now?"

He made a pinched face. "You asking as a shrink?"

"No, as a friend." Maybe I wasn't the only one who could use someone.

He took a few bites of food before finally sighing. "Yeah, it's hard. Sucks because I am damn good at what I do on the sub and I've been at it over a decade now." His ever-present smile was gone, and his eyes were tight. "I love the pace of the sub, the focus it requires. Everything feels important."

"You'd be a good surgeon." Trying to lower the tension, I smiled at him. "Adrenaline junkie, life-or-death decisions, long hours. You'd be perfect."

"Thought you weren't going to analyze me?" he teased, stealing another shrimp dumpling. "But you're not wrong. I don't like being bored, and I like responsibility while still being part of a team."

"And you don't have that now with what you are doing on base?"

He groaned even before I finished the question. "This assignment isn't terrible. This week I got to work out an urgent supply situation. That was good. But there's talk about extending my time on shore, and I'd rather be where I can be most useful and that's on a sub."

"I get that." I used a soothing tone, regretting bringing up an uncomfortable subject for him. But curiosity got the better of me. "Are they worried about your health on the sub?"

"Probably." He stabbed some seaweed salad with his fork. "A repeat concussion would suck, and falling is always a risk on the sub."

"But one you're willing to take?" I wasn't a neurologist, but I knew plenty about the aftereffects of a head injury. They weren't anything to mess around with.

However, Calder simply made a dismissive gesture. "Life is a risk. Bottom line, I can do more good deployed and be less bored, so win."

"Winning is good." I was more of the opinion that life was a series of compromises that kept us safe and relatively healthy, but I wasn't going to argue with his life philosophy. And I admired his work ethic and commitment to his job. "I see with my patients how important it is to be able to keep doing what you love, so I understand you wanting to be back out there."

"Yeah. Tell me more about how you keep your patients working longer." It was a clear bid to move the conversation away from himself, but I didn't mind. I loved how easily we could flow from trivial to serious and back again and how intently he listened to all of it.

And like how I enjoyed performing stories for the girls, I enjoyed sharing about patients, warming to the audience with little details and anecdotes. Making Calder laugh was the best feeling.

"I'm sure you're an awesome doctor, but man, you could also be a comic. You're too good at the doctor humor and impressions."

"Eh. I enjoyed drama class and high school and college theater. Making people smile is fun." I met his gaze so he'd know that the pleasure truly was in making him specifically smile.

"Couldn't you do local theater? My brother Roger's wife has done some community theater. Small productions, but she has fun."

"I haven't done much since college, but maybe when the girls are older." It would be different if I had more help with them, but I didn't, so I tried not to dwell on hobbies I'd had to let go of. The girls were more than worth the sacrifice of a little free time.

Calder kept me talking through dessert of a ginger sorbet, and we were both smiling as we ventured out into the chilly night.

"My parking garage is near here." I pulled out my phone for exact directions, and Calder peered over my shoulder.

"Good." He gave me a lightning-fast kiss on the neck before I could object, then set off in the right direction.

"You memorized the map that quickly?"

"Yep. When I'm properly motivated, there are not many logistical challenges I can't meet."

"I'll keep that in mind." I sped up to match his strides. How he could make map reading and logistics sound so sexy, I had no clue. Heat gathered low in my gut as we neared the garage. I hadn't made out in a car in years, yet Calder had me craving it.

He must have been anticipating it too because his movements took on a quiet efficiency, like he'd already mapped out the best route to my lips.

Sure enough, as soon as we were both in my SUV, he swiveled in the passenger seat. "My kiss."

"I thought you wanted one at the pier?" I felt free and flirty and at least ten years younger.

"There too." He licked his lips but didn't reach for me. That was cute, how he waited for me to make the first move. It was a departure from his ordinary in-charge self, and I liked seeing him with his guard down, not afraid to let someone else lead.

The power he bestowed on me made me giddy, almost giggly as possibilities raced through my mind. I wanted to make this good for him. Memorable even. Maybe sex wasn't on the agenda, but I could be the best damn good-night kiss he'd ever had.

That in mind, I leaned over the console and claimed his mouth. Softly, like he had kissed me in the elevator, and unhurried, like we had all night, not a few stolen minutes. If it was slow he enjoyed, then slow he would get, a gradual build from featherlight brushes to little tongue and lip teases to tiny nips before finally slipping into deeper forays.

He'd said things felt different with me. Better. My ego liked being special for him and that made me both more aggressive and more inventive than usual. He tasted sweet and gingery, cold lips from the night air, hot tongue, and I couldn't get enough. Trying things to see what he'd like best—a bite here, a suck there—was fun.

Fun.

Maybe there was something to his worldview after all because right then fun felt like the only thing that mattered.

"Oh fuck. You're too good at this." Groaning low, he reached for my collar, running a blunt finger all along my neck. "This has been driving me wild all night. You all buttoned-up and professional while I remember how wild you went for neck kisses."

"Yes." I sucked in a breath, waiting for him to put me out of my misery as he kept fiddling with my collar and tie. "I want—"

Buzz. My phone cut me off with an insistent message alert. And it didn't matter what I wanted from Calder, I had to check and make sure it wasn't something wrong with the girls.

"Sorry." I wiggled so I could fish my phone out of my pocket.

"It's okay. You're an in-demand guy." He fell back against his seat. "I'll keep."

For how long remained to be seen. There was only so much patience for kid interruptions most fun-loving singles had.

"It's my stepmom." I looked up from scanning the message. "They're back at the house. I should—"

"Go. You can't miss bedtime." He gave me a rueful smile.

"I'm sorry."

"Don't be. You've got a command story performance to deliver. Or rather, be sorry and make it up to me next weekend." He leered wickedly at me.

"Maybe I will." My whole body thrummed with everything I wanted from him. That determination of his was going to get him everywhere.

Chapter Fifteen

Calder

See you soon. Funny what a difference one text could make. My drive to the cabin for the work weekend with Felix and the girls felt far less lonely than my first trek there. Felix and I had been texting on the regular all week, silly stuff like food memes and cute kid stories and flirty things like veiled references to kissing, but his hopeful text that morning had buoyed me the most. I liked not being the only one counting down until we could see each other again.

Even with weekend traffic, the drive seemed to go faster this time and even the bear sign looked a little friendlier as I turned into the drive. Felix's SUV was already parked in front of the cabin, and he must have just arrived because the girls were still unbuckling as I pulled up alongside him.

"Calder!" Charlotte had many bags and belongings as she climbed out of the car. "I brought my book of bones."

"Excellent." I relieved her of two of the backpacks. I might not understand her interests, but her enthusiasm was infectious. Setting her bags on the porch, I returned to help Felix, who was unloading the rear hatch.

"Hi." His smile was warm, but his eyes were slightly shy as if he were remembering that parking garage kiss and unsure how to greet me. "How was the drive?"

"Not bad. No sign of a storm this weekend." I'd spent all week and most of the drive replaying that kiss myself, but the girls were racing back and forth, retrieving bags and asking questions, so it wasn't like I could simply plant one on him right there. I'd told him I could wait, but my gut still fluttered every time my eyes landed on his lips.

"Whee." Twirling down the steps, Charlotte interrupted my staring contest with Felix. "I wish it would storm! I like snow."

Felix saved her from colliding with the car by redirecting her toward the open space in front of the cabin. "Do a good job of helping with the work, and maybe I'll take you up to the visitor center to the snow play and sledding area. They have snow tubes and things like that."

"That sounds fun." I grabbed some grocery bags from the back of the SUV.

"You can come." Charlotte offered first, but Felix nodded as well.

"I might." I followed Felix into the cabin and set my load of bags on the kitchen counter. "Think you brought enough groceries, Doc?"

He laughed, a real chuckle, some of the awkwardness draining away as we started putting stuff away. "Couldn't risk having to live on jerky and eggs. Or pancakes. I thought we could make pasta tonight."

"You remembered that I can do spaghetti?" My ego perked up right along with my posture. I liked how he truly listened to my stories, remembering even small details.

"I didn't want to miss our chance to have your specialty."

"Oh, you've got more than one chance." The girls were nowhere to be seen, so I risked a suggestive tone and look to match. Prowling closer, I reached for him, but he stepped back.

"Did you know you have bones in your ear?" Charlotte popped up over the breakfast bar.

"Really?" Felix shot me an apologetic smile, but I shrugged. If the kid interruptions were the price I had to pay to get him alone later, I didn't mind. And honestly, Charlotte was rather cute, the way she knew so many big facts. Madeline was far less talkative and seemed less happy to see me, but I liked her too, the way she was talented at sliding her own requests or observations in between Charlotte's monologues.

"Should we start dinner or do we have time to start on my list?" I asked Felix once the last of the food was put away.

"Your list, huh?" Both of Felix's well-groomed eyebrows went up.

"Well, you sent it to me." He'd sent me the list as a picture on the phone so that I could see what needed doing this weekend. The grainy image with its cluttered bullet points had practically screamed out for my talents. I retrieved a couple of printouts from my bag and handed one to him. "I might have improved upon what the management company sent you. I organized it into subtasks and things that might be kid-appropriate. Their column is pink."

Felix tilted his head like I'd grown a second nose. "You made a spreadsheet for the weekend?"

"Overkill?" I rubbed the back of my neck. I was so used to organizing as part of my job that I forgot that not everyone shared my love of planning.

"No, I'm impressed."

"Told you. I'm good at logistics." I might have a fun-loving rep, but organizing spreadsheets and having clear tasks always made me happy. I could think on the fly, but I kept my sub running with my advance planning. "And speaking of supplies, I picked up a few things to supplement the toolbox."

"You didn't have to do that. I can pay you back."

"We can work that out later." I made a dismissive gesture and could practically hear my brothers laughing at me. Me not care about repayment? Yeah. I had it bad for Felix.

"All right. But we will settle up at some point." Felix wagged a finger at me. "Now, what's first on your chart?"

"A number of the items have to do with loose things like cabinet handles." I dug around in my bag until I came up with a roll of yellow tape. "So I want the girls to go test every handle in the cabin and put a piece of tape on the loose ones. You and I will follow behind with screwdrivers."

"Yay!" Charlotte cheered while Madeline took the tape from me, and we all spent a fun hour testing doors and tightening screws.

"That was a brilliant way to involve them." Felix patted my back. We'd ended up back in the kitchen, working on adjacent cabinets while the girls checked the bathroom for other loose handles. "Didn't you say you thought you were bad with kids?"

"It's not that I don't like them." I leaned into his touch, and he took the hint, rubbing lightly. "I'm always afraid of squashing or dropping the tiny ones. Or scaring them. Or making the bigger ones laugh because I did something stupid or didn't get a pop culture reference. And even older, well-behaved ones like yours are a lot of responsibility. I worry about screwing up."

Wow. I couldn't believe I'd spewed all that out loud, and I had to look down, closely examine each screw to see if it was stripped. I wasn't sure what it was about Felix that got me talking. Even family members and longtime acquaintances couldn't get this sort of deep thinking out of me.

"Calder. They're people. Small people." Felix's tone was patient and kind, but firm. Maybe that was part of why I liked talking to him so much. Felix never judged, but he also wouldn't let me get away with BS either. He moved his hand from my back to massage my tense neck. "Some kids are smart and funny and amazing. Most are good-hearted. A minority are mean-spirited or more challenging than others. A few will make you tear your hair out, but it's not that complicated to be good at interacting with them."

"It's not?" I all but purred at how good his touch felt.

"Simply keep doing what you've been doing. This idea of yours was great."

"Thanks." I tipped my head back, seeking a kiss, but right then Madeline came down the hall and Felix dropped his hand.

"I'm hungry." She glared at both of us. This was part of what I'd meant. Some kids I simply couldn't seem to charm.

"Dinner is spaghetti. Why don't you go pick out a book for tonight while Calder and I cook? It's your turn to pick." Felix gestured at the stairs and the girls clattered up them, bickering over what sort of story they were in the mood for later.

"Sorry. They seem to have impeccable timing today." Felix's tone was weary, and his eyes were apologetic when I spun to face him.

"Can I kiss you?" I pulled him closer and this time he let me. "Please?"

"Since you asked so nice..." He stretched to brush a light kiss across my lips. His mouth was familiar and warm, and I groaned low. Something about that sound must have done it for him because he deepened the kiss. We went from chaste and friendly to burn-the-kitchen-down hot in three seconds flat.

His mouth was urgent against mine and the gasp he made when I used my tongue against his went straight to my groin, but I was also on red-alert for noises from upstairs. Reluctantly, I released him.

"Wow. Um. Food." Felix rubbed his mouth with the back of his hand.

"Yes. We need to cook." I grinned because it was nice to see Felix as flustered as me. And also because cooking together was almost as fun as kissing, and getting dinner over with got us that much closer to bedtime.

I lined up ingredients while Felix retrieved a pasta pot and a skillet.

"Did you intend to arrange things by size order or was that a happy accident?" he teased as he set the skillet on the stove.

"Sorry. Organization just seems to happen with me." My neck heated.

"Don't apologize. I think it's cute. And a good trait."

"Thanks. Part of it is always having cramped shared spaces, both on the sub but also growing up and sharing small rooms in base housing. I got good at squeezing my stuff in."

Felix's admiring glance went a long way to making me less embarrassed. "I should have you come do our pantry at my house. Or maybe my closet."

"Is the closet in your bedroom? If so, sign me up." I leered at him, loving how he laughed. "Seriously though. I enjoy tasks like that. Invite me over sometime."

"Calder..."

I had a feeling he was about to lecture me about the inadvisability of a continued friendship between us. He was wrong, but before either of us could continue, Charlotte trotted down the stairs.

"I want Calder hot chocolate for dessert," she announced.

"Calder hot chocolate?" I looked over at Felix, who was filling the pasta pot with water.

"Apparently, you put in *two* marshmallows." He shook his head. "We've had to hear all week about how you do the best cocoa."

A soft spot deep in my chest pinched. "Yeah, I can do that again tonight."

"Good." Charlotte clapped her hands. "And then I want ten stories."

"Ten?" I echoed weakly, sensing bedtime slipping further away.

"How about two?" Felix suggested before lowering his voice to me. "I think they had soda at school. Or sugar. Maybe both. She's rather wired, whatever it is."

"I know the feeling." I'd been hyped all day myself. All week if I were honest. And even if it took ten stories and all my patience, I couldn't wait until Felix was all mine.

Chapter Sixteen

Felix

I hoped I wasn't too late. The girls had taken forever to settle. Two stories downstairs with Calder, another upstairs in the loft, several complicated questions from Charlotte, and a couple of deep thoughts from Madeline, and finally I was able to slip away. I fiddled with the woodstove and cleaned the kitchen until I was reasonably certain they were asleep and then at last I tapped on the bedroom door.

"Sleeping?" I asked in a low voice.

"As if." Calder lay on the bed, still fully clothed, reading one of the books I'd rejected as Charlotte's choice for story time, a compendium of unsolved mysteries. Probably my grandmother's, judging by the yellowed pages. Even though she'd had no love lost for my father's side of the family, Grandma would have liked Charlotte. Calder, too, for that matter, a thought that both made me smile and gave me pause.

"Too bad you're not looking for work," I teased him as I entered and shut the door. "You'd make a good after-school nanny for us. You and Charlotte could binge true crime shows and eat spaghetti every night."

"Ha. Navy might have something to say about that career shift. But when she gets older, I'll introduce her to the best of the horror genre." Calder laughed and so did I.

I didn't want to ruin the light mood by pointing out he likely wouldn't know us then. It was a nice image, even if it wouldn't come true, Charlotte having someone who shared her appetite for the spooky.

"Now, come over here. Please." His tone was commanding, but the *please* was utterly adorable, that hint of uncertainty he seemed to have around physical affection like catnip for me.

Locking the door, I quickly crossed to the bed, where he was patting the spot next to him. I liked how he didn't only seem to enjoy going slow but also seemed to need it on some level. He made even simple acts feel brand-new again.

Like the humble pleasure of stretching out next to someone, anticipation building, but nearness alone thrilling. And comforting. Lying down next to Calder reminded me how long it had been since I'd had someone to cuddle with. For all he loved sex, Tim was often hurried and goal-oriented, so cuddling had fallen off the agenda even before we split.

With Calder, though, nothing was rushed. His happy sigh as he pulled me closer was mirrored in my soul, a sensation of coming home. I snuggled in, simply soaking in the closeness. He smelled sporty, some trendy aftershave popular with the jock crowd, but on him the crisp scent was endearing. And his big arms were strong and warm around me.

Ripped had never been that much of a turn-on for me, but I couldn't deny his aesthetic appeal. Stroking his muscled forearms, I wrapped him more securely around me.

"This is nice." I rested my head on his shoulder.

"It is." He hummed contentedly, and we hung out like that for several long minutes, like electronic devices recharging their batteries. Utter bliss, absorbing his quiet energy.

"If I get any more relaxed, I'm going to drift off, so apologies if I start snoring." I faked a giant yawn, but genuine tiredness wasn't that far off.

"Feel free. I know you have to end up back on the couch, so I set an alarm for you, but I wouldn't mind holding you exactly like this until it buzzes."

"Exactly like this?" Tipping my head back, I found his mouth for a clumsy but sweet kiss. Speaking of sweet, he got major bonus points for being thoughtful about the alarm.

"Yep." He swept a broad hand down my front. "Of course, if you need help getting sleepy, I'm game for that too."

"Mmm. I like where this is heading." I preened into his touch.

"Yeah?" He pulled my shirt loose from my jeans. "I like this sweater. It's soft."

"Glad you approve." I sucked in a breath as he worked his hand under both my sweater and T-shirt. "I was half tempted to not change after seeing some patients this morning, let you have your fun with my tie."

"Darn practicality." He nipped at my neck. "This is sexy too, you all fuzzy and cuddly."

His lips and teeth felt so good on my skin that I groaned low, cock already throbbing. "It can be fuzzy on the floor too."

"That a hint?" He pushed my shirts up higher, palm skimming over my ribs and chest.

"If you want it to be." I could joke, but I had no interest in pressuring him further than he wanted to go. Like him, I was already high on the closeness, and much as I craved some skin, I'd be okay if this didn't end in orgasm.

My cock twitched impatiently in my jeans, objecting to that idea, but my brain was much more about figuring out what Calder wanted and needed. And maybe he didn't entirely know the answer to that because he took his time, playing with the edge of my sweater as he kissed my neck, delicious torture. Goosebumps multiplied on my arms and legs with each lick and tease.

"Fuck." I moaned softly. His thumb moved idly against my nipple, random sparks that joined the shower of sensations stemming from the neck kisses, and the combo was almost enough to get me there with zero friction or clothing removal.

"Okay, yeah, I want your collar out of the way." He rolled away enough so that we could both sit up and pull off our shirts. I toyed with my belt, not wanting to rush him, waiting until he nodded at my hand. "Jeans too. I want to see if the neck trick works a second time."

"Neck trick, huh?" I chuckled as I pulled off my pants and he did the same. "And, yes, it will work. I'm kind of embarrassingly easy."

"I love that about you." He grinned broadly. "Be easy all you want. Anything else unusual that gets you off? I want to know all your secrets."

"All of them?" I faked shock, eyes going wide, like I had anything worth hiding.

"All of them." Tickling me lightly, he tumbled us back onto the bed, naked now, and I groaned from how damn good his bare skin felt against mine. He had more body hair than a lot of fair-skinned guys, fuzzy chest and abs, which rubbed deliciously against me as he returned to spooning me. "Tell me everything."

"Uh… I'm pretty tame, honestly. Kiss my neck and give me anything resembling friction and I'll get there. Or grinding and kissing. Give me a steady diet of making out, and I'm a happy guy."

"What about the other stuff?" His hold on me tightened, and I could practically hear his frown. Heck. Maybe I'd misread him, and he wanted something other than fooling around and kissing endlessly. Most guys eventually did, so I made sure my smile didn't dip.

"It's all good. I'm not always the most on bottoming, but I will if that's what you're up for. I like oral too, giving especially." I started to turn in his embrace, but he held me fast.

"I wasn't hinting at wanting either of those things." His tone was still too serious as was his heavy sigh. "I love what we've been doing. Can I tell you something?"

"Absolutely." I had a feeling that if I looked up at him, he'd stop, so I let him talk into my hair.

"Sometimes I have a really hard time getting off. I hate disappointing people. Like oral is amazing but then I feel bad because someone's jaw is locking up and I'm nowhere close. Or we do all the prep and buildup for fucking, and then I still need my hand to climax. I feel like such a buzzkill."

"You're not," I hurried to add, but he was already shaking his head.

"Yeah. I kind of am. There's lasting a long time like sexy endurance and then there's marathon slog where I can legit sense that the other person really just wants to be done and go to sleep. So you being super easy to make come, that's amazing. I love that. Makes me want to get you off over and over."

"Well, I knew having a hair trigger would come in handy sometime…" I waited for him to laugh before getting more serious. "There's no one right way to have sex. Including not having it. If it doesn't feel good or does feel good for a while and then stops feeling good, it's okay to switch to things that do feel good. I'm not feeding you a line when I say that I really would be okay with kissing for the next three hours, even if neither of us comes. I can give myself orgasms. But self-cuddling is way harder."

"Isn't that the truth." He chuckled more freely now. "I

love cuddling. I miss being a teen when all the expectations for what comes after weren't there yet."

"They don't have to be there now. I am way too old to give a fuck about other people's expectations—"

"You're not old." He tickled me until I giggled. "See? Not old. And you're right. Maybe that's why it feels different with you. The pressure to fuck you through the mattress doesn't seem to be there."

I gulped because I honestly wouldn't turn that down, but I also meant what I said about liking other things more and about us setting our own rules. Seeing him so down on himself made my voice firmer even as my heart went that much more tender. "If you got to decide, like ordering at an ice cream place, no expectations or pressure, what would you like most right now?"

"Hmm." He kissed my neck in between making thinking noises that made my spine vibrate. "I want to kiss your neck while you tell me where else to touch you that makes you feel incredible, and I want to keep kissing you until you come, and then I want to cuddle you all boneless and happy. That was the best last time."

"Yeah, it was." My throat was strangely tight. His wants were so simple and so nicely aligned with mine that giving him this was ridiculously easy. "Let's do exactly that. And if you want to come too, I found it hot as hell when you stroked off last time, but I'm also cool if you don't want that."

"Not sure what I want. Rubbing against your ass feels good right now. I like lying like this."

"Me too." I tipped my head back for a leisurely kiss. The angle wasn't the best, but the gentle gratitude of his mouth more than made up for any neck strain. "We'll figure everything else out as we go."

Chapter Seventeen

Calder

I was naked in a bed with another person, and it was apparently A-OK if no one came. Well, Felix was going to come because getting Felix off was fun, all his little reactions and sounds. But I didn't have to, which was weird, but also freeing as hell. For all that I told others to have fun, shutting off my own inner perfectionist was hard.

Felix made it easy to let go though. I ran my hands all over his lean body. He was slim and strong, but not wiry or muscle-bound. I liked the softness to his belly and the downy hair on his thighs. I liked even more that he hadn't tried to use doctor or therapist talk on me when I'd told him about the unique way I seemed to be wired.

I wasn't clueless. I knew that sex drives came in many flavors and strengths, everything from ace to hypersexual, vanilla to kinky sprinkles, and lots of combos, but my body wasn't so easy to classify. I did have a sex drive, but I got randomly horny in hard-to-predict ways. And for whatever reason, friction or familiarity, I found it far easier to climax from my own hand. And Felix had taken all that at face value, made me feel normal even, and not tried to pin a label on it.

He seemed genuinely into my idea of me getting him off too, squirming to get closer and arching up his neck like a touch-starved cat. Careful to not leave any hard-to-explain marks, I resumed licking and kissing his neck.

"Yes. Like that," he said, head falling farther forward, opening more real estate for me to explore. He smelled like woodsmoke and expensive shampoo and something sweet that made his soft skin that much more fun to nibble.

My hands skimmed up and down his ribs in time with his sighs until he grabbed one of my hands and dragged it to his chest.

"Want something?" I nipped at the top of his spine.

"Yeah. Nothing too rough, but I love your hands on me while you attack my neck."

"I can do that." Closing my eyes, I let myself drink him in, one kiss at a time, one flick of my finger on his nipple at a time, his reactions streaming through me. He rocked against me and the friction against my hard cock made me throb. I wasn't near orgasm, but simply allowing the sensations to build without getting hung up on how long I was taking or other pressures was like flying, a soaring sort of pleasure almost better than being on edge.

"Please, Calder," Felix begged, moving shamelessly against me. The way he allowed himself to ask for exactly what he wanted was awe-inspiring, seeing someone let go like that.

Opening my eyes again, I slid a hand down to hover near his straining cock. "This?"

"Yes, that." He thrust up, dragging his cock along my palm. *Message received.* I smiled before resuming my neck kisses. Nipping at his shoulder, I experimented with tweaking his nipple more firmly to make him gasp. I countered those more intense touches with light strokes of his cock. His cock felt weighty in my hand. It had a natural curve that mine didn't and a flared, cut head that made him fun to play with. Pushing insistently against my hand, Felix made it clear he wanted a tighter grip, but I wanted him that much more desperate for it.

"Please. Need..." He trailed off on a near-whine as I finally gave in and stroked him in earnest now. Watching his face, I found a grip and rhythm that seemed to suit him. Less friction than I would have needed and slower paced, more time to use my thumb or a flick of my wrist to tease.

"Close?" I licked the side of his neck. "I wanna see you go."

"Yeah. God. Keep doing that," he panted. The way he kept wriggling and thrusting into my fist had me groaning too and rocking forward to meet his motions.

"Here. Let me show you something?" He reached back between us, hand brushing my cock as he angled it more down, between his thighs.

"Oh." Now I was the one to gasp.

"Good?" He moved his hand out of the way as I tried out thrusting like this.

"Yeah. Totally." This was a new one for me, but I liked it a great deal already. Not fucking, but way more pressure and rub than a hand or mouth.

"Sometime, we can try this with lube, but I'm way too close to go search some out." His breath came in small huffs.

"No, I like this. Tight." The drag of his skin against me made my whole body buzz. And when he tensed his legs, I groaned right along with him. "Wanna get you off."

"You are." He shivered as I sped up my hand and neck attention both. "That's it."

"Yeah." I could feel his body spiraling higher, the way his back went taut, muscles straining, abs clenching. My body vibrated with our shared energy as I pinched his nipple while raking my teeth across his shoulder.

"Calder. Going to..." His back arched and his thighs tightened as he shot creamy ropes all over my fist. I thrust harder against him, all of a sudden so close, his moans pushing me higher along with the tight pressure of his thighs. Not quite there, but almost, his heavy breathing having my balls lifting.

Almost. I made a frustrated noise.

"It's okay. Go on." Felix rolled away slightly, and that was all the permission I needed to get a hand on my cock.

"Kiss me," I demanded. And he did, mouth finding mine in a hungry, possessive kiss. One stroke became three became me coming in a single heartbeat. A nuclear warhead could have ripped through the room, and I wouldn't have noticed. I was that wrapped up in how damn good climax felt. Felix swallowed my moans and stroked my hair and face, kiss gradually gentling.

I still didn't know why it felt so different with him, but it did, and this part at the end where he took care of me on the way down was a big part of it.

"Thank you," I gasped when he finally released me.

"No need to thank me. Pretty sure we both won big there." Giggling like I'd tickled him, he used his discarded undershirt to clean us both off before settling back next to me. He yawned and rested his head on my shoulder. "You sure you set that alarm?"

"Positive." I reached for my phone on the nightstand and showed him before wrapping him in a tight embrace.

"Good." He kissed my neck before pulling the covers up around us both.

"Stay here a little longer," I whispered. He was a busy guy with a lot competing for his attention, but in that moment, he was all mine and I was keeping him as long as he'd let me.

Chapter Eighteen

Felix

"Exactly how good do I have to be to go to the sledding place?" Charlotte was in a bargaining mood after a morning of cleaning and repair work. She had a purple headband holding back her curls and her nose was dusty.

"I'll ask Calder where we are on the list," I offered, looking up from wiping down a baseboard near the stairs.

"Can he come with us?" she asked.

"We'll see. He might be wanting some alone time." Standing up, I patted her head. Calder had been excellent about involving the girls all morning, but since he wasn't used to kids as much, he was undoubtedly craving a break.

"Nope. I don't do alone time." Proving me wrong, Calder came down the stairs, carrying his drill and looking far sexier than he had any right to. His heavy tread matched the little hitch in my pulse at his appearance. "The snow sounds like a fun break. Maybe we can get lunch out, skip cooking."

"I'll tell Madeline." Charlotte raced away before I could disagree. Not that I would. Having Calder along would be more fun than me on my own with the girls. And the more time we spent together, the more I was coming around to his way of thinking that fun mattered.

Perhaps some of that shift was discovering that Calder was

actually a lot more complex than his good-time guy persona. He had a serious side with a perfectionism I rarely saw outside of medical school. That intense drive to succeed made him a great organizer and also explained a fair bit about his character, and it made him more likable and relatable for me. And like him, I did, especially after the night before. He'd been honest and real in a way a lot of lovers weren't, and that had made the whole experience that much more powerful.

"We got a lot done this morning." He smiled at me, eyes bright and way more alert on low sleep than me. I'd intended to drift off next to him, let the alarm send me back to the couch, but we'd ended up having a sleepy meandering conversation about everything from first crushes and awkward first times to more recent relationships and even some about our jobs. I'd felt like I was back in college, the urge to get to know him better beating out sleep, and we'd both been startled when the alarm had buzzed.

And now I had to pay the piper, so I yawned and headed toward the coffeepot.

"We did good. We earned a break for sure. I can drive if you want to ride with us?"

I half expected him to want to drive himself, but he nodded agreeably. "Sure. Let me change into pants better suited for playing in the snow and we can go."

In short order we were all in cold weather wear and headed up the mountain to the visitor center parking lot, which served as a hub for snowshoeing and cross-country skiing enthusiasts out to enjoy the trails while young families headed to the snow play area with its groomed sledding hills.

Being a Saturday, finding a parking spot was a challenge and the trek to the snow play area was crowded with lots of happy faces coming and going. Calder insisted on carrying the plastic toboggan we'd brought, and he and Charlotte marched ahead of us.

Hands on her hips, she surveyed the area like a pint-sized mountaineer. The area featured a number of sledding runs of various lengths and inclines from places for the tiny tots to higher hills that had even adults whooping and hollering as they slid down on sleds and inner tubes.

"I'm going to do the biggest hill." Charlotte turned her conquering gaze back to us.

"I'm not doing it." Madeline wrinkled her nose. "Look how fast they're going."

"I know! It's awesome!" Charlotte spread her arms wide like that might let her capture more of the experience.

"Why don't we start with one of the smaller ones?" I suggested, trying to keep the peace, but also find something that might tempt Madeline into trying.

"Yeah, work up to the bigger runs. That's smart." Calder nodded before we walked toward the nearest hill.

"Thanks for backing me up," I said to him in a low voice as we found places in line. "Sibling harmony is hard."

"Don't I know it. Roger, my oldest brother, always wanted to do the hardest hike, the biggest dirt bike ramp." Calder adjusted the sled to his other arm.

"Not you?" I kept an eye on the girls, who had started playing in the snow with some of the other kids in line. "I would have thought you'd be the adventurous one?"

"Eventually. I do love adrenaline." He grinned broadly. "But early on, they had to use all sorts of dares and bets to get me to try new things that I ended up loving. I used the same tactic with my younger brother, not sure he appreciated it though."

"That's the one dating your best friend?"

"Yup. He hates bets. Thinks I'm obsessed with winning.

He's a musical genius and all about celebrating differences and everyone having a good time. We haven't always gotten along."

"It's almost our turn!" Charlotte turned toward us before racing back to the other kids.

Even as the kids pulled my attention away, I still wanted to offer Calder some reassurance. "Perhaps it'll get easier hanging out with him now?"

"Yeah. In some ways things are better now. But they're stationed in Connecticut, and mainly, I just miss them both. And sounds like I'd better come up with an idea for a wedding present quickly. But I am *not* a shopper."

Luckily for Calder, I did like to shop. And maybe I couldn't offer a way to improve the past with his brother, but I could offer help. "Something handmade. There's a website with all handmade gifts that I use for weddings and appreciation gifts for our office staff."

"You can help me find something." His fast smile was undoubtedly because I'd given him another excuse for contact. But before I could waffle, he gestured to Charlotte. "Come on! You're next. You ready to go?"

"Hold on tight!" I reminded her as she got settled in the toboggan. Then we hurried back to the base of the hill as Charlotte gleefully sped down, chortling the whole way.

"Way to go!" Calder clapped her on the shoulder as she returned to us.

"Thanks." She beamed at him before thrusting the sled at us and taking off after the bigger kids. Calder watched her go, a strange expression on his face. Maybe he was still thinking about his brothers, another layer to him, the brother trying hard to do better. And perversely, the more complex he became, the more interested I was, and that was fast becoming a problem.

"Maybe I do want to try." Madeline came trotting back up to us, cheeks pink and voice breathless.

"Awesome news." Calder gave her a high five. "Do you want me to carry the sled up for you?"

She nodded. "I'm going to try being brave because everyone else is having fun."

"You don't have to do something simply because everyone else is," I reminded her, which earned me an epic eye roll.

"I *know*. But I want to see what it's like." She drew herself up taller, a stoic set to her chin that hadn't been there before. A tight place in my chest twinged.

"That's the spirit." Calder swooped up the toboggan and headed back toward the line for the easy hill, coaching her as they went. "Now what you want to do is relax, don't worry too much about steering. Don't forget to look around you on the way down."

"Now that's a good dad." A woman standing nearby stepped closer. "Your husband is a good guy."

"My… *Oh*." My eyes were likely dinner-plate huge as my jaw dropped open. I closed it and gave the woman what I hoped passed for a casual smile. "He's not mine. But thanks."

The woman's assumption wasn't that unreasonable. Calder did look like the girls, what with his fair coloring and long limbs, and he'd been doting on them the whole time we'd been at the play area. Even now I could see him joking around with Madeline in line, making her laugh. And if I had a moment—a microsecond—when I wished for the impossible, well, I certainly wasn't confessing that to a stranger.

I'd spent so long telling myself that I didn't need a partner and that solo-parenting was the path for me, that I didn't exactly welcome the reminder of how nice it could be to have someone to share the work and joys.

Like the triumphant way Calder raced back to Charlotte

and me, Madeline fast on his heels. I'd had my heart in my throat her whole ride down the hill, but Calder did a terrific job of seeming like he'd believed in her the whole time. "She did great!"

"That was amazing!" Madeline crowed, arms wide and voice loud, more like her sister's usual mode. "I want to go again!"

"Me too!" Of course, Charlotte was game and the girls took several more turns on the small hill before gamely tackling a medium-sized one.

"I wanna see Calder go!" Charlotte demanded after another successful trip down the hill.

"That I want to see." I pushed on his massive shoulder, not that I thought it would take much to convince him to take a spin.

"And you, Uncle Felix," Madeline added.

"Oh I don't think I should..."

"Sure you should." Shoving the toboggan at me, Calder steered me toward the slope. "Here you go. Have at it."

Both girls cheered as I made a show out of groaning and being all reluctant to get more laughter and cheers from them. "Okay, okay. One time."

In reality, I probably would have agreed even if Calder hadn't been along. He didn't have a monopoly on having fun with the girls, but he certainly did have a way of amping my enjoyment way up.

"We'll cheer for you," he called after me. The line moved crisply, and my turn arrived before I could talk myself out of this idea. The three of them stood at the bottom the slope, faces turned toward me.

Pushing aside my worries about looking silly, I took a deep breath. I launched myself down the hill, zipping along at a skin-stinging clip. My lungs burned, like my oxygen levels were soaring right along with me. All too soon I arrived back at the bottom and stumbled toward Calder and the girls on shaky legs.

"You did great." He threw an easy arm around my shoulders. Maybe he *was* mine. Only for a second. But it counted.

"Thanks. I lost my hat though." I patted my bare head, hair undoubtedly sticking every which way.

"Here. Have mine." Calder stuck his cheerful orange hat on my head. "My brother's wife knits whenever he's deployed, keeps us all in hats. Looks better on you anyway." He winked at me before grabbing the sled. "My turn. Let's see if I can beat your time."

"Always a race." Chuckling, I shook my head at him. His long strides easily carried him back up the hill, and it wasn't long until he was speeding back down to us, big grin on his face.

Mine. Only for this moment, but mine. I got to claim him, and today that was enough, the rush of pride and happiness making me feel like I was back skidding down the slope myself. Who needed adrenaline when they had Calder?

"Way to go!" I cheered when he returned to us.

"Who's ready for lunch?" He accepted high fives from both girls. "Bet we can find something with bones for Charlotte."

"You're silly." She giggled and poked his sleeve. "I want a burger."

"Me too." The moment might not last, but I sure was going to enjoy it.

"Sounds good. Lead the way back to the car, Miss Charlotte." Calder made a show of following Charlotte, making all three of us laugh.

"Thank you," I said to him as the girls raced ahead.

"For what?" His brow wrinkled.

"For being so good with them."

"Eh. I'm just having fun." He put his arm back around my shoulders.

"Me too." And I was. As long as I remembered that fun was all this could be, we'd be fine, and I wasn't going to let weighty questions distract me from enjoying how damn good he felt by my side.

Chapter Nineteen

Calder

"I should be sleepy." Felix yawned against my chest. It was late, and by all rights we should have been sleeping hours earlier, but we kept thinking of new things to talk about. "I'm gonna regret this tomorrow."

"Me too," I groaned and held him closer, no intention of actually going to sleep before he did. This was simply so good. I wasn't sure I'd ever enjoyed talking with another person this much. Somehow we'd slid from another molten make-out session into a discussion of basic training versus medical school. Spirited debates were always going to win out over sleep for me, even if I'd need more coffee in the morning.

"You?" Felix lightly elbowed me. "You're like the star of a battery commercial, never losing your charge."

"Hey, you wore me out today." I rolled my neck from side to side. My whole body had a well-used feeling that made my chest lift.

"Yeah, I did, didn't I?" Felix smirked before dropping his gaze to our naked bodies. Neither of us had bothered getting dressed after making out earlier, choosing to do the bare minimum of cleanup and snuggle under the covers instead.

"You're cute smug. I meant the work around the cabin and the sledding, but yeah, make it about the sex." I pretended to be put out when actually I too was rather proud. I'd gotten him off in record time. Win.

"Sorry." He blushed adorably, looking far younger with pink cheeks, reminding me of how he'd looked flying down the sledding hill. Man, that had been a sight. Almost as good as watching him come. Felix enjoying himself was never going to get old for me.

"Don't be." I kissed his forehead. "Keep talking long enough and you can go for doubles."

His cock had perked back up the longer we cuddled. The only thing better than getting him off once would be doing it twice. As nice as it felt to climax while he kissed me and I touched myself, I loved his orgasms most of all.

"Now who's sure of themselves?" Felix tilted his head up, clear invitation.

"Me." I kissed him long and tender. Impossibly, he still tasted sweet, better than the chocolate ice cream we'd had for dessert.

He sighed happily when we finally came up for air. "See, this is why I can't sleep. I'm stockpiling kisses."

"Until the next time we can be together?" I asked carefully. We'd been inching toward this topic all evening while also avoiding the issue like it was surrounded by hazard tape.

"Calder..."

"Tomorrow doesn't have to be goodbye." My voice was firm. I did have to leave by midmorning to be back on base in time, but I was already full of plans for Felix, and I wasn't giving up easily.

"It should." Eyes serious, he rolled so he could peer down at me.

"You promised to help me find a wedding present for Derrick and Arthur," I reminded him. I wasn't above using his help, especially if it got me more of those kisses. "Also, you've got a pantry for me to organize. And we don't need a lawyer meeting to decide to have dinner. This doesn't have to be complicated."

"But it is." Felix groaned and flopped back down next to me.

"You're overthinking it." I stroked a hand down his torso, trying to smooth away his growing tension. "You'll need to give me the keys for the weekend I'm borrowing the place, right? So we meet up, maybe for ramen this time, exchange keys, make out in your car a little. Easy."

"You're all-in on the friends-who-kiss plan, aren't you?" His eyes narrowed, but his tone said he was at least a little impressed.

"It's a good plan." I kept my voice even and casual, not wanting to let on how desperate I was to see him again, and we hadn't even parted yet. "I like you. I like hanging out together. I don't see a reason to stop."

"I can't start dating. It's not fair—"

"I'm not asking you to date." Actually, Felix was rapidly making me rethink my own stance on dating. If it got me more late-night conversations and leisurely make-out sessions, I'd be game to try. However, he'd been so adamant on this point that I was pursuing the friends-with-benefits angle harder. "We're friends, remember? And we kiss as long as kissing seems fun, and if you meet someone you do want to do the serious relationship thing with, we dial back the kissing."

I'd probably hate that person even more than I hated his ex, but I also was a realist. I wasn't the best relationship bet, even if I was willing. I'd take what I could as long as it made him happy, and step back when it didn't.

"I don't want either of us to get hurt." His tone was all adult and reasonable, and irritated me to the point that my fists clenched.

My voice shifted from light to pointed, honesty seeping past my frustration. "I don't want anyone hurt either, but *I'm* gonna be hurt if you don't want to be friends at all. And I think *you're* going to be hurt if you continue to tell yourself you don't have room for adult fun or friendship in your life."

"You're not wrong." Rather than getting angry, Felix deflated and so did I. Not wanting to fight more, I kissed his temple.

"I'm smarter than I look."

"You are." Turning his head so we could kiss for real, Felix sighed against my mouth. "I guess if I have to get you the keys anyway..."

"Exactly." I sure as hell wasn't going to point out that Felix could simply give me back Tim's set of keys, which I'd returned to him at the lawyer's office. He could send me home with those, but then I wouldn't get my date. "I'll start researching places to eat."

"When do you want the cabin? In two weeks?"

"Yeah, that sounds about right." I stretched, way happier to talk practical details than trying to convince him that we made excellent friends with benefits. "Max will need to get leave. They work the cranes lots of weird shifts. We'll probably get another buddy or two to join us."

"I hope you have fun." Felix's smile was fond and something about it made a bright new idea march through my brain.

"Hey." I rolled onto my elbow, looming over him. "You could come."

"I could what?" He blinked up at me.

"Come hang out and play cards and ski with us and give me a reason to be the one who claims the bedroom." Oh, I loved this idea. Loved it. I beamed at him, but he continued to stare at me like I'd sprouted horns.

"You don't seriously want me along."

"I think we just established that I do." I kept my voice even, but I was rapidly losing patience for needing to prove to him that I really wanted him in my life.

"Thanks." His voice softened right along with his eyes as he touched my shoulder. "I can't leave the girls, and you need an adults-only weekend, not more family fun."

"Debatable." I did want the weekend I'd promised my friends, but I'd had a ton of fun that day with Felix and the girls. I wouldn't be opposed to more days like this at all. However, I was also firmly Team Felix Needs a Break as well. "If you did get a sitter or arrange a sleepover for them, you could come alone, grab some kid-free time with us. Even short notice. It would be more fun with you along."

Felix studied me intently for a long moment. "You really mean that, don't you?"

"I like you," I said softly, grabbing his hand.

"I like you too." He squeezed my hand before groaning dramatically. "We are so screwed."

"Nah. I've been in no-win situations before. This isn't one of them." I made myself sound way more confident than I felt, a talent that had gotten me far in the military and that worked here, earning me a cautious smile from Felix.

"I hope you're right."

"I usually am." I puffed up my chest because we both needed a laugh.

"Humbleness is an excellent friend trait."

"Hey, I know what I'm good at." Still looming over him, I dropped my head to kiss him softly, and he welcomed me eagerly with a hungry noise that made my own cock pulse with renewed interest.

"Well, you are good at that at least." He tossed his head back, expression all dreamy.

Damn, I did love when he praised my kissing. “You sure? Maybe I need more practice.”

“Well, on second thought…” He pulled me down to him, and I went happily. I’d won. I got more Felix. Now to make sure he didn’t regret it.

Chapter Twenty

Felix

"There's somewhere you'd rather be." Gabrielle regarded me with shrewd eyes over the rim of her wineglass. It was an exceptionally nice pinot noir from the Willamette Valley, assertive cherry notes along with subtle hints of marzipan, lemon, and black tea, and I'd barely touched my glass.

"Nope," I lied. Maybe if I said it loud enough, I'd start believing it. But Calder was at the cabin with his friends and I was here in Seattle having dinner with my stepmother and the girls at her house. We'd finished the food and the girls had run off to the TV, leaving us to our wine. And pointed questions I'd rather not get into. "Long week. The nanny I thought we hired two weeks ago didn't work out."

"Again?" Gabrielle raised a sculpted eyebrow. With her fluffy ash-blond hair and high-maintenance makeup and nails, she looked closer to my age than she actually was. "What decrepit object did Charlotte show them this time?"

"For once, it wasn't Charlotte." I glanced at the dining room archway, not wanting either kid to think the ongoing nanny crisis was their fault. "Or ants. Or even my unpredictable work hours. The nanny's boyfriend got a transfer to San Francisco and she wants to go too."

Of course, her decision to accompany him might have been

hastened by Charlotte explaining all the steps for an appendectomy, but I wasn't going to risk Charlotte hearing that complaint. I loved how into collecting medical facts she was, and the rest of the world could adjust its expectations accordingly rather than try to force her into some box.

"Do you think you'll have someone by next weekend?" Gabrielle tapped a pink nail against her glass, the sharp sound putting me on edge as much as her question.

"Why?"

"I had an idea." Tone crafty, she leaned forward, silky top swishing. My back stiffened. Her ideas were usually expensive or impractical or both. She'd received the bulk of my father's estate, and tended to forget that the rest of the world had rules and budgets.

"I'm worried already." I kept my voice light but wary.

"I want to take the girls to Vancouver. There's a play an old friend is producing—very kid friendly." She smiled broadly, but I wasn't buying it.

"You said that about the one you took me to as a kid where everyone died."

"Not everyone, darling." She gave a dismissive wave of her hand. She hadn't been a terrible stepmother and she had instilled my passion for the performing arts in school, but she'd also had rather flexible ideas about what was age appropriate. "This one is more for families. There's singing and dancing and big set pieces. Even Miss Hard-to-Please Madeline will love it. And we can do Granville Island and Forest Park and a bunch of other sights."

"I don't particularly crave a weekend of sightseeing." Damn it. I *did* want to be somewhere else. I wanted to be at the cabin, cooking for the kids, snuggling with Calder, and even the social aspect of meeting his friends and playing cards sounded better than traveling with Gabrielle. I liked her, but we had way different ideas of fun when it came to places to eat and how jam-packed to make a schedule.

"Oh, I didn't mean *you.*" She took a sip of her wine before continuing. "You'd be miserable. A girls' weekend for me and them. We'll do high tea, get our hair done, and I know just the place to stay..."

"You want the girls for the whole weekend?" Such was my life that this offer had come for next weekend, not this one, when I might have been more tempted.

"That is what I said, is it not?" Tilting her head, she regarded me like I might be feverish.

"You'd fly?" I bit my lip. Madeline was a nervous flyer at the best of times, even with me there to coach her through it.

Gabrielle grinned like Calder did when holding a winning card. "The train. More fun with the girls."

"Well..." I drew out the word. Madeline was far better with trains, and Charlotte loved the whole experience from getting the tickets to the dining car. She would love this trip with Gabrielle.

"You're considering it." Her eyes went wide, thick lashes fluttering.

"Don't look so startled," I teased her because we both knew my practicality compared to her starry-eyed ideas was legendary.

"Darling, you put the *over* in overprotective parent." She laughed along with me. She was right, which was why I'd probably end up vetoing the idea or reluctantly going along. But Gabrielle wasn't giving up easily, sliding the platter of gourmet cookies closer to me. "Let me do this, please? You need a break and you never ask me to take them."

I pursed my mouth because I *could* have asked for this weekend. I'd known she was back from Aspen, and for all that she was flighty, she did love the girls and they adored her and her whimsical ways. If I'd asked, then I wouldn't have to be here now, missing Calder something fierce.

"I don't want to overburden or overly count on you." That wasn't the only reason I hadn't asked and I knew it, but I didn't want to dwell on the other reasons I'd used as excuses to not go with Calder.

Gabrielle frowned. "That's not fair. I'd drop everything if you needed help, and you know it."

"I know." I patted her hand. She was a help, and it wasn't that I didn't trust her with the girls. I had custody because she hadn't been up for full-time parenting and had made noises about sending them to boarding school as she'd done with my half sister, collecting her for whirlwind trips on breaks. I'd wanted more stability for Charlotte and Madeline, more of the traditional home life I'd had with my grandparents. However, Gabrielle was excellent in the fun-time grandma role and I shouldn't discount that.

"You're always telling me everything is handled." She wagged a manicured finger my direction. "When it rather clearly is *not*. This lack of a childcare solution is running you ragged."

"It hasn't been easy," I admitted. I'd been calling in favors at the practice, working fewer hours so I could pick them up from school, but taking more on-call hours in exchange. I'd also been relying on piecemeal solutions of play dates and after-school activities, but those also weren't long-term fixes.

"Let me give you a weekend off and the girls a fun break."

"You do seem rather enthusiastic about the idea." I was wavering and I knew it.

"Of course, I'm the glam-ma. Sprinkling fun is what we do!"

Shaking my head, I chuckled. "The fact that you just called yourself the glam-ma should disqualify you."

"Felix. You're the day-to-day guy. Let someone else handle the fun?" She was smiling again, likely because she knew she was close to winning this battle.

But before I could give in, Charlotte wandered into the dining room. "Calder is fun. He can be in charge of fun."

"Charlotte," I groaned, but was too late because Gabrielle's eyes were already lighting up, a terrier spotting a treat.

"Who is Calder?"

"Uncle Felix's friend. We thought he might be a burglar, but it turned out he's nice."

Gabrielle tugged Charlotte over to her lap and slid the cookies back in front of her. "Do tell me more."

"He got Uncle Felix to ride a sled down a big hill." Charlotte helped herself to a cookie, totally oblivious to my please-stop-talking vibes.

"Did he now?" Gabrielle shot me a knowing look. For all she could be impractical, she was also one of the sharpest people I knew.

"Gabrielle." I so was not having this conversation in front of Charlotte. Or at all.

"This is another reason why you should let me have the girls for the weekend. Go out. Be an adult. Get drinks. Go ride a sled." Her smile was downright devious.

"Nana wants to take us on a trip?" Charlotte bounced off Gabrielle's lap.

"*Nana.* I thought we discussed making plans firm before we tell the kids something." I tried to spear her with a hard stare, but she waved away my lecture.

"Oh, you were about to agree, and you know it. You're the one feeling guilty for letting go for a weekend."

"Please, Uncle Felix." Charlotte grabbed my hand and swung it back and forth. I was outnumbered, and Gabrielle wasn't wrong. I had been about to say yes. And if I was feeling guilty, it had less to do with concern for the girls than feeling conflicted about how much I did want a weekend to myself.

"All right. You can go. I guess I'll find something to do to keep from getting lonely." I made a pouty face for Charlotte's benefit, but my brain was already racing ahead, an image of Calder glowing neon-bright.

"Yay!" both Charlotte and Gabrielle cheered.

My eyes flitted to where my phone lay on the table. Maybe he wouldn't even be free, but I couldn't deny the way my pulse thrummed. We'd had two dinner meetings since our weekend at the cabin, and the stolen kisses in my car had been delicious desserts, but I wanted more. Damn it. I liked him too damn much and should work on distance, but I was already mentally composing an invite.

Forcing my attention back to the matter at hand, I pointed at Gabrielle. "And I'm going to want an itinerary and phone numbers for the hotel and the theater and—"

"Yes, yes, darling. All of that." Making a vague gesture with both hands, Gabrielle continued to beam.

Calder would be good at a trip schedule. Again, I glanced at my phone. A vision of the two of us taking the girls somewhere had my eyes fluttering shut, taking a second to appreciate something that wasn't ever coming to pass. But he was adorable with his spreadsheets, and unlike Gabrielle, he was realistic with time estimates. He wouldn't overcommit, yet he'd schedule in plenty of fun.

"I'm going to go tell Madeline!" Charlotte raced away as I opened my eyes. I didn't have room for such fanciful thoughts or this new yearning in my chest.

"I hope you're happy," I said to Gabrielle.

"Very." Her expression turned sly. "Is there a doctor-related reason you keep looking at your phone?"

"I'm waiting on some test results." It wasn't a complete

untruth. I was on call for the weekend, which meant more patient phone calls even if I didn't get called in.

"Liar." Her eyes sparked like a cat with a shiny new toy. "Tell me about this friend."

Trying to make my face impassive, I shook my head. "Nope. Nothing to tell."

"Bring him around. I'll be the judge of that."

"You got your way about the trip. Be happy with that." Grabbing my phone, I pushed away from the table. The idea wasn't terrible. Calder was effortlessly charming, and he'd make enduring Gabrielle's whims way more fun. But introducing the two felt distinctly like the relationship territory we were trying to avoid. Nope. Not happening. "Girls! Let's get ready to go."

"Go on now. Be sure to check on those…test results." She waved me away. And despite all the reasons I should temper my expectations, my pulse was already galloping as I counted down until I could text Calder the news.

Chapter Twenty-One

Calder

"You win." Max folded his arms and leaned back against the wall. We were playing cards in the dining nook, which seemed so cozy with Felix and the kids but felt cramped with four adults.

Our other buddy RJ untangled himself from the bench. "I'm bushed. Tonight I'm gonna try pushing two of the smaller beds together upstairs. I think you were expecting Gremlins, buddy."

"They're great fun for kids," I said absently as I shuffled the deck.

"Yeah? You expecting some anytime soon?" Max laughed like such a notion was high comedy. A month ago it would have been, but strangely, I'd been missing the girls all weekend. They appreciated my pancake efforts and laughed at my jokes and gave me excuses to play, whereas lately my crew seemed to live to give me a hard time. And shop talk about work seemed to have an edge that hadn't been there before.

"Boy. You and kids. That would sure make your mom happy." RJ joined Max in chuckling.

"Don't remind me." Yet even as I groaned, I could totally picture my parents around Felix and the girls. My mom would love the girls and dote on them, and even my stoic dad would get a kick out of the things Charlotte said. Parental approval was a crap reason to start dating, but if I could convince Felix to keep this friendship going, it might be a nice side benefit.

"We're going to turn in too." Max's friend, Ember, slid out of the bench, followed quickly by Max.

"Really? We were just getting started!" Setting aside the cards, I frowned at the three of them.

"We're getting old, dude." Max clapped me on the shoulder.

"Never." I laughed but it sounded forced, even to my own ears.

"It was all that mountain air." RJ shook his head before stretching his back and legs. "I'd forgotten how hard skiing is on the knees."

"Okay, maybe *you* are old." I rolled my eyes at him. Privately, though, I agreed. My ankle had recovered from its sprain, but skiing had woken the injury back up, and it had ached all evening. I'd thought about messaging Felix to ask if I should ice it, but I didn't want to worry him. It was my own fault for letting myself get talked into one more run.

"You are too." Max nodded sagely on his way down the hall. "Father Time comes for us all."

"Go take your pop psychology truisms to bed." I waved all three of them away to a chorus of good nights. Maybe they were right. Maybe we were getting old and that was why the weekend didn't seem as fun as it would have even a few months ago.

I quickly cleaned up from the poker game and put the kitchen to rights, wishing I had Felix to clean with. Wishing again that he'd been able to come. I understood that the girls had to come first, but I was still disappointed. Worse, I wasn't sure that he was as bummed as me. Hell, maybe he was relieved to have had the excuse.

A heaviness settled over my shoulders, lingering as I checked the woodstove and settled in on the couch. However, the second my phone buzzed with a message, the weighty feeling lightened. Finally. Felix and I had texted most nights the last few weeks, and I'd hoped he wouldn't skip tonight.

How is it going there? Felix asked.

Good. But it would be more fun with you here. I could have lied or not admitted to missing him, but honesty tended to get me further with Felix.

Flatterer. You're probably busy taking all your friends' money at poker. He added a laughing emoji.

There were cards earlier. But apparently we're getting old and a day on the slopes means early to bed. Now I'm all by my lonesome on the couch. I found an emoji that was close enough to puppy dog eyes and hit Send.

The couch? You didn't take the bed?

I stretched my legs out on the couch, trying to pretend it was a comfortable fit for a night's sleep. Max brought a date. Seemed only fair to let them have the bed. Besides I would have been all lonely without you to come visit me.

Poor Calder. No midnight kisses. Felix was apparently in a flirty mood, which I could work with. I licked my lips before replying.

If you really feel sorry for me, you'll tell me which night this week you could do dinner.

Hmm. About that... Felix didn't finish the thought, which had me frowning to the empty room. The low light from the woodstove kept reminding me of Felix reading stories and made me miss him that much more.

Felix. We've been over this. We're friends. And I want Thai this week.

To my surprise, his reply came super fast. Me too. But I can do you one better if you're free Friday or Saturday. I'll cook for you. My stepmother is taking the girls to Vancouver.

Oh hell yes. A weekend with only Felix. As much as I did like the girls, I liked the sound of this even more. My fingers flew to try to get a response before he changed his mind.

Both. I'm free both nights. Want to head to the cabin?

Felix's reply opened with a sad face. Can't. I'm on call again. But I could meet you at the ferry Friday and make us something nice for dinner?

Yeah, I could do that. I slapped my thigh. It's okay. I'm stoked to get an invite to your house. Please say there's a sleepover involved.

That earned me an eye-rolling emoji and an even better response. There's a sleepover involved.

Knew I loved you. Wait. I couldn't text that. I meant it in the casual *love you, man* sense. I loved cards and spicy food and good beer and my friends. Of whom Felix was one. But I didn't *love* him.

I inhaled sharply. I liked him. A lot. I thought about him all the time, and I didn't mind admitting that I missed him. I wanted to keep our friendship going, sure. But love? That would be all kinds of complicated, and neither of us wanted that, especially Felix. So, no, I couldn't text that.

Instead, I erased and retyped. Sounds awesome. See you then.

There. That was better. We could have fun, but feelings were absolutely not part of my plan.

Chapter Twenty-Two

Calder

"You brought a toolbox on the ferry?" Felix narrowed his eyes at me as I tossed my stuff in back before sliding into the passenger seat. He was parked in the pickup lane near the ferry, and he'd evidently come straight from work if the tie was any judge. We'd texted or talked on the phone every night that week, but seeing him in person was damn nice. I'd forgotten how hot he looked dressed up.

"Yeah, I brought tools." I shrugged because I'd seen far stranger things on the ferry over the years. Felix had insisted that I keep the drill and other things I'd bought for the cabin, and it wasn't like they got a ton of use in my room at the barracks. "I wasn't sure what you had at your place, and depending on what we end up doing to your pantry and closet, I figured the drill might come in handy."

"I'm not sure whether to crack a joke about things that need drilling at my house or sit in shocked silence that you were serious about organizing things for me." His chuckle had a dazed edge to it.

"Of course I was serious." It occurred to me a little too late that maybe he was not and he might not want someone poking around his stuff. "Wait. Do you not want to?"

"Oh I want to." He leaned across the console to brush a

kiss across my lips. "Home repair is my second-favorite thing to do with you."

Reassured, I tried to pull him back. "How about another of those?"

Honk. The car behind Felix was apparently even more impatient than us.

"Oops." Felix put the SUV in drive. "At my place. Promise."

"You better." I settled back for the drive to Queen Anne, a picture-book perfect neighborhood of old but stately homes that went for bonkers prices because of the area's proximity to downtown.

I liked it when Felix drove. As much as I considered myself a car guy and loved mine, I enjoyed being able to relax, let someone I trusted worry about Seattle traffic. Soon enough we arrived at a two-story mid-century brick home with a bright blue door on a nice corner lot. He parked around back, near the detached garage, and we entered through the kitchen door.

The main floor was bright and open, dominated by a modern kitchen with dark cabinets and gleaming counters. A long breakfast bar looked like a fun spot for the girls to hang out and a little dining alcove with a black table was already set for two. The restaurant-worthy stove was likely capable of far more than pancakes, unlike the tiny older model at the cabin.

I whistled low as I set my stuff down near an antique hutch. "This is nice. Whoever did the kitchen renovation must have had fun."

"I hired most of it out, sadly. And the remodel isn't done." Frowning, he hung his jacket on a hook near the back door on a rack crowded with kid coats and bags and random items. I put my own coat on the last available space as Felix continued, "Having to buy Tim out of the house and cabin means that the lower level is a mishmash of decades and styles. And the master bath is lovely, but the one the girls share still needs to join this century."

"I could help."

"Maybe." He gave me a tight smile that said he wouldn't take me up on the offer but that he was trying to avoid a lengthy discussion about what type of friends we were. I'd just have to convince him later that we were totally the type of friends who helped paint or tile.

"Maybe," I echoed far brighter as I followed him on into the kitchen.

"And I'm sorry for the mess." He gave a sweeping gesture to encompass a housekeeping style my dad would have jokingly called "there appears to have been a struggle." Primary-colored bins in the dining area overflowed with kid art supplies while a doll family appeared to have taken over part of the leather sectional. Legos were scattered across the coffee table, and someone had left a cereal bowl on an end table. "I tried to pick up before we left for school and work, but a backpack emergency took precedence."

"I love it when you use big words, Doc." I pulled him close for quick kiss. And he felt so damn nice that I kept right on holding him. "Don't worry about any mess. I like a lived-in place. Makes it feel like a real home."

"But there's kid stuff everywhere," he protested.

"I'll help you pick up and organize," I offered, nuzzling his temple. My parents did have rather high cleaning standards, but I'd spent enough time with other families to know that clutter was a byproduct of happy living. And an organizational opportunity waiting to happen. "You might need more bins and hooks."

"I'm totally ending up at the home improvement store with you tomorrow, aren't I?" He flopped his head onto my shoulder, so I squeezed him all the tighter, let him lean on me.

"Yup. How else are you going to keep me from getting bored?"

"Oh, I have some good ideas." He twisted so he could kiss my jaw.

"I bet you do." I found his mouth for a kiss because I had all sorts of ideas myself. "But we can do that and get your place in order. It'll be fun, and if you get a work call, I'll have a project to occupy me."

Felix had warned me that him being on call meant he'd probably have to answer a few medication-related questions or urgent patient needs, and I was actually kind of looking forward to getting to hear him do his doctor thing.

"Well, I guess it's that or make you play solitaire." Laughing, he kissed my neck, making my recently shaved skin glow, along with the rest of me. I simply liked being around him so much.

"Exactly. I did bring a deck too, though, in case we run out of things to talk about."

"Somehow I don't think that's going to be a problem." His gaze was hot enough to fry a steak.

"Nope," I agreed happily before I kissed him again. These little hello kisses were so much fun. I liked the hot and heavy stuff too, but simply getting to touch him and be affectionate was a novel pleasure. "Getting enough sleep, now that might be an issue."

"Promises, promises." Felix stroked my forearm. Even on the phone we had a hard time saying good night, and we'd had more than one instance of being totally shocked at the time after talking for over an hour at the end of the day.

"You could show me the bedroom now." I was absolutely on a mission to see exactly how many orgasms I could give Felix before Sunday, and I didn't mind starting right then.

"Or I could feed you first." Felix glided out of my embrace

and bent to retrieve a bottle from a small gourmet wine-cooling fridge near the actual monster sized refrigerator. "Gabrielle had this amazing pinot noir last weekend, and I picked up a bottle for us."

"Fancy." I moved so that he could retrieve two wineglasses from an upper cabinet. "I'm usually more of a beer drinker, but if you like something, I'll happily try it."

"Good. And I'm looking forward to cooking something other than nuggets and endless cheesy pasta dishes. Neither girl will eat fish or mushrooms, so I'm doing a glazed salmon, mushroom risotto, and a salad."

"Sounds delicious." I followed him on his trek back to the fridge after pouring the wine. "Tell me how I can help."

As always, cooking together was fun, lining up ingredients and taking directions about what needed rinsing and chopping.

"Can you get me the arborio rice from the top shelf in the pantry?" he asked as he grabbed a saucepan.

"Sure thing." I opened the door on the other side of the fridge to reveal a small walk-in space that looked like it had been hit by both an earthquake and a cyclone. Dry goods haphazardly stacked on the shelves, kid-friendly snacks everywhere including escaping bins on the floor, and no order to anything, boxes of pasta intermingled with cereal selections. "Oh, this pantry is going to be a project."

"Sorry." Felix cringed as I emerged with the rice.

"Don't be." I kissed the top of his head. I was legit excited. "This is going to be fun. We're totally taking before and after pics."

"You do have some unique ideas of fun."

"Like this one?" I turned him so I could kiss his mouth. The rice could wait a minute. "And I'm serious. I'm gonna need to make a sketch of the space, maybe take inventory of what's already in there..."

"Oh, baby, talk organization to me." Chuckling, Felix returned my kiss. He tasted like red wine and happiness and I wanted to stay in that moment forever.

Chapter Twenty-Three

Felix

"I'm not sure inventory is something most people do on two glasses of wine," I complained, but only mildly, to Calder while holding a pen and a clipboard from some pharmacy company giveaway. He'd enjoyed my drawer of random promotional giveaways almost as much as my cluttered pantry.

"If I know what you already have, then it will be easier to see what you need," he said all reasonably while counting single-serve chip packets. "Oops. Another for the out-of-date pile."

"Sorry." I accepted the bag and added it to the trash bag at my feet. We'd found more than a few items that needed pitching. My skin flushed from more than overindulgence in the wine that had tasted far better with Calder. Dinner had been truly lovely. Nice piece of wild-caught Pacific salmon, risotto that no one had interrupted me while making, and wonderful company. Calder was by far the most fun person I'd cooked with in a long time, helpful without being in the way, and delightfully appreciative of the results. We'd lingered over the wine and a cherry tart I'd nabbed at the bakery.

But now, somehow we were doing inventory rather than canoodling on my couch.

"Felix." Calder looked up from his sorting, voice gentler.

"Quit saying sorry. You're an overworked guardian without a ton of help. So your pantry got a little scary. You keep the kids happy and fed. That's what matters. And now we get to fix it."

"I guess that's one way to look at it. Glad we have mess to keep you from boredom." I wished I could be as stoked as him about attacking all the clutter that was threatening to overtake the house.

"Hey, come here." Backing out of the pantry, Calder started to straighten but hit his head on a low shelf. "Ouch."

"Are you okay?" I pulled him the rest of the way out of the pantry so I could see him better in the kitchen light. "Bleeding?"

"It's just a bump." He twisted his mouth in what might have been frustration, I couldn't tell. "I'm okay."

"Let me feel." I reached for his head but he dodged my fingers. "Dizzy at all?"

"No, Doc, no concussion." Stepping farther away, he made a dismissive gesture. "I got a clean bill of brain health last week. I'm good."

"You had a doctor's appointment?" In all our hours of phone conversations he hadn't mentioned that. I bit my lip, trying not to feel hurt.

Still frowning, he shrugged. "It was no big deal."

"But now you can go out on the sub again, right?" A boulder landed right in the center of my chest. No more nightly calls. No spontaneous weekends like this. No organization projects. No Calder.

"Not that easy." He paced over to his abandoned wineglass on the counter, took a sip. "The detailer—personnel in charge of assignments—and higher-ups apparently like me on shore duty. Guess I'm too good at what I've been doing, and they want to extend the assignment."

"Oh. That must be disappointing for you." Trying not to show my own relief that he was not imminently about to be deployed, I followed after him and put a hand on his shoulder.

"Eh. It is what it is." He exhaled hard but didn't shrug my hand off. "Not something I get a lot of choice over. Higher-ups would like me to apply for a special duty rate dealing with operations management."

"Maybe that would be more interesting than your current assignment?" I started rubbing his shoulder.

"Yeah. Probably. I'm not uninterested, but I'd have to agree to adjust my re-up timeline, and it would mean more shore duty." Humming softly, he leaned more into my massage. "Faster pipeline to senior chief or a limited duty officer, but way less chance of a sub assignment."

"But you'd still be assigned to Bremerton?" I added my other hand to the massage. Why him staying local mattered so damn much was a point better left unexamined. Calder being happy in his job should be my main concern as a *friend*, not any personal benefit to me or our…friendship.

"Yeah. I'd be working with the command on base that supports both the deployed subs and the ones in port. I have a call with the detailer next week about my options now that I'm medically cleared, including the special duty assignment or the chances of getting reassigned back to sub either now or with an upcoming deployment."

"Tell me how the call goes?" I was proud of how casual I sounded, but he still tensed under my hand.

"I don't need to bore you with a bunch of shop talk." Turning back to face me, he pursed his mouth.

"I don't mind. I like hearing about your work. And if we're friends, how about being the kind you tell about a bad day or a big decision?"

That got a half smile. "Yeah. Okay. I'll keep you posted."

"Good." I rubbed his biceps, wanting more than that partial smile from him.

"But right now, imagining your finished pantry is way more interesting than thinking about my job."

"Well, by all means. Don't let me keep you from your inventory." I trailed after him back to the pantry. His eagerness to help me made a lot more sense now. It wasn't necessarily about *me* or whatever we had going here, but rather a distraction from his work stress. Understandable. Relatable even. And absolutely no reason for my jaw to go tense. I rolled my neck to try to loosen my muscles. "You sure your head is all right?"

"Yeah. Doesn't even hurt anymore." Calder touched his fingers to the crown of his head then frowned more. "Heck. I got some sort of dust or plaster in my hair."

"Oops. I warned you it was scary in there."

"I'm not afraid of some dirt." He handed me my clipboard again, clearly impatient to get the focus back off himself, but I wasn't done trying to make him feel better.

"What do you say we finish up here quickly and then you can take a shower? A bigger water heater might be my favorite renovation thus far."

"Yeah. That sounds good." His smile was still two sizes too small, but it was a start. Sensing that he needed some time to himself, I didn't try to invite myself into the shower either. Him enjoying one of my favorite spots in the house was its own reward, and thinking about him warm and soapy and all relaxed made me double down on finishing the pantry inventory quickly.

Calder insisted on doing some measuring and making a list of items to purchase at the home improvement place in the morning, but finally I was able to herd him upstairs and toward my master shower. The connection to my grandparents was the main reason why I'd fought so hard to keep the house, but the renovated master bath was definitely on my list as well. Large, with stone tiles and a built-in seat, it gave the room a spa vibe that never failed to relax me, and I hoped it did the same for Calder.

"I put out fresh towels earlier," I said from the doorway, ushering him and his backpack ahead of me into the bathroom.

"Ah. Thanks." He glanced around before looking back at me, cheeks pink. "You…uh…join me?"

"Nah." I liked the idea of him all soapy very much, but his body language was still rather tense, and I didn't want him offering out of obligation. "I think you'll get cleaner without me distracting you."

"Fair enough." He gave me a fast kiss before turning toward the shower. Him not pursuing the idea of me joining him showed that I'd made the right choice there. Besides, there were other ways to be romantic and take care of him than soaping his back. I turned back the bedding, lowered the lights to a rosy glow that reminded me of candlelight without the fire hazard, and put on some soft music.

I debated what to wear to bed far longer than I needed to, but lounging naked or in my boxer briefs felt a little presumptuous and sexual pressure was the last thing I wanted to inspire. So I pulled on a pair of the flannel pants I normally wore and had to smile when he emerged from the bathroom in a near-identical pair, simply a different shade of plaid. He had a towel around his neck and a way more relaxed grin.

"You weren't kidding. That water pressure is so much better than the barracks. I do feel better. Thanks." He crossed over to the bed, and I patted the spot next to me.

"Good."

"This is nice too." He gestured at the room before stretching out next to me. The bed creaked. It too wasn't used to the extra occupant. However, having someone next to me was cozy, a pleasure I hadn't allowed myself to miss.

"You want to watch something before sleep?" I reached for the remote that controlled the flat-screen TV mounted over the dresser.

"You. I want to watch *you*." Giving me a heated look, he rolled onto his elbow.

"Flattery will get you everywhere, but we don't *have* to have sex." I turned so that we were face-to-face. "I truly am happy simply with you here."

"I'm happy too." Face softening, he stroked my cheek. "Sorry if I got moody earlier."

"It's okay. Sounds like you have good reason to be frustrated or whatever you're feeling." I glided my hand down his bare arm. "You don't have to always be in fun mode. I like talking to you, even the serious stuff."

"I like talking to you too. Feels sometimes like fun mode is what everyone expects of me." His expression turned cloudy and he glanced away, but I cupped his chin, brought his gaze back in my direction.

"Yeah, well, I'm not everyone."

"I know." He kissed me, a surprisingly serious gesture that felt like compliment and promise both. I met his unexpected solemnness with the gravitas it deserved, kissing him slow and deliberate.

Eventually though, we caught fire, same as always, heavy mood giving way to something lighter and sexier, but still tinged with an emotion that hadn't been there before. However, his agile tongue and roaming hands made it hard to think about anything other than how damn good he felt.

"I wanna set a new record." Pulling back, he had a predatory intent in his eyes that made more heat pool low in my gut. He skimmed his palm down my ribs.

"Hold on there, speed demon." Chuckling, I stopped him before his hand could reach my waistband. I loved how intent he always was on getting me off and how he delighted in doing it fast or multiple times, but tonight I had a different agenda. I wanted to take care of him in a way I hadn't craved in far too long. "You're not the only one who likes to play and explore. My turn."

Chapter Twenty-Four

Calder

"Your turn?" I bit my lip to keep from frowning because I wasn't entirely sure what Felix was after.

"Yes. I want to touch you. Taste too, if you're up for that." Felix playfully licked at my neck, intent clear, and simply the rasp of his tongue against my Adam's apple had my cock taking notice.

"Oh, I'm up." I pulled him closer so he'd see what I meant. However, as nice as his tongue all over me sounded, I also didn't want him wasting his time. "But I can't generally get off that way."

"Is that the only goal?" Felix tilted his head, giving me a searching look.

"No, of course not." I did feel like a lotto winner every time I made him climax, but we were both big fans of cuddling and things like making out in his car. Affection felt nice even without orgasms attached. And affection came in various forms too—like Felix making his room here all cozy for me and insisting I shower in that gorgeous shower of his.

"Then how about letting me make you feel good, and when you can't stand it any longer, you can take over, finish the job so to speak." He winked at me, seeming downright eager to fool around even knowing I'd probably need to be the one to get me off.

"You wouldn't mind that?"

"Mind?" Chuckling, he gave me a fast, hard kiss. "Hardly. Watching you stroke yourself is hot as hell. I only want a chance to play with you first, ramp you up."

"In that case, have at me." Arms over my head, I flopped back against the pillows. Unlike my narrow bed in the barracks, this was like a hotel luxury suite bed—thick, pillowy mattress, crisp white linens, small mountain of pillows behind us with a sturdy upholstered headboard. Combined with the muted indigo walls, it was a very adult, elegant space, and one I wanted to be invited back to. If Felix wanted to play, I was more than happy to be his pawn.

"Don't mind if I do." Felix quickly took advantage of my position, straddling my hips and pinning my arms before capturing my mouth in a blistering kiss that made me forget all about whatever objections I had to this plan.

"Mmm." I made a happy noise as we kissed and kissed. Damn. Felix really was the best at this, more intoxicating than that wine of his and sweeter than any dessert. I couldn't get enough of him, but when I freed my hands so I could touch him too, he pushed my arms back down.

"Not yet." He gave me a stern look that did flippy things to my insides. Power games were not my thing, and if he asked to tie me up, I'd be out, but apparently my cock liked him bossy plenty. "Your only job right now is to tell me what feels good."

"You. You feel good." Letting him keep me pinned, I rocked my hips, trying to encourage him to grind on me.

But all he did was laugh and settle his weight more firmly against me, making clear he was in charge. When I stopped trying to move, he beamed down at me. "Good. We'll get there, I promise. Now, how about this?"

Dipping his head, he started licking and kissing my neck which had me moaning softly in short order.

"Feels good." If he found giving me this sort of attention fun, I sure wasn't going to discourage him. But I also wasn't squirming and panting like he always did when I attacked his neck. "I'm not sure I'm going to light up like a Christmas tree from it like you do though."

"I think we just haven't found your light switch." Seeming undaunted, he winked before stroking my arms, deliberate touches as if he were testing some sort of theory. Sure enough, as soon as I groaned when he rubbed my biceps, that area got a kiss.

Exhaling softly, I shut my eyes and let myself drift on the low music while he kept finding new places to bless with kisses. Like the room and the wine, the music was more upscale than I was used to, but I liked how the rich instrumentals made me feel all peaceful and floaty. His lips were soft against my shoulders, and each kiss lured me further into an almost meditative space.

"Sorry," I mumbled. Putting me to sleep was probably not part of his plan.

"Don't you dare apologize." He nipped at my collarbone. "Seeing you this relaxed is a gift. Quit thinking you need to be on the verge of spurting to make me happy or satisfy some imaginary timetable."

"I'll try." Keeping my eyes shut, I made an effort to get back to the floaty place, breathing like we were in a yoga class until I didn't have to think at all, simply slide from kiss to kiss and touch to touch.

Once I let go of the idea that I needed to be getting off, I could wallow in how good Felix felt. His weight on me tethered me to the bed and his hands were endlessly fascinating, soft yet callused in different places than my own. Bristly cheeks contrasted with lush lips that made electricity jolt in unexpected places—my hands, my sternum, even my ribs. He kissed my nipples, which made my cock twitch, but then he raked his teeth across one and my back bowed.

"Oh. That's…different." My voice sounded all drugged.

"Good different?" Felix's superior tone said he already knew the answer.

"Very." I dragged his head back down and he let me, repeating the gesture on the other side. And again, little bites alternating with soft sucking that had me moving restlessly against the sheets, until I was panting and trying valiantly to avoid reaching for my cock.

I could end this with about three strokes, but I was also super curious to see where this was headed. And apparently, so was he, as he abandoned my nipples to kiss his way down my stomach. Not as electric, but still nice, the rasp of his cheek against my abs.

"Can these go?" He plucked at the waistband of my sleep pants.

"Yeah." I scooted out of them, still all drunk on his attention, and not really picking up on what he was after until he dropped a kiss right next to where my hard cock lay on my stomach. "Oh. You don't have to…"

"I want to." He stroked my thighs with soothing hands. "Do you not like how oral feels?"

"No. I love it. Feels amazing. Just can't come from it, usually." Tension in my back started to chase away the floaty feeling, but he grounded me with a stern tap to the center of my chest.

"We're not worried about that, remember? Not trying to get you off, just trying to light you up." With that he kissed the tip of my cock and I hissed because it did feel damn good, more so since I wasn't worried about taking too long. Instead of tensing my muscles and reaching into my bag of tricks to try to get closer, I followed his orders.

No worrying about orgasm. Just letting it feel fucking great, the warmth of his mouth taking me in, the slick glide of his lips, the teasing flick of his tongue. He didn't seem in any hurry to take me deep either, playing with shallow sucking and licking and—

"Ah. Oh. Fuck." I gasped as he found a place on the underside that legit had me seeing twinkling lights.

"On switch?" He chuckled against my thigh.

"Cocky bastard. You know damn well you're good at this." I pet his hair appreciatively and he hummed around my cock.

"Always nice to hear it."

"Yeah. Do that again," I demanded as he worked that spot like it actually was a sensor of some kind, licking and flicking. But right as I was about to think maybe I'd been wrong about not being able to climax, he slid lower. My cock popped free of his mouth with a lewd sound that made me groan right as he licked my balls. A current raced up my spine. "Fuck. That. Damn."

"Ah." Felix made a highly pleased noise. "I think we found some more lights…"

He proceeded to tease me there with more licking and gentle touches until I was rocking toward him. And then with a move a lot of wrestlers would probably envy, he wiggled between my legs, pushing my thighs wider before licking lower.

And lower.

"Fuck." His mouth felt amazing, but this was rather uncharted territory for me and my skin heated with the knowledge of exactly where his lips were. "You don't need to…"

"I know I don't. But you smell like my favorite shampoo, and you've got me all kinds of turned on to try. Please?"

"Yeah," I whispered. The please did it for me as did his happy noises as he settled himself more firmly against me, spreading me wider. I'd assumed that rimming was really only a porn thing. Definitely not a straitlaced doctor thing. Except apparently it was, and every flick of his tongue had me groaning. "Oh God. That feels…so good."

"Excellent." Felix went back to work, idly stroking my cock while giving lavish attention to my balls and rim.

"Fuck. Want…" I didn't have a fucking clue what. Something. Then Felix's thumb brushed my hole and my brain lit up like an entire receiving station. "That. That. More."

"Yeah?" His finger was rougher than his tongue, but he must have licked it because it was also slick as he rubbed little circles around my rim. Thinking of him licking his finger made my cock pulse.

"God." My head thrashed against the pillow and I didn't dare open my eyes. But every pass of his finger drove me higher. "Why does that feel so… *Damn.*"

"Don't think. Let it feel good." His finger was back now, slicker, pushing inside enough to have me gasping. Apparently whatever nerve endings I lacked in my neck had all made their way to my ass because even the faint burn of the intrusion was a fucking revelation.

"It does feel good. Fuck. It really does." I sounded all rough with a mix of surprise and need.

"Calder? Do you ever bottom?" Felix's voice was as gentle as his touch. And when I didn't answer right away, he stroked my thigh. "It's okay—"

"I want to." The words came out in a hell of a rush because I could sense the moment slipping away. If I hesitated too much, the offer might be off the table, and given how good his mouth and finger felt, I simply had to know. It was like being confronted with a giant water slide. I couldn't not try.

And it was Felix. If I'd misjudged and didn't like it, he'd laugh with me at my brashness and we'd try something else. He was the perfect person to try this with, in large part because he'd removed all expectations.

He sat up to reach for the nightstand. His hair was a mess and his lips swollen, and I'd never seen him so turned-on looking, a faint pink sheen to his skin and glassy glow to his eyes. Fumbling around, he came up with a tube of lube and tossed it on the bed.

"I can stick with fingers if you've never..."

So damn polite and giving. If I didn't ask outright, he wasn't going to take it. I took a deep breath. "No, I want it. Fuck me."

"Whatever you want." The sincerity in Felix's voice was exactly why I wanted this with him right here and now. He was all about what I needed, what would make me feel good, and he made it safe to want this too.

"I want you." I held his gaze as he added a condom next to the lube.

"You've got me." He dropped a tender kiss on my chest before settling back down between my legs. Teasing some more with his mouth, he didn't make me wait too long before a slippery finger joined the mix, him licking at my balls while he slowly pushed in.

"Oh. Damn." Unlike earlier, he didn't stop, pressing deep in a smooth stroke that stole every last drop of oxygen I had when he brushed a particular spot. I surged toward his hand. "Fuck. More."

"Easy." He made a soothing noise before he grabbed my hand, led it to my cock. "Here. Touch yourself. Don't come yet."

My chest hurt with how damn good that felt. Not his finger

on my prostate, although that truly was amazing. Him getting what I needed and giving it to me so effortlessly. I kept my grip on my cock loose, wanting to prolong this as long as possible, even as he added a second finger and the fullness and pressure increased to a point where all I could do was make inarticulate noises when both fingers found that spot. Forget Christmas tree. This was a whole fucking light show.

"Again," I demanded, voice a low rumble.

"Greedy. Fuck. I love you like this." The wonder in his voice was even better than driving the good doctor to cursing. I was giving him something too. And I wanted to give him even more.

"Do it. Now. Fuck me."

"I can do that." Felix moved so he could take care of the condom, shedding his pajama bottoms with comical speed.

"Need me to flip?" Watching him unroll the condom and add lube was making my pulse thrum.

"No. I want to see you like this, make sure you're doing okay." His serious expression was exactly why we were doing this at all. He wore his caretaking like a second skin. I still wasn't used to it. For years now, I'd been the big guy looking out for everyone else. Having someone take such careful care of me was novel, but I liked it, like an extra layer of warmth I hadn't realized I desperately needed.

"I'm doing fucking amazing," I said and meant it. Felix knelt between my thighs, arranging my legs until I got the idea and drew them up and back. Then he was pushing in, an unfamiliar pressure, different from a finger. Not bad. Just… different.

"Breathe," he encouraged, reaching a hand out to stroke my stomach.

"I am." Porn made this look a lot simpler, and breathing was a challenge when my whole body kept wanting to tense.

"It's okay. Not a race. We can go slow."

I wanted to level up fast, tell him I didn't need training wheels, but I nodded, something in me trusting him to know best. He rocked forward in shallow little thrusts, and I finally remembered how to exhale. I closed my eyes, stopping my body's chase for more thousand-watt sensations, instead seeking the floaty place where Felix knew best and where it was more about feeling good than any particular destination. Maybe I'd come. Maybe he would. I let go of the last of my expectations, let this be about how good and close I felt to Felix, how taken care of.

And then a funny thing happened along the way to my newly enlightened state. The fucking started feeling a lot better, less of an intrusion, more of a welcome fullness, all those nerve endings lighting back up until the whole room seemed brighter. I had to be glowing, it felt that damn good.

"Think we found that on switch." Opening my eyes, I managed a strangled laugh before moaning again when he pressed even deeper still.

"We did." His expression was both proud and tender, eyes still glassy with pleasure, but somehow he kept himself in check, setting a steady rhythm that seemed to hit that spot every damn stroke. He dragged my hand back to my cock. "Touch yourself. Make it feel good."

"It does," I assured him, right before he went harder and I had to groan. "Oh, fuck, it really does."

"Make it better," he demanded, all stern and bossy again and so fucking hot. My cock pulsed even before I gripped it. Felix taking over was the hottest thing I'd ever seen, even without the pyrotechnics happening inside me. He made an approving noise as I started to stroke. "That's it. Fuck, Calder. You're so sexy."

His eyes made me burn that much brighter. "You like watching me?"

"So much." He pushed my thigh back a little more and the new angle had us both groaning. Shameless now, I wrapped my other leg around him, tried to pull him even deeper. The deeper he thrust, the higher I flew, my hand moving in tandem with his rhythm.

My balls tightened in a way that was both familiar and brand-fucking-new. "Oh fuck. Felix. Fuck. I think I can come."

My surprise must have come out in my voice because he laughed. "Do it. Please."

"Yeah? You want that? Me to come for you?" Knowing he was watching made my abs quiver. So fucking hot, his intense gaze boring down on me.

"Yes. Come for me." The little hint of sternness there, a command, made my ass clench. And then he fucked me harder and that new tension spiraled into something amazing.

"I'm close." My whole body was trembling, more on edge than I'd ever been. My cock had never been this hard before, this urgent. I reached for the edge, but climbed higher instead, some new place where need seemed to build and build endlessly.

"I've got you." Felix held me closer even as he kept fucking me, like there was no place I could go where he wouldn't follow, no height that he wouldn't catch me from. Nothing was too big or scary for Felix. I could shout myself hoarse, and he'd be right there, that patient voice.

He had me.

And with that, the edge stopped slipping away and instead crashed into me, my cock shooting so hard, the first shot hitting my chin. The pleasure overloaded every damn circuit in my body and I welcomed it.

"Coming." Like he needed the advisement. But instead of laughing at my ridiculousness, he groaned low, hips pistoning faster. Oh. He really had gotten off on watching me go. That was enough to make my ass clench again, one last spurt escaping my cock as he came too.

He gave a few last lazy thrusts, riding the pleasure out for both of us, before he withdrew to flop next to me. After taking care of the condom, he cuddled close to my side, still breathing hard.

"Oh damn." I sounded dazed, half laughing, half groaning. "Damn. I had no idea..."

"None?" He raised an eyebrow at that like thirtysomething men did not suddenly wander into their prostate for the first time. He wasn't entirely wrong.

"Little bit of fooling around on my own, but nothing like that. No one ever asked me to bottom before." I shrugged, arranging my hands behind my head. "Just not what people seem to want from me."

"I want you. All of you." His intent stare was back. Maybe it never left.

"Good." I licked my parched lips, not sure what to do with how much I liked that nothing about me seemed to faze Felix. And this thing had never been about what I could give Felix, what he needed from me. He was a pretty damn complete package all on his own. And that he seemed to enjoy me was a fucking gift. "I like that."

"I like *you*, Calder." Still so serious as he stroked my face, touch so reverent that it had to be leaving a mark on my soul. Good. I hoped it would. I wanted him too. All of him. Whatever he could share with me.

"I like you too, Doc," I whispered, voice thick as I gathered him even closer. This wasn't supposed to be this damn good. The heaviness in my chest also wasn't supposed to be happening. But hell if I could stop any of it. All I could do was try to keep him right here next to me as long as I could before the world tried to steal him away.

Chapter Twenty-Five

Felix

"It's too big. It won't fit." I tried to tease rather than whine, but I'd lost track of which aisle of the home improvement store we were in, and Calder's enthusiasm for complicated shelving systems hadn't dimmed a bit.

"No, it's not too big. Or too many pieces." Calder knew me well enough to predict that was likely my next objection, and he wasn't wrong. Despite the weekend crowd at the store and my attitude issues, his smile was broad as ever. "Trust me."

"I do." I rubbed the bridge of my nose, promising myself a coffee at the place near the exit if I could find a fraction of Calder's patience and interest. He was trying hard to make this fun for me. For us, really. It was a nice weekend project and I needed to get over whatever issue my brain was having with accepting his help.

"Then trust my measuring."

"All right. Put it in the cart." I tried for a smile.

"Good." Calder hefted multiple boxes into the cart. The flex of his muscles was a pleasant distraction, but then he paused with one box still in his arms. "Wait. Should I be concerned about your budget here? I know Tim did a number on your finances."

"This is fine," I assured Calder, hating that we even had

to have this conversation. "The divorce was expensive. But that has to do more with big picture finances, like needing a home equity mortgage and liquidating a bunch of investments to buy him out. I'm good for some storage bins, even if I wish I didn't need them."

"Why?" Calder saw this whole thing as a lark. Sorting was fun. Measuring was fun. Power tools were fun. A trip to the store was an adventure. And meanwhile, I was over here trying to not feel like a failure.

"I don't like feeling like I've dropped the ball," I admitted because I knew he'd just chase me down if I didn't give a real reason.

"You said something similar last night before I hit my head." After putting the box in the cart, Calder rubbed my upper arm, apparently caring not that we were in a busy shelving aisle. "Felix, you've had two years from hell. If your pantry and closets suffered, be glad that's all that needs overhauling."

"I know." I huffed out a breath. He was right. And he was kind and generous, doing this with me. "I just hate needing help."

"You don't," he said firmly.

"I don't?" I was pretty sure my search for an after-school nanny alone revealed how much I couldn't do it all on my own.

"It's what I like about you. You're so damn self-sufficient. You take pride in taking care of most things yourself. And that's great. I admire that."

"Thank you." I looked down at the scarred flooring. I liked that he saw me that way, as someone who could handle problems.

"But your independence is what makes helping you so fun. You letting me help with something feels like a win. Like I scored, getting to do something for you."

"You do like to win." And I didn't mind being able to give him that feeling. Like the sex last night, being able to do things for him that made him feel like a winner was immensely satisfying. His surprise when he realized he was about to climax was one of my all-time favorite sights, ever. "I like helping you win too."

"And I like being able to choose. My mom is similar to you in being able to handle a lot on her own, and if I stumble on a gift or a favor that actually matters for her, that's a bigger victory than the times she tries to guilt me into something or where I feel there's no choice."

"I guess that makes sense." I understood what Calder was saying. There was no obligation between us, and the worst that would happen if he didn't help was that a few more random dry goods would go out of date, lost in a sea of chaos. And I liked doing things for him as well. I could get the appeal in wanting to do something for me, even if I was having strange guilt over it. "Thank you. I'll try to be more gracious."

"You're plenty gracious. Just let me do this for you." Calder still had his hand on my arm, and his eyes were softly beseeching. Big, hot guy begging me to let him do home repair. How did I luck into this?

Heart thumping harder, I nodded. "Okay. No more grumbling from me. And having you here is far better than when I brave the store on my own."

"Good." Calder pushed the cart farther down the aisle, glancing back over his shoulder and slowing until I caught up. "Let's pick up lunch on the way back. Get something spicy you can't do with the kids around."

"You sure you want me eating something spicy?" I raised an eyebrow. We'd gotten a late start thanks to a good-morning kiss turned four-alarm fire, not that I was complaining about that development one bit.

"Oh, I'm gonna keeping kissing you even if I need a hazmat suit." He winked at me and the thumping in my chest got louder. The easy way Calder went from pacifying my bad mood back to flirting was something I'd never had with Tim. Calder was so damn fun and refreshing to be around that I was having a hard time reminding myself this was supposed to be super casual.

Friends.

But few friends could make me feel this good. And all I could seem to do was nod. I'd keep kissing him too. As long as he'd let me, and undoubtedly way longer than was smart.

Chapter Twenty-Six

Felix

"All right. So you'll try the new dosage, and we'll see you in the office this week for a follow-up to discuss what effect the changes are having." I tried to wrap up my call with a patient's spouse, knowing Calder was in my pantry with a drill and feeling guilty I wasn't more help.

"Thanks, Doctor Sigund. You're the best. Enjoy what's left of your Sunday."

"I will." I hoped I didn't sound *too* eager, but Calder and I had indeed kissed our way through the weekend. Light kisses in the parking lot. Spicy kisses after takeout for lunch. Sneaky kisses in the pantry and my closet as we worked on the organization projects. Long, lazy kisses watching a movie in bed. Brunch kisses. All the kisses until I lost track and I had a closet and pantry worthy of a magazine shoot.

"Okay, my call is done. Sorry for taking so long. What can I help with?" I asked Calder as I returned to the pantry.

"Don't apologize. Listening to you talk doctor is sexy," Calder teased, then sobered. "Seriously, man, everyone should have a doctor as caring. You spelled out the medication name three times and you never once sounded put out that you had to stop your weekend to deal with the questions. I'm impressed. Seriously."

"Thank you." I rubbed the back of my neck, not used to this kind of praise. "It was a spouse who's trying to keep their partner home as long as possible. There are hard conversations we're going to have to have in the coming months, but if I can help push those decisions off a little longer, I'm happy to do it."

"And I am happy to help you here while you make that possible. Doesn't it look good? I think we're done." Calder stepped back to admire the finished pantry, and I took advantage of his proximity to give him a hug.

"It looks amazing. You were right. This was a fun project," I had to admit. The pantry looked three times as large now, with airy shelves and neatly labeled bins and large glass jars. Even the lighting had received an upgrade from a single bare bulb to a nice fixture that made it possible to see everything, even the far corners. I squeezed Calder closer. "I'm going to be able to send the girls in to get their own snacks so much easier now."

"Excellent. Parenting win." Calder kissed my temple. I liked how he often referred to me as a parent, no hesitation, simply accepting that the girls and I were a permanent unit. So many people treated my guardianship like a temporary babysitting gig, but Calder seemed to instinctively get that I was raising them. They were my kids, no qualifiers needed.

"Thank you." I turned so I could kiss him more thoroughly on the mouth.

"Oh, that's nice." He gave an exaggerated shiver that did splendid things for my ego.

"Not too spicy?" We'd cooked together for brunch, including some spicy Bloody Mary drinks and pepper bacon I'd had in the freezer.

"Try me." Eyes flashing, he pulled me flush against him

for a kiss that made my bare toes dig into the hardwood floor. His agile tongue had me panting in no time flat.

"Feeling dusty after all that work?" I licked my lips as he released me. "I could show you the benefits of the second head in my shower."

He fondled the curve of my ass through my jeans. "You can show me—"

"Uncle Felix!" A gleeful shout echoed from the front of the house. Damn whatever impulse had led to me giving Gabrielle her own key.

"Crap. They're back early." Stepping away from Calder, I patted my hair like I could smooth away evidence of what we'd been up to. Heck. I'd planned on taking Calder to the ferry before Gabrielle and the girls were back, no one needing to know how I'd spent the weekend without them.

But now here was Gabrielle breezing in, coat that was closer to a cape flapping behind her, makeup predictably perfect despite the long train ride. The girls were right behind her, racing to tackle-hug me, and then Calder, happy squeals all around. They, at least, didn't seem all that suspicious of his presence, but Gabrielle was a different story.

"Oops! Didn't realize you had company." Her shrewd gaze swept over Calder and her sly smile said she was busy drawing all sorts of conclusions. "I did text."

Oops. Looking around, I discovered my personal phone on the counter near the work phone. I must have neglected to put it back in my pocket after taking some pictures of the pantry progress.

"Sorry. Is everything all right?" My self-recrimination came out in my tone. Damn it. I should have known better than to lose track of my phone. What if the girls had truly needed me? It was one thing to enjoy Calder's company and another to get so distracted that I lost track of my real priorities.

"Everything is splendid." Gabrielle slipped out of her coat, clearly planning to stay. The girls raced upstairs, dragging their overstuffed bags behind them. Clearly Gabrielle had ignored my plea to not go overboard on the shopping.

"You're earlier than I expected." I couldn't shake the feeling that I'd narrowly dodged missing something critical.

"Maybe a little, but darling, it's almost three." Gabrielle waved at the clock on the microwave.

Sure enough, it was far later than I'd expected. Double damn. I really had lost track of everything other than how good hanging out with Calder felt. Another few moments and we would have truly been in an embarrassing situation, and it was all my fault for getting so wrapped up in him.

"Now I'm the one saying *oops*. Guess we lost track of time." Calder laughed like this lapse was no big deal. And I supposed for him it was a minor thing. "I better get to the ferry."

"I can take you," I offered, even though logistically it was more complicated now with Gabrielle and the girls here. But I couldn't simply abandon Calder either.

"Nah. I'll sort out the bus. It's not that far." He gave me a fast kiss on the cheek, almost absently. We'd been sharing easy affection all weekend. It wasn't surprising that he forgot we weren't alone anymore, but my skin still went ghost-pepper hot.

Not trusting myself to speak, I managed a nod.

"I'll grab my stuff." He headed for the stairs, taking them two at a time, good mood not flagging in the slightest.

"Well." Gabrielle drew the word out. No chance she'd missed any of the subtext there. "Seems like you took my advice. Any…sledding this weekend?"

"Gabrielle." At least the girls hadn't seen the kiss. I could do without more awkward questions and assumptions. Gabrielle's smug look was bad enough.

"What? I'm happy for you. You need a—"

"Friend. He's a friend who helped me with some home improvement projects this weekend. Come see the pantry." I ushered her closer so she could see that I'd been busy, not having an orgy in their absence.

"Lovely." Gabrielle dutifully admired the matching bins and baskets. "After Tim, it's nice to see you with someone who can earn their keep."

"He's a friend. I'm not with anyone," I said firmly as steps sounded on the stairs.

"Okay, I'm out of here." Calder came into the kitchen carrying his backpack in one hand and Charlotte on his back. "Found this one lurking in the hall."

"I was looking for a mouse," she explained as Calder gently set her down. If he'd heard my denial that we were together, he didn't show it, ruffling Charlotte's curls and grinning at her.

"Mice? You have mice?" Gabrielle, who lived in a slick modern condo, sounded predictably horrified.

"No, of course not," I assured her. Actually, I didn't know. It was an old house. Mice happened, and with Charlotte it was a toss-up as to what was imagination and what was based in fact.

"You could get a cat," Calder suggested casually as he scooped up his bag again.

"I want a cat!" Charlotte crowed.

"Thanks." I gave Calder a pointed look, and he at least had the grace to blush.

"Sorry. Didn't mean to create trouble."

"It's okay." I forced a smile as I waved him to the door. "Go, before you're late."

In reality, he had created a heck of a lot of trouble and not simply with the cat suggestion. I needed him gone before he said something else. And before I could care even more. As it was, I sighed softly as he retreated, unreasonably sad at no goodbye kiss, even though that would have been ill-advised. Looking away, my eyes landed on his toolbox near the pantry. I could dash after him. But it wasn't like he needed his drill on base. I could let it be an excuse to see him again.

There was only one smart choice, and even knowing that, I still stayed rooted to the spot. Trouble, indeed. I wanted all the trouble he could create.

Chapter Twenty-Seven

Calder

"You're a miracle worker, Euler." Coffee cup in hand, Senior Chief Feinstein leaned on my desk in the admin building on base. He was a great guy, inching close to his twenty and retirement, and he'd taken a shine to me ever since I'd arrived on light duty in his department.

"I try. It wasn't just me either." I had to give credit to the personnel I had working under me as well. A good chief was only as effective as their ability to lead. "I had Allen and Slade on it too, trying to make stuff happen. I take it the order went through?"

Feinstein whistled low, like I'd unveiled a new car. "You cut through all that red tape like butter."

"Good." I was pleased that all my time on the phone and in emails had paid off, and staying busy this week hadn't been nearly as difficult as when I was first handed the assignment. I'd found a rhythm and a purpose, but some of my contentment was also having memories of the prior weekend with Felix to keep me company. It was hard to work up much resentment over being on shore duty when I had such a fun distraction anchoring me. I handed Feinstein the stack of papers he'd actually stopped by for. "And you correctly anticipated the delay with the sanitation shipment, but I'm on it. Delay should be thirty-six hours or less, not the week they tried to tell us."

"Damn. Excellent work." Feinstein raised his coffee cup my direction. "Not sure how you manage to be part-wizard, part-fortune teller."

"You're just throwing me a glitter parade because you want me to take that assignment the brass is so keen on." I could be honest with Feinstein, at least to a point. He was a straight shooter, the sort who invited candor, and he simply laughed off my assessment of his motives.

"You got me. But I'm not going to serve forever."

"Of course you are." It was the only acceptable answer with personnel approaching their twenty. Either he'd gun for master chief and stay in, in which case I couldn't be too eager to see the last of him, or he'd head to civilian life content with the knowledge he was indispensable to the rest of us still serving.

"Ha. I got a fishing boat with my name on it." Apparently, Feinstein had already picked his path. Must be nice to have that sort of clarity about one's future. My back tightened with more envy than I'd ever admit. I was tired of wrestling with my future in my head, considering all the angles like it was a supply problem.

"Hope you catch a lot of big ones." I made my voice way heartier than I felt.

"I will. No worries there. But first I gotta ensure my favorite protégé makes senior chief himself. You're on track, Euler. You could do it ahead of schedule even."

"It's not about making rank." I did like the idea of making senior chief, a long-held goal, but even that incentive didn't give me that clear-cut of an answer. "I like being…"

I trailed off as I realized too late that I couldn't complain about not being out on a sub to a man who'd made most of his career on shore, and who was damn proud of the fine job he'd done rising through the ranks.

"Needed? Useful?" Feinstein filled in the blanks I hadn't been willing to, direct as always. "You trying to tell me that the only way you feel needed is on a deployment? You've got three different crews singing your praises today, with two chiefs of the boat and one commander telling me how you're the best thing to happen to this department. Hell, maybe you do need that glitter parade."

Rightfully chastised, I hung my head, studying the top of my scarred desk. Careers were earned here. Missions were saved here. Disasters averted. I was the one clinging to a single definition of success, and I deserved the rebuke. "Sorry, sir. I didn't mean to disparage what we do here. I just miss my crew."

"So you do." Voice pragmatic, Feinstein shrugged. "But you've got a hell of an opportunity here. That's all I'm saying."

"I know I do." I had to admit I'd been more than my share of whiny over my impending decision, and the reminder that a lot of people would love to be in my shoes was both necessary and welcome.

"Don't be hasty." He waved the papers at me.

"I won't." Even if thinking things over was killing me, I owed it to everyone, not simply myself, to consider all the angles. It was easy to pine for my old life, but it was past time that I acknowledged that even if I were deployed, things would be different now. No Derrick. Possibly an entirely new crew. Change was inevitable and I didn't want to miss out on the chance for something new and perhaps even better by trying to pretend it wasn't happening.

"This thing is fast spiraling out of control."

"Uh-huh." I could laugh because Derrick meant his impending marriage, not the current state of my life, which did seem to presently hinge on a lot out of my control as my earlier conversation with Feinstein had illustrated. But Derrick wasn't calling to hear about that. I shifted the phone so that I could adjust the towel around my waist. "You're the one who wanted a wedding."

"I did." Even with an entire continent between us, his happiness still came through crystal clear. He sounded more bemused than genuinely put out about planning. "And first it was going to be an elopement. Then maybe a quiet thing with your folks."

"Nothing is quiet where the Eulers are concerned." I finished toweling off my hair. I was back in the barracks after finishing an early shift, doing a hard workout, and showering. At some point I'd have to think about hitting the chow hall for dinner, but I was happy for the distraction of Derrick's call in the meantime.

"As I am learning." The line crackled as he laughed, a reminder of how rarely I got to hear that familiar chuckle these days. The changes Derrick's transfer had meant for me pushed down heavily on my shoulders. I didn't begrudge him and Arthur any happiness, but I could also admit privately that I missed my best friend, missed working with him especially, and missed his dry sense of humor.

"And Mom was never going to let you get away with some little ceremony in their living room or something." Delaying getting dressed, I sat on my bed instead.

"I know." There was a rattling sound on Derrick's end as something hit a skillet. It was three hours later there, and he'd called me while making dinner because my brother was busy with a work project. "And this new plan of everyone meeting in Chicago since it's in the middle and a few people

I knew growing up can come isn't a terrible idea. But things keep getting added to the itinerary."

"Your problem may be having an itinerary in the first place." I stretched my legs out, connccting with the edge of my closet. My narrow room felt so much smaller after the weekend at Felix's spacious house and his bedroom which, unlike mine, didn't resemble a dorm room in the slightest. Even my unframed posters felt more shabby this week, and I missed that big bed something awful.

"Says the guy who never met a situation a spreadsheet or flow chart couldn't fix."

"You have me there." I was good at that, wasn't I? My plans for Felix's closet and pantry had gone perfectly. Having a clear checklist had helped, even if it did earn me some teasing. People like Derrick could rib me all they wanted, but they were the ones who praised my organizational skills when my spreadsheets save their asses a lot of work. Feinstein's earlier praise rang in my ears too. I was good at what I did, and there was no shame in owning that.

"Anyway, since apparently we've expanded from close family only for the wedding, did you want to bring a date?"

"A what now?" Having just wrapped my head around needing to travel to Chicago for this thing, I had to blink. Also, I'd been trying so hard to stealth-date Felix that the word *date* caught me by surprise.

"A plus-one." Derrick's tone was patient as he chopped something. "Someone to keep you company on the flight maybe? I know how you hate traveling alone. I don't care if it's Max or another friend if you're not seeing someone special. But I don't want you bored in the hotel room all weekend."

"I won't be." I flopped back against the pillows. Derrick wasn't wrong. I'd much rather travel with someone else. But dragging a buddy along to the wedding held limited appeal.

An image of how damn good Felix looked in a tie crept through my brain. Damn. Him all dressed up for the wedding would be exactly the distraction I needed. "And yeah, I might bring…someone."

I could ask at least. He'd probably say no, but maybe if I got extra persuasive, I'd have a chance. Heat rushed south at the mere thought of how I could persuade Felix, and I almost missed Derrick's reply.

"Good." Derrick laughed before his tone shifted to more coy. "Are you wanting me to pretend I didn't hear that pause or should I ask what's new with you?"

Even though he couldn't see me, I still waved away the concern. "Oh, you know me. I keep busy."

"I know. And I can't wait to hear all your latest adventures and wins."

Hmm. Not many wins lately. The last several weeks, I hadn't had much time for cards or other games. I chatted with Felix most nights instead of hanging out in the lounge with the guys. Any adventures I'd been having were of the more domestic variety, but I also wouldn't trade the last few weeks since meeting Felix for anything. We were rapidly approaching spring now, and I had no desire to go back to my old routine.

"We'll catch up." I kept it vague, then changed the subject. "I know you don't want a typical bachelor night—"

"A night of cards is fine. Bring some decent beer and I'm good." Derrick chuckled like he knew me so damn well. And he did. I wasn't incapable of planning some pub crawl or bigger party, but given permission to keep it small, I was rather predictable. But this time, I was already picturing Felix at the poker table with us, the secret looks we might share, counting down until later…

Yeah. I had to bring him along. Thinking of Felix reminded me to be nicer as well. After all, it wasn't only Derrick getting married. "Arthur can come. It's his bachelor night too."

"He'll probably tell us to have fun without him, but I'll ask." There was a fond familiarity to Derrick's tone that I truly envied. For the first time, I wanted that. Wanted to need to check with someone before making plans. Someone to cook for. Someone to come home to.

"You do that. Tell him I hope he's settling in well." I tried to make my brain move on from thoughts of Felix and how much I wanted him to come along, but then I bumped into my mini-fridge. I needed out of the damn barracks. Okay, yes, I definitely wanted a home. A place I could spread out. A place with…

Felix. Again he took over my brain, and I sighed, probably audibly enough for Derrick to hear.

"I'll tell him. You sure you're okay?"

"Me? I'm great." I did an excellent job of faking a hearty tone. "Have a good rest of your day—night." I'd forgotten the time difference again. And maybe there was more than three hours separating us these days. Funny that I'd intentionally gone the whole call without talking about Felix or anything else important going on in my life. But Felix was too new, like a fragile plant I needed to protect before sharing with the rest of the people in my life, even if I was rapidly starting to want that. And as to everything else going on, well, talking wasn't going to help there.

So, I ended the call with Derrick, happy for having gotten to talk to him but not feeling any more settled myself than I had when the phone had rung as I got out of the shower. And here I was, still in my towel. I went to stand in front of my closet, debating whether to put on a uniform and head to the chow hall or lounge in something more casual a little longer.

Right as I reached in the dresser for a T-shirt, my phone buzzed again. It said a lot about my mood that I, the king of socializing, wasn't in the mood for another conversation. I almost let it go to voicemail, but then I saw the pic I'd assigned Felix pop up. I'd taken a few of him while working on the pantry and closet, and I'd spent more time than needed deciding which to make his profile pic.

And I'd always answer the phone for him.

"Hey, there." I kept my tone light as I pulled on a T-shirt. He knew that I'd been working an earlier shift this week, and we'd had several pre-dinner calls like this as he waited for the girls at some activity or friends' house. "What pickup duty are you on today?"

Felix's answering laugh was the best thing I'd heard all day. "New after-school program we're trying out. Lots of art and creative fun. If they like it, I may be able to get by without a permanent nanny a little longer. Madeline should enjoy it at least. I hope it's not too boring for Charlotte."

"Anything short of observing surgery or scaling a mountain might be too boring for her."

"You know her well." Felix was joking, but I did. I knew his kids better than any of my nieces or nephews, knew the girls' likes and dislikes and little quirks. Man. I really was getting domestic. And I couldn't say I hated it either. I rolled my shoulders as Felix asked, "How was your day?"

My back tensed right back up again. "It was a day."

"Oh? Tell me about it. Distract me from this traffic jam."

"Nothing big." I wasn't going to unload on him, but I also couldn't lie to Felix. Even when I tried to make light of something, the truth had a way of slipping out around him. He made talking feel good in a way that few others in my life ever had. "Shipping snafu to sort out for supplies for a sub deploying end of the week. We got it handled. Senior chief was pleased."

"Ah. That's good." Felix's tone was sympathetic. Maybe a little too sympathetic. "But you have mixed feelings about them deploying without you?"

How did he do that? Cut right to the heart of what I was dealing with. All damn day I'd been on edge, not even sure why. I'd passed by a homecoming celebration on my way to the barracks, and nearly cracked a tooth from gritting my jaw so hard. As I'd tried to articulate to Feinstein, I didn't like not being out there. But at the same time, I also liked being right *here*, talking to Felix, and hell if I knew what to make of the swampy soup of feels I kept seeming to need to wade through.

"Yeah. But being on shore duty, at least I'll get to go to Derrick and Arthur's wedding. Speaking of, you said you'd help me pick out a present?"

It was a change of subject but also a sneaky segue into my plan to ask him to go with me.

"I did, didn't I?" His tone was fond. Like Derrick's when he'd talked about Arthur. My chest expanded, shoulders lifting too. Damn but I liked Felix and liked being the reason he was smiling in his car in rush hour. I'd heard him telling his stepmother that he wasn't with anyone, and maybe that was technically true, but the tenderness in his voice said I might have a chance of changing his mind.

"Any evening you might be free for dinner? We could shop afterward."

"Sounds lovely, but I'm not sure when I can get kid coverage, and unless you're in the mood for spaghetti—"

"I'm always in the mood for spaghetti," I said quickly, sensing an opening. "That on the menu tonight?"

"Yes, actually it is. That you angling for an invite?" He

seized my bait so beautifully I had to stifle a chuckle as I pulled on jeans, not a uniform.

"More like offering to come help you make it. If I hurry, I can catch one of the fast rush hour ferries."

"Well..." Felix drew out the word, and I could sense him waffling even from here. More and more his reluctance felt like an inside joke between us. He called and texted me every bit as often as I did him, and he was quick to reveal whenever he had kid-free time. "You did leave your tools behind. Come collect them and we can do some online shopping while the girls do homework."

I had every intention of leaving my tools right where they were. The more visits I got, the better. And this felt significant, him inviting me over while the girls were around. Grinning, I put my shoes on. "Sounds great. I'm on my way."

"Excellent." Felix's pleased tone warmed me all the way down to my shoelaces.

And just like that, my bad mood was gone. *Poof.* I got to see Felix and the kids. My step lightened, the way it sometimes did on my way to my parents'. Weird how much like home Felix's place already felt. As I grabbed my keys and wallet, I tried to remind myself to not get in over my head. Somehow, though, I knew the lecture would fail.

Chapter Twenty-Eight

Felix

"Is Calder your boyfriend?" Charlotte asked from the back seat, voice at such a high volume passersby probably heard.

I made a choking noise. "What? Why do you think that?"

We were in the pickup line near the pier waiting for Calder. He'd caught one of the fast rush hour ferries, and it had worked out well for us to pick him up on our way back home. But the wait time meant dealing with Charlotte's endless questions and observations.

"He comes over a lot and he makes you smile."

"Lots of friends make me smile." It was true that Calder did more than most though. Simply hearing his voice earlier had brightened a crappy day. I still wasn't entirely sure why I'd invited him to dinner, but needing a smile was certainly part of it.

"And Calder did a sleepover when we were gone," Charlotte pointed out. Of course the junior detective hadn't missed that little detail. "Flora says her mom's boyfriend stayed over all the time and then he did a proposal. Now Flora gets to be a flower girl."

"Good for Flora." I rubbed the back of my neck with one hand.

"Will you marry Calder?" Charlotte clearly wasn't done with the questions. "I like poofy dresses."

"I am not marrying Calder," I said firmly. God, the thought of marrying anyone again was terrifying.

It was.

I refused to entertain the image of Calder in a tux that tried to pop into my brain. Not welcome. Calder, married? Never. Even if he would make someone a far better spouse than I'd originally thought…

No. Still not going there.

"Good." Madeline was rather emphatic from her seat next to Charlotte.

"Madeline? Don't you like Calder?" Maybe inviting him for dinner had been a big mistake. I didn't want to make the kids miserable. This was their time with me, not my own personal happy hour.

"Oh, he's nice. And funny." Her laughter went a long way to reassuring me that he wasn't the most unwelcome of guests. "But you don't need a boyfriend."

On that we were in agreement. It didn't matter what fanciful thoughts insisted on dancing in my head. It wouldn't be smart or fair to the girls to date anyone right now, even someone who made me smile as much as Calder. But I also couldn't have Madeline down on all relationships regardless of whether I was having one.

"Calder is a friend. But it wouldn't be terrible if he was a boyfriend. Many boyfriends or girlfriends or partners are good people. Sometimes grown-ups like having another grown-up around."

"I know that." Madeline sounded all worldly. "But Tim made you sad. I don't like you sad. Divorce sucks."

"Don't say sucks. But agreed." Tim had never been Uncle Tim, had never enjoyed being around the girls even on a part-time basis, and he hadn't done anything to make a better impression on the girls.

And this was an excellent reminder that even happy couplings ended, and those endings were hard on kids, even if they didn't like one of the parties. Madeline didn't need to see me all down in the dumps over another breakup.

"I'm never going to get married," Madeline announced, followed quickly by an indignant noise from Charlotte.

"You should want a wedding—" An argument was about to erupt in the back seat right as Calder was walking toward the car. I whistled sharply and held up a hand.

"Enough. No one is getting married. It's just a guest for dinner."

That was all it could be. A friendship, some benefits we both enjoyed, but only a friendship. And then he smiled right at me as he slid into the passenger seat and my whole body heated, like I was standing in front of the woodstove at the cabin. Friends didn't usually invoke such a visceral reaction, but maybe we were simply...*warm* friends.

"Hey." Calder's smile widened as he buckled up. No kiss, but I almost felt like I'd received one with him radiating so much joy at seeing me. "Hope you weren't waiting long."

Only my whole life. Damn it. Why couldn't I have met Calder five years ago? Or three years from now? Or any other time when feeling like I'd waited my whole life for someone like him to come along inspired happiness, not dread.

"No, it was fine." I swallowed back all that internal drama, gave him a return smile. "Gave us a chance to have a nice chat. Now, let's get to cooking at home."

"Sounds good."

It did. And that was why I'd invited him. Oh, I'd let him think he was doing the inviting, but I'd been more than okay with the idea after another day spent craving his in-person presence. Cooking with him after a long day sounded lovely. Someone to chat with while the girls got settled with homework and electronics. Someone to appreciate my cooking. Someone to smile at me like he did.

And maybe not someone in the vague "anyone will do" sense, but someone like Calder specifically who joked with the girls and who made the transition to the dinner routine easier, hanging up backpacks and chasing down pencils while I quickly changed out of my dress shirt. He even lined up ingredients while I settled the girls with their homework assignments at the dining table.

"Ooh, fancy sauce tonight." Calder held up a bottle with a gold lid that I'd picked up at a specialty store some time back.

"Shush." Glancing back at the dining area, I dropped my voice. "I'm hoping they don't notice it's not the basic marinara they usually insist on."

"I won't tell." Calder smiled as I stretched. Even the switch to more casual clothing hadn't eased my mood much. "You doing okay? You seem tense. Did me coming over add to your stress?"

"No, you're my stress relief." I might not like needing him, but there was no denying that I was calmer and happier around him. "It was a day. Like you said about yours. I'll be glad when it's the weekend."

"Tell me about it." He touched my shoulder as I grabbed a pot for the pasta.

"Well, first, we got off to a late start because of missing shoes." The pantry was the bright spot in the chaos that was living with kids. Somehow a pink sneaker had gone missing, and of course, Charlotte had needed that pair, no substitutes.

"We can do their closets as our next project if you want." Calder made the offer like he was truly looking forward to the challenge. "Fewer missing items."

"You're the best." I'd probably turn him down. I couldn't keep taking advantage of his organizational skills. However,

I didn't want to start an argument by refusing right then. Instead, I admitted to another one of my stresses. "Then one of my favorite patients took a turn for the worse health-wise. The one I had to take the call for over the weekend. The patient won't be able to stay at home much longer. It's an expected part of my job, helping patients and their families navigate those transitions, but it's still hard."

"I bet." Calder moved to rubbing both of my shoulders, and it felt too damn good to make him stop. The girls were already done with homework and had scooted off to the lower level to the TV. "What else went wrong?"

Damn man was a clairvoyant. I groaned and leaned more into him. "And I had to deal with Tim's lawyer on the final property tax numbers. I directed him to my lawyer, but it still was a hassle my day didn't need."

"How much longer until everything is actually final as in done and over?"

"The divorce decree has been final awhile now." That was part of the stress. We were divorced. That part of the ordeal was supposed to be behind us. And yet the headaches persisted. "This should be the final request for modification. I hope. I'm ready to move on from all the money talk."

I was ready to put Tim in my rearview, get back to my life with the girls and being happy, not so stressed all the time. Heck, maybe I'd even take Calder's and Gabrielle's advice, look into some way to be involved in the performing arts community again that wouldn't take me away from the girls too much.

"I hope it's the last time you hear from them too." Calder dropped to a knee in front of my wine chiller. "Which of these should I open to go with the pasta?"

"Oh, I probably shouldn't drink." I waved away the suggestion even though I was sorely tempted to share a glass with him. Introducing him to new wines was fun, and he wasn't wrong about me needing the relaxation. "It's a weeknight and I'll need to run you back to the ferry and—"

"And you had a day." He looked up patiently at me, not moving from the spot. "That's reason enough. I was already figuring on finding my own way back because you'll need to do bedtime for the kids. But you deserve to unwind a little after a day like that."

"You do make a good argument." Somehow I always seemed to give in far too easily around him. As much as I didn't want to admit it, he was part of why I was ready to move on, but the one thing I was not ready for was figuring out where Calder fit into my plans for future happiness. Best to focus on tonight only. "Grab the second bottle on the top right."

After handing him a wine bottle opener, I retrieved two wineglasses as he smirked. "I'm good at being persuasive."

He was. And the glass of wine definitely did the trick, eased the cooking time and smoothed the transition to eating dinner with the girls. I was still nursing my first glass at the table, nowhere close to tipsy, simply relaxed and happy to be sharing a meal with the kids and Calder. The atmosphere was so cozy and natural I had to keep reminding myself not to get used to it. Moving on from Tim without counting too much on Calder felt like the key to balancing all my conflicting emotions.

"Did you like your new after-school program?" Calder asked the girls. The pleasant warmth in my chest that the wine had started continued to build watching him making an effort.

"It was fun!" Charlotte reported. "And next week we're showing off a special dance at Friday pickup. You should come!"

"Well..." Calder stretched out the word, probably searching for an appropriate excuse. I had his back there.

"Calder probably has work."

Calder shot me a look I couldn't quite read. "I'm not sure what my duty schedule is yet, actually. I'll try to see what I can do."

"Good." Charlotte nodded sharply before the subject shifted to the art project she'd completed that afternoon. And I wouldn't lecture Calder too much about making promises he couldn't keep. I could still use the work excuse for him, and being around kids was still new for him. He didn't know that Charlotte would take his maybe as a yes. But he likely had zero interest in the kids' dance, and he'd been plenty nice already, paying them both a ton of attention all evening.

After dinner, Calder insisted on doing the cleanup while I herded the girls through the nighttime routine of laying out clothes for tomorrow, showers, a quick story, and leaving them to read quietly before lights out. By the time I made it back downstairs, the kitchen was sparkling and a second glass was waiting for me with a ginger cookie by its side.

"Okay. You coming for dinner was a fabulous idea." I took a bite of the cookie.

"Good. I like being your stress relief." Hugging me from behind, he rested his head against mine. So damn sweet it hurt.

"Sorry that we can't..."

"Don't be sorry. Aren't you the one always telling me that we don't need a certain goal in mind or even a destination like your bedroom? I'm happy holding you a few minutes." His tone was sincere and he squeezed me tighter to make his point.

I suppressed a sigh because he really was that perfect. "Well, at least I can make good on the present help. Let me grab my laptop."

We took our wine and cookies to the couch where we snuggled with the laptop between us. Calder's arm around me felt so good as we scrolled through options that I could forgive him a lack of enthusiasm.

"All wedding gifts start to look the same to me." He frowned as we made our way through the happy couple's registry.

"Says the guy who showed me fifty million shelving options. Such a romantic."

"Hey, I'm plenty romantic. I'm just saying that if I ever did get married, I wouldn't register for the same stuff everyone else seems to. There's nothing romantic about dishes." Something in his tone gave me pause. He sounded different than he had that first night at the cabin, less adamant, more speculative.

"I thought you were rather dead set against relationships, let alone marriage."

"Oh, I don't know. I might be softening." He gave me a lazy smile, light and teasing, and my body had no idea how to react, back tensing even as my stomach flipped.

"So, I think what you want for a present is something personalized for them."

Calder had an arch look for my abrupt subject change. He knew what I was doing. So did I. No way could I discuss Calder's changing stance on relationships right then because that would mean reexamining my own and…

No. Better we get back to present looking.

"Personalized is good." Calder followed my lead back to the gift shopping. "It needs to be either shippable or portable though, as the plan is everyone meeting in Chicago for a wedding weekend, and I don't want to have to check luggage."

"Fair enough."

"There is something I want to bring along." His tone was so full of good humor that I was instantly curious.

"Oh?"

He grinned broadly as he spread his hands wide. "You."

Well, hell. I stumbled right into that. "Bringing me is probably not a good idea."

"Why? The girls can come. All the nieces and nephews will be there, so they won't be bored. And don't most little girls like an excuse to wear fancy dresses?"

Thinking of Charlotte's comments in the car, I had to nod. "They do."

"See? It will be fun. Don't make me go alone." He made an exaggerated pouty face like asking him to go alone was the same as telling him to eat his vegetables.

"That puppy-dog face doesn't work on me," I lied, because he actually was rather adorable in his enthusiasm for this terrible idea. But I also wasn't sure that latching onto this plan was the healthiest thing. "And you wanting a distraction from your feelings about the wedding isn't a great reason."

Losing the comical expression, he frowned. "I'm not brokenhearted about it or anything."

"I'm not saying you are." We'd talked about the situation enough that I knew he wasn't jealous of his brother landing Calder's best friend, but there were certainly some complex emotions, especially around missing them after the cross-country move. "Not all uncomfortable emotions need distraction. Sometimes it's better to sit with your feels."

Calder's mouth twisted. "Good advice, Doc. But there's a fine line between healthy coping and wallowing. Why let the negative stuff win? Acknowledge it, sure, but sometimes moving forward is the better option."

My back tingled as Calder dropped his gaze to my balled-up hands. Maybe we weren't only talking about the wedding anymore. Did he think I was wallowing in my post-divorce feelings? Returning to my earlier thoughts about moving on, I had to wonder about my motives for insisting that we couldn't date. *I don't like you sad.* I had to think of the girls. I clenched my hands tighter. His views on relationships might be changing, but mine couldn't.

I deliberately kept my voice more doctor-like than usual. "Focusing on the positive is good. Perhaps the distraction element isn't such a bad thing. But possibly you inviting another...friend would be the better option?"

Exhaling hard as if I'd kicked him, Calder grimaced. His eyes were so sad and disappointed that my insides trembled.

"I don't want another friend. I want you." The stubborn set of his jaw made me want to kiss his foolish lips. This was madness but I still let him continue. "Why can't we be the sort of friends who take a trip together?"

A pained noise escaped my throat. "Because—"

The sound of little feet on the stairs cut me off. Madeline poked her head into the living room, Ellie the elephant under one arm. "I can't sleep. My room is too hot."

This was a frequent complaint, right up there with being too thirsty or too cold for sleep, and usually meant that she had something big on her mind she needed to talk about before she could sleep.

"That's too bad. I'll be up in a second to see what we can do." I turned back to Calder after she'd headed back upstairs. "Sorry—"

"Don't be sorry. Go." He gave me a tight smile. "Take as long as you need. I'll be here."

But would he really? Notwithstanding the fact that he needed to catch one of the late ferries, would he keep coming around if I kept digging in my heels about not dating? He'd dropped enough hints all evening that he wouldn't mind a change in status. Heck, he'd invited us to a major family event. Eventually, he was going to find someone more free to embrace his newfound domestic side. And I missed him already.

Chapter Twenty-Nine

Calder

"Whoa! Take any more frustration out on those weights and the steel might bend." Max strolled over to me as I finished my last set of free weights in the gym on base. "Luckily I have the answer for you."

Frowning, I put the weights back on their rack. "I haven't told you the problem yet."

"Doesn't matter. I have the solution for all your ills." His dark eyes flashed as he made a gesture like he was about to offer me a gift.

I highly doubted that. Max couldn't magically make Felix ready to date me for real nor could he fix any of the other dozen things on my mind. However, I owed him for not asking a ton of questions when I'd fessed up that the cabin wasn't legally mine after all. My relief over not being teased was something a psych like Felix would have a field day with. Still, Max deserved way more than a brush-off, so I stepped closer. "I'm listening."

"Highly exclusive poker party tonight. Catered foods. Experienced players only." Max was coming off a treadmill run, and he paused to wipe his face with his shirt. "It's exactly what you need for whatever funk you've been in the last few months, and I scored us both an invite at the last minute when spots opened up."

"You didn't ask me first."

"Dude. It's cards. You're off tonight and tomorrow. What more do you need to know?" Heading toward the locker room, he motioned for me to follow him.

"I have plans."

"Change them." He paused at the locker room door to give me a mock stern look as if he were a CO giving me an order.

But this wasn't a mission-critical situation no matter what Max seemed to think, so I shook my head. "Can't. Char—someone is counting on me."

"A new girl?" Max raised an eyebrow as we both grabbed towels from our lockers.

"Guy. Felix. Charlotte is his kid. It's complicated." I didn't want to get into the whole tale right then, but I also wasn't going to lie to my friend. Felix would probably object to being labeled as my guy, but unlike him, I wasn't invested in keeping up the fiction that all we had going was a close friendship. If that's all Felix truly wanted, then so be it. I'd be happy to be his friend, but I also was done being scared of the *relationship* word.

"Sounds like it. Sure you can't get out of whatever it is?" He stripped off his shirt. Attraction was such a funny thing. Max and all his muscles did nothing for me, but Felix and his slim body and bookish silver fox looks made my pulse hum like nothing else.

"I already told him I'm coming." Toting my shower stuff, I followed Max to the showers.

"I'd say bring him, but I'm not giving up my seat."

"It's not his style anyway. And the thing is for his kid, so I doubt he can get away tonight."

"And you're staying in all night too?"

"Yup." I nodded even though Felix didn't know that yet. My plan was to offer dinner help and wrangle some time with him as a bonus after the dance performance. Things had been tense all week even though we'd still talked most nights. He wouldn't agree to Chicago, but he also hadn't totally slammed that door either. More like the door was cracked but he refused to step through. No matter. I had a plan to coax him into giving things between us a real try, Chicago trip included. And me taking off for a night of poker didn't enter into my goals.

Even if I was tempted. Cards sounded way more fun than a kid dance that Felix had only grudgingly given me the details on. He rather clearly expected me to bail. He wouldn't be at all surprised or upset if I canceled. Which was why I had to go.

If I went with Max instead, I'd be right back where I'd been a few weeks ago at the cabin with my crew. Missing Felix. Lonely even with my buddies around. Something had been missing from my life for some time now. I'd thought it was connected to my career, but I was increasingly sure that the missing element was a person, not a thing.

And I had to prove it to him by showing up. So I shook my head again as Max opened the curtain to his shower. "Sorry. I bet you don't have a problem finding someone else to go."

He whistled low. "Damn. Suit yourself, but never thought I'd see the day you turned down a chance to win big."

Join the club. But here I was, showering fast so I could catch the ferry in time to catch the right bus to the community center with the girls' after-school program. I could have driven, but the ferry was actually the faster option, and part of my plan to spend more time with Felix involved not having my car with me.

"You made it." Exactly as I'd predicted, Felix seemed surprised as we met up outside the community center, my bus arriving shortly before I spotted his SUV.

"I said I'd try." I sounded defensive, but he could pretend a little harder to be happy to see me. He looked damn good in his doctor attire with a crisp white shirt and green tie that seemed ready to welcome early spring. I wanted to touch him in the worst way, but I couldn't risk him shrugging off the touch.

"You did say that. I didn't..." Felix shook his head before giving me a smile that didn't reach his eyes. "Charlotte will be excited. And I appreciate it. You took the ferry?"

"Yep." This stiff formality was killing me. You'd never know this was the guy who two nights ago had debated the merits of various true crime shows while we lingered on the phone. But get us in person and suddenly we had nothing to say as all the tension from our last meeting shoved out our usual easiness with each other.

"I can give you a ride to the pier after if you need."

"Was hoping you'd let me give you a helping hand with dinner first." Giving him what I hoped was a winning smile, I kept my voice light but determined. I wasn't giving up. We only needed a chance to talk things through, and then we'd be back to the cozy fun and warm touches I craved.

Felix's face softened as if he were tempted even as his shoulders stiffened. "Calder..."

"Well, this is a pleasant surprise." Felix's stepmother arrived, heels clicking against the sidewalk and wearing an elegant silver top way nicer than anything the other people milling around the entrance had on. She swept an appraising gaze over me. She seemed like the type who didn't miss much.

"Likewise." Felix gave her a fast hug. He was stiff with her too, which strangely reassured me. Maybe it wasn't only me that he had a hard time letting in. His voice was still all doctor-formal as he asked, "I thought you had some sort of charity meeting?"

"It finished early." Gabrielle made a dismissive gesture that had her open jacket swishing in the breeze. "Besides, Charlotte asked me specially."

"She was rather enthusiastic with her invites," Felix agreed, sparing a fast glance for me. "But I'm pretty sure this is a rather short performance."

"It'll still be fun." Gabrielle linked arms with Felix. "Calder, nice to see you again."

"You too." I hadn't missed her emphasis on *again*. And I matched her smile because I liked being a regular part of their lives even if Felix didn't seem to quite know what to make of that development.

"Let's go in and find seats." He gave a resigned sigh like Gabrielle and I were marching him toward a high dive he'd be expected to leap from.

"Sure." Meeting his gaze, I tried to tell him with my eyes that this didn't have to be so scary. I believed in him. Believed in us. And I believed this thing could be a lot of fun if only he'd let it.

At the front door, we all had to show IDs and get checked in before we were led to a gym with a few rows of folding chairs set up. The chairs were too small for most adults, but we found three together. I didn't even mind being cramped because it meant rubbing shoulders with Felix, which I'd take any day.

"Here they come," some other parent whispered as a group of around twenty kids of assorted ages came in through a side door. Their young dance instructor bubbled with enthusiasm as she introduced the song, an upbeat pop number getting a ton of recent airplay. Arthur would tease me relentlessly if he knew, but I already had all the words memorized.

Accordingly, I forgave the tinny acoustics of the gym and hummed along as the kids danced to the song. They were charmingly off-rhythm and Charlotte kept stopping to wave at us. Madeline was there too, serious expression on her face as she and some older girls put more effort into following the instructor's moves. Watching them both up there trying hard made my chest do this strange squeeze. Was this pride? I wasn't sure, but I'd been feeling it more and more lately.

"Now for the fun part!" The instructor stepped back to the front to address the audience. "We're going to do it again, but parents and visitors, you can join in!"

Join in? They wanted us to do a silly dance too? In public? It was one thing to goof around with the kids at the cabin or Felix's house and another to make a fool of myself with an audience. And dancing type of coordination was never my strong suit.

"You don't have to," Felix whispered as some of the adults started reluctantly shuffling forward. Gabrielle ventured up there, heels and all. Yet again, he was assuming I wasn't up for a challenge. I was damn tired of it. Fuck public humiliation. I wanted his faith in me more.

I stared him down. "I will if you will."

Chapter Thirty

Felix

"I will if you will." Calder had a stubborn set to his chiseled jaw. He had a point to prove. What, I wasn't entirely sure. But he was here at the community center when I'd expected him to find an excuse to avoid the kid event. All week I'd been waiting for him to pull away because I wouldn't agree to Chicago, bracing myself for him to invite someone else or otherwise move on from our friendship. But he hadn't. And now here he was, the guy who really didn't like eyeballs on him, daring me to go to the front with him.

I opened my mouth to tell him we could both stay put, but Charlotte chose that moment to crow, "Come on, Uncle Felix! Come dance!"

"Coming!" Damn it. Now I'd trapped both of us because of course Calder was right behind me as I went to stand near Charlotte. Madeline and her friends surrounded Gabrielle, who was listening intently to them and the dance instructor, who was demonstrating some of the steps. Gabrielle had always had a natural grace, and she made even the silly moves look elegant.

I, on the other hand, undoubtedly looked like a broken puppet trying to copy the instructor. Calder didn't fare much better, bumping into me twice as we went through a practice run with the rest of the grown-ups who had chosen to join in. But he was here and he was trying, which was more than a lot of people would do.

About half the adults remained in the audience, some taking pictures of their offspring and laughing at those of us fumbling our way through the dance.

"Isn't this fun?" Charlotte grabbed both my hand and Calder's, swinging herself between us.

"Yep. Sure is." Calder gave her an indulgent smile. His cheeks were pink though. Charlotte probably couldn't tell how hard he was working to not be embarrassed, but I could and the urge to rub his arm or something was strong.

"Calder came! Nana too! Everyone I like is here." She did a wiggle that wasn't part of the dance, simply Charlotte being happy. Her unrestrained joy at Calder's presence made my chest ache. What was it that I'd told Calder about uncomfortable emotions? I'd told him not to shy away from complex feelings, but right then, I wanted no part of the way pride and sentiment were battling it out with anxiety in my brain.

It was going to hurt when Calder stopped coming around either because of a deployment or because he moved on to someone more able to give him what he needed and deserved. Charlotte was going to miss him. Me too. So much. Him being so good with the kids only made it that much worse. We were all getting too damn attached.

"Now with the music!" The instructor called our attention back to the front as she fiddled with her phone, which was controlling the portable speaker.

"Come on, Uncle Felix! Smile!" Charlotte demanded.

I tried. I really did. But my head continued to churn even as the song started. I stumbled over my own feet, and Calder steadied my elbow.

"Careful. Don't want to fall."

I already had. I'd fallen for him even when I hadn't intended to, and now I was falling for him all over again as he grinned at Charlotte and tried to copy her hand movements, making her giggle and giggle. He even sang along like he knew the lyrics. Being silly didn't come naturally to Calder at all, and here he was, yet again making a big effort with the girls. He was so damn fearless, putting himself out there.

I simply wasn't sure I had the same sort of bravery in me.

Instead I tried to endure until the end of dance, fighting a losing battle to not succumb to Calder's charm. Despite a steady stream of lectures to myself, I still found myself smiling at the end.

He was wearing me down, and that was only going to make things that much harder when we inevitably crashed and burned.

"So about dinner?" he asked after the instructor dismissed the kids and went over checkout procedures.

"Yes, about dinner." Gabrielle strode over before I could explain what a bad idea that was, Madeline trailing behind her. "Let me take the girls? I have the worst pizza craving."

"Liar." I gave her a pointed look. She would have a side salad and pick at a breadstick while the girls devoured the treat. And in typical style, she was making an offer I couldn't refuse without disappointing the girls, who were already clamoring to go.

"Can we sleep over?" Charlotte asked Gabrielle, all heart eyes at the concept.

"That's a splendid idea." Gabrielle didn't bother glancing at me before she answered. "Then Uncle Felix and Calder can have a nice grown-up evening."

I should have known matchmaking was behind the pizza offer. "We don't need—"

"Please." Charlotte turned those big eyes my direction.

"Can we watch that circus musical again?" Even Madeline appeared to want to go, which I hadn't expected. All around us families were departing, full of Friday plans of their own, making my reluctance to agree feel more Scrooge-like. I didn't like depriving them of fun.

"You want a sleepover?" I asked Madeline, trying to give her space before Charlotte steamrollered her into going along with her.

"Sure." Gold curls bouncing, she shrugged like the change of plans was no big deal when only a few months ago it might have meant a lot of tears. "I want pizza. And Nana let us watch musicals on the train. That was fun."

"Please," Gabrielle added, teasingly. "Come on, Uncle Felix. Have some fun."

Fun. That was what this thing with Calder was supposed to have been. Fun. A lark. Not serious. Not something to ache over. Not something to pine for. But now things were too damn complicated, and we needed to talk, something best accomplished without an audience.

"All right." I reluctantly nodded, not because I was truly worried about the girls with Gabrielle but because part of me wanted to delay that talk as long as I could. The distraction of the girls would have helped with that, but they looked so eager to go with Gabrielle. "You go with Nana, who will call me if anything comes up. Right?"

"Of course, darling. I'll call." She patted my cheek. "You and Calder have a lovely evening."

I highly doubted that was possible, but Gabrielle and the girls were looking at us all expectantly. I forced a smile. "We'll try."

Chapter Thirty-One

Calder

After the girls departed with Gabrielle, I half expected Felix to dump my ass back at the pier, no dinner, no chance to talk. He hadn't seemed happy the whole evening, and not even the cute kid performance had cheered him up.

However, as we walked back to the SUV, I was still riding an adrenaline rush from getting up there. I'd been so tense, all my old hatred of being the center of attention coming back, those long-held worries about people laughing, but then I'd realized that they were going to laugh whether or not I got up there. A bunch of adults trying to do a kids' dance *was* funny. So, why not have fun with it? I was able to make Charlotte happy by participating, and if the people who remained in the audience had wanted to laugh at the big guy with two left feet, let them.

In fact, when someone in the audience *had* laughed when I'd stumbled early on, I'd actually relaxed. The worst had happened. Now I could move on and enjoy myself, not let those ancient fears hold me back from doing something. And making the kids smile was worth letting a few folks chuckle at my expense.

"That was actually kind of fun," I remarked to Felix as he unlocked the car.

"You knew the lyrics." He laughed as he slid behind the wheel.

"Guilty." My neck heated. Maybe I wasn't completely beyond the fear of embarrassment after all.

"Don't be shy. You're cute." He smiled at me, but his tone was more wistful than teasing.

"I try." After buckling my seat belt, I turned toward him. "Can I be cute over dinner? I promise to discuss other overplayed pop ballads I know by heart."

"I'd like to see that playlist." Felix laughed then sobered. "We need to talk."

"And we need to eat." I didn't like the way he said *talk* as I was pretty sure he had a different objective than I did, but if he'd agree to a meal, I'd have that much more time to win him over.

"We do." A muscle in his neck jumped like he was doing intense calculus, trying to weigh the risk of public argument against a desire for dinner.

"We can get takeout." I made the math easier for him. "Tell me what and I'll do an order from my phone."

"I guess we can eat at my place." His tone was resigned, but then he brightened. "There's a Cajun place near the house I keep meaning to tell you about since you like spice as much as me. Incredible barbeque shrimp. And there's coffee beignets for dessert."

"You planning on keeping me around until after dessert?" I kept the tease light, but I honestly wasn't sure what the odds were of the conversation going my way.

"Yes. I wish—"

I held up a hand. "No sad wishes. Not until after we eat, okay? Now, let me call in an order."

"Aye, aye, Chief."

While he started driving back to Queen Anne, I got the

information for the place, discovered they had an online ordering option, and completed the task quickly.

"I got extra beignets in case you want some for the morning. Make this a sleepover and I'll make sure you have an appetite." If optimism alone were enough, my hope could power a small city.

"Calder..."

"Look, you have a kid-free Friday night. Even if we do need to talk about some things, we don't have to go all heavy and serious the entire evening. I like hanging out with you. That hasn't changed."

"I like hanging out with you too." While stopped for a red light, he touched my hand.

"See? We can still have a good time. Even cranky and needing to talk with me, I still like you better than Max and his poker party idea."

"You turned down a poker party to go to a kids' dance recital?" Felix's eyebrows went up. Oops. I maybe shouldn't have revealed that.

"Yeah, I know, I'm shocked too."

"You should have gone." His face was impassive as the light changed and we crept forward with the rush hour traffic.

"What? Why?" Not that I wanted heaps of praise for showing up, but him pushing me away so blatantly stung.

"You're a young single guy who can have his pick of Friday-night fun and companionship. You don't need to be stuck with us."

"Way to value yourself," I shot back. "And I'm over thirty. Not some kid. A lot of my buddies have left young and single behind. And because I too can be mature, maybe I picked you because you are the fun I want tonight."

"This is fun for you now." His too-patient tone was grating on my last nerve. "But for how long? The kids are getting attached to you, and I'm getting worried for how they are going to react if you stop coming around."

"The kids?" I gave him the most pointed of looks as we stopped for yet another light. I wasn't going to let him get away with hiding behind the kids. "Really, Felix? The kids are getting attached?"

"Well, they are. Charlotte was delighted to see you." His hand clenched around the steering wheel, shoulders stiff. "Too delighted. She'll be hurt if you move on."

"Charlotte will be hurt?"

"All right, all right. Me too. I'm getting too attached. I'll be hurt. Is that what you want to hear?"

"Yes!" I dug my fingers into my thigh as we arrived at an upscale Cajun place not far from Felix's house.

"Oh?" Felix crept forward, trying to find a parking spot on the crowded street. I waited until he'd found one and I had his full attention again before I continued.

"Yes. Because I have the solution." Shifting in my seat, I turned toward him. He might have that professional doctor tone of his, but I had my chief voice, the one I used for delivering a plan of action. "I keep coming around. Then no one's hurt when I stop because there is no stopping. Date me for real, Felix."

His eyes went so wide I worried he might sprain something. "Cal—"

"You think on that while I grab the food." I kissed his cheek and quickly slid out of the car, heart hammering. I had more to say. Much more. And leaving him alone with his thoughts was a calculated risk, but I was betting on him being more amenable to the idea when fed. And also, my logic was sound.

He was worried about being hurt and me leaving. If I didn't leave, then he didn't need to worry. Problem solved.

I grabbed our food order, which smelled divine, and hurried back to the car where Felix still looked as stunned as when I'd left him.

"Wow, that's a lot of food," he said as I climbed back into the passenger seat.

"Yeah, well, I'm hungry and I'm planning to stay awhile."

"You certainly do seem convinced about this dating idea." If nothing else, he seemed impressed by my stubbornness, and he put the car in drive without further argument.

"We've been dating." The obvious needed to be pointed out. "We talk almost every night. We see each other whenever we can. I think about you all the time. I want to take you to my brother's wedding and other places. We *are* dating. Just make it official, so you're less worried that I'm about to ghost you."

"Officially dating wouldn't make me any less worried." He headed away from the bustling Friday-night traffic into the residential streets.

"Why not?"

"I understand that you've had a change of heart where dating and relationships are concerned. But I can't be your trial run—"

"Whoa." I held up a hand as he turned onto his street. "Who said trial? I'm in this thing, Felix. This isn't some starter package. I want you, specifically, not a partner, generally."

"I appreciate that. But, Calder, you're going to get bored or frustrated with the amount of baggage I bring to the table. The kids. The house. The divorce. The unpredictable doctor hours." He let out a miserable sigh as he parked at his place.

God, I wanted to shake Tim all over again for putting the idea in Felix's head that he might be too much for someone. "Your baggage doesn't scare me. I have work stuff too. I understand what it means to be on call."

"I know you have work obligations as well. And that's the other thing. You could be deployed at any moment."

"No, I couldn't." I exited the car because the space was starting to close in on me, and he followed me, leading the way to his back door.

"The whole time I've known you you've been itching to get back on a sub." Even after unlocking the door, he continued to stare me down, pale light from the hall giving him an ethereal glow. "You're telling me you're not going to leap for joy the first deployment that comes your way?"

"No." My heart started hammering because I'd been circling this answer the last two weeks or so, but this was my first time giving voice to the decision aloud. "I'm going to take the training opportunity. Stay on shore duty."

Chapter Thirty-Two

Felix

"Ah." Head spinning, I made a knowing noise. I should have known something like this was behind Calder's newfound domesticity. I slumped against the mudroom wall as Calder shut the door.

"That's your reaction?" His tone was more resigned than angry, as if I'd let him down on a personal level. My chest felt like something large and angry had stomped on it.

"Sorry. I didn't mean to make light of your decision." Squashing Calder's feelings wasn't something I wanted to do at all. However, I also couldn't give him the overjoyed response he might have been hoping for. "But your sudden interest in dating makes a lot more sense now."

A frustrated sound escaped his throat. "I'm not going to deny that having you around made the choice easier. But I think it's something I've been working my way toward even before you."

"That's good." I was hiding behind my doctor voice and I knew it. Overly professional seemed preferable to letting my emotions overtake me, even if Calder's frown deepened with every careful syllable of mine. "But I can't be your consolation prize for not getting what you truly want. Or your backup plan."

"Give me more credit than that." He stalked into the dining area with the bag of food, which he set on the table. "Me being around more does make it easier to pursue a long-term relationship, but I'm not over here sulking and using you to make myself feel better."

"Really?" I couldn't believe that. "You've been mad about being on shore duty since we met."

"You should eat something." He pulled out a chair for me and pointed at it.

My head swam. I had no idea what to make of him caring about my hunger level in the middle of an argument as it was outside of my realm of experience, where fights were typically louder with more pouting and personal attacks. This was downright civilized, but I wasn't sure I trusted his motives.

"Don't change the subject." Oops. There went some of my professional tone. I sat down in part to try to bring my voice back to even. "Something happened to make you feel better about this choice."

"Well, I got happy. And I know you don't want to hear it, but you did have something to do with that." Calder too sounded like he was working at not snapping. He divided up the food on the plates the place had provided. "I realized I could be as happy and fulfilled away from the sub as I was on it."

"Happy is good," I whispered. My traitorous heart thrilled to know I made him happy even as my stomach twisted. Making him happy also meant the power to make him unhappy, a responsibility I wasn't sure I wanted.

"This training opportunity is a great chance to meet my goal of making senior chief before I hit my twenty years. It's the sort of advancement and opportunity I've wanted." He paused to place a plate of food in front of me. "I did, however, have to let go of my attachment to being deployed."

"I don't want to be the reason you made peace with that," I said as he sat next to me.

"Sorry. I'm not going to lie. You showed me I can love other things as much as I love being deployed."

All he had to do was hint at the *L*-word and my pulse sped up. I made a pained noise and shook my head, not trusting myself to speak.

"Don't look so horrified. That's not a bad thing. It's a win-win. I can get the career advancement and I can have a relationship that matters to me. I'm not going to apologize for having feelings for you."

Much as I liked hearing about those feelings, I frowned because I wasn't sure I wanted to be another *win* for him, a way to maximize benefits from a tough decision.

"I'm not asking you to apologize. I care about you too." I might be frustrated and conflicted, but I couldn't let him think all those emotions of his were one-sided. He deserved that much honesty from me. "And because I care, I don't want you sacrificing anything for me."

After finishing a bite of food, he shrugged. "Every relationship involves some amount of sacrifice."

"Exactly. And most fail." Still not eating myself, I gestured with my plastic fork.

"And some don't." He sounded awfully pragmatic for the guy that a couple of short months ago had been rather resolute that relationships were a bad bet he wanted no part of. "My parents made it work. Your grandparents did too. It's not always doomed. Maybe sometimes it's worth it."

My heart swelled with the memory of my grandparents taking long walks together right up until the end. There was a time when I'd wanted that kind of love for myself in the worst way, but now I wasn't sure that kind of relationship was possible. Trying for something with terrible odds was the sort of foolishness I couldn't afford. "And other times sacrifice breeds resentment and hastens the inevitable end."

"You keep assuming that I'm going to bolt at some point. Give me a chance." Leaning toward me, he took my hand.

"It's not about only me." My throat was raw and scratchy and his hand felt too damn good against mine. "I have to think about the girls too. I can't have them getting attached and then disappointed when we break up. And it goes the other way too. I have to put them first, and that's not fair to you. Eventually you're going to be disappointed and want a situation where your needs can be top priority."

Grimacing, he dropped my hand. "I'm not Tim."

"I know that." I felt the loss of his touch on a visceral level.

"I'm not sure you do." For the first time in this long conversation, he sounded genuinely angry. "You think I'm so selfish that I can't understand your commitment to the kids. And you assume I'd ghost on them too if things went south between us. You're so worried about the chance that I'm going to turn into Tim that you don't want to give us a chance to be different."

"I know you're not Tim. And you have a tremendous amount to give a potential relationship. So much." I started out with a patient tone, but the facade dropped as an image of Calder with another person blared in my head. My voice wavered to an embarrassing degree. "But I don't know if I can give you what you need in return. A relationship is a risk I simply can't take right now."

"Bullshit." His eyes hardened right along with his voice. "You know perfectly well that you have plenty to give me. You care. You show it all the damn time. What you are is scared."

He wasn't wrong, but I couldn't admit that. "Maybe I'm worried—"

"You're scared and it's okay. I'm scared too. But maybe we can be scared together?"

All my oxygen escaped all at once. His expression was as vulnerable as I'd ever seen it. My throat had never been this tight in my life either. "I—"

Buzz. Buzz. Right then at the worst possible moment, my phone vibrated nosily in my pocket, clanging against my keys and utterly paralyzing me. Calder, however, simply sat back and gestured at my lap.

"Check your phone. I'm not going anywhere." How he could be so calm and patient when I felt ten cups of espresso worth of jittery was beyond me. Maybe he was that certain of the outcome of the conversation. Must be nice. Myself, I had no clue, didn't even know what I'd been about to say.

And looking at my phone was as good a stalling tactic as any. But then I had to groan as soon as I saw the message.

"Crap. It's Gabrielle. She's bringing the girls back because Madeline threw up all over her car before they even made it to pizza. And now Charlotte doesn't feel well either." Food and conversation forgotten, I pushed away from the table, mind already racing ahead to how to manage this new crisis.

"What can I do to help?" Calder asked as the front door sounded.

"You don't need to stay for this." My evening had gone from terrible to even worse, but maybe his was still salvageable. He could go to the poker party, leave me to deal with this latest disaster. That would probably be best even if it did make my chest hurt cardiac-event levels of bad. My heart might not survive Calder, but the rest of me would have to go on.

Chapter Thirty-Three

Calder

I wasn't going anywhere. Felix seemed more than ready to shuttle me out the back door, but even if we weren't in the middle of one of the most important conversations of my life, I'd still want to help. No matter what he thought, I couldn't simply leave and go on about my Friday night.

"I ruined everything," Madeline wailed as she, Charlotte, and Gabrielle entered the house. None of them looked in great shape. Madeline was covered in puke, but Gabrielle looked decidedly rumpled too and Charlotte was clutching her stomach.

"You didn't ruin anything," Felix assured her as he rushed to her side. "You're sick. These things happen."

"I'm sick too," Charlotte moaned, then dashed for the stairs.

"I made a mess in Nana's car." Madeline was full-on crying now, face flushed like she might have a fever on top of everything else.

Felix put an arm around her, mess and all. He was such a good parent. "Nana's car will clean."

"Hopefully," Gabrielle muttered, looking rather pale herself and not at all like she wanted to deal with puke.

"I could handle that mess for you," I offered to Gabrielle, not Felix, who was busy shepherding Madeline up the stairs.

"You're a blessing." Gabrielle was all wide-eyed gratitude. I'd known she'd say yes, and the task bought me a little time to be useful to Felix later on too.

"I'll grab the cleaning supplies." I'd taken care of drunk friends enough to have the art of vomit removal down.

"Thank you, darling. I'll see what I can do here." But she didn't head for the stairs, instead striding toward the dining area. "Maybe I can pack up this lovely food for you?"

"That's probably best." No one was going to eat anytime soon, and since she didn't seem inclined to go on hazardous waste duty upstairs, I let her handle the remains of our dinner. Meanwhile I tackled her car, which was indeed gross, but I'd dealt with way worse. Felix helpfully kept rubber gloves along with the cleaning supplies. With any luck, maybe I'd avoid getting sick myself.

And after the earlier tense conversation with Felix, cleaning was soothing. Taking an awful mess and returning Gabrielle's car to a pristine state made me feel good. Like I'd done something important.

"Charlotte threw up too," Gabrielle reported as soon as I was back in the house and washing my hands thoroughly at the sink. She'd packed up all the dinner food and found a glass of water for herself.

"Oh man." I groaned as I washed my hands an extra time. Whatever I'd managed to do for Gabrielle, it was nothing compared to what Felix was dealing with. "Poor Felix. Poor her."

"Seldom have I been so grateful for the nanny we had when Courtney was little." Shuddering as she set the water aside, Gabrielle tugged her flowy jacket more tightly against herself. "I already feel like I need three showers."

"Why don't you go on home?" I suggested because it was pretty clear she didn't want to deal with all this. "I'm sure

Felix will text you an update, and that way you're at home if it's food poisoning and you're next to feel ill."

"Perish the thought." Holding up both hands, she took a literal step back. "We never made it to the pizza. We were stuck in traffic and then disaster happened. More than once. Charlotte said there's a bug going around the school."

"Ugh. That must have been hard on you." Aiming for a sympathetic tone, I patted her shoulder. "And a bug at school explains why it's both of them."

"Yes, and I shouldn't leave Felix to deal with it all alone." She shot a longing glance at the back door.

"He's got me." I gently steered her toward the door. "I'll help and I've got a cast-iron stomach. I'm not leaving."

"No, you're not," she said slowly as she studied me intently. She nodded like she'd come to some important conclusion about me. "He'll tell you he has it handled."

"And he does. I'm still staying." I drew myself up taller under her shrewd gaze.

"You're the right man for the job." She said it solemnly, like she meant more than simply puke duty.

"I hope so." I wasn't staying to prove to Felix that I was a worthy partner, but after this was all over, we did need to finish that talk. Maybe he'd come to the same conclusion as Gabrielle. Maybe.

"I think I will sneak out." She gave me a small smile as she pulled out her phone. "I'm going to give you my number though because I don't trust Felix to call me back if more help is needed."

"I'll text you," I promised as we exchanged numbers. After seeing Gabrielle out, I grabbed some empty mixing bowls and headed upstairs to see what else I could help with.

"How are they?" I found Felix looking harried with wild

hair and askew dress shirt in the hallway between Charlotte and Madeline's rooms.

"Not the best." He made a pained face. "You're still here?"

"Yep. Gabrielle's back seat needed cleaning, so I helped her out. She headed on home to shower, but I promised her updates."

"I'll text her in a while." Felix pulled at his collar.

I didn't tell him that I too planned to text her, instead holding out the bowls I'd brought upstairs. "Here. These should help if the vomiting keeps up. What else needs doing now?"

"Calder. Thank you, but you don't need to stay." He'd gone back to the too-patient doctor tone, which he tended to revert to when highly stressed. "I appreciate the gesture. But I have this."

"I know you do." I glanced around the upstairs, looking for a task because Felix sure wasn't going to assign me something. There was a mound of dirty clothes outside of the girls' bathroom. "But let me at least start a load of laundry for you. You're not going to want those clothes to sit."

"God, no. I was contemplating pitching them, to be honest."

"It's Madeline's favorite sweatshirt." I'd seen her in the hoodie advertising a cartoon franchise at least three times prior. It was a good guess that she'd miss the thing. "I'll put a load on for you."

"Uncle Felix!" Charlotte bellowed from her room. She might be sick but her voice box was working fine.

"Coming," Felix called back before returning his attention to me. "I guess laundry would be good. You know where the machine is downstairs?"

"Yeah. My mom made sure that I can handle some dirty clothes. I've been doing laundry since I was Madeline's age. I've got this," I assured him before he headed into Charlotte's room, and I got another pair of gloves and a plastic bag to collect the messy pile.

It wasn't my first time doing puke-stained laundry, and I had the machine loaded and running in short order. Still down on the lower level, I pulled out my phone to message Gabrielle to make sure she made it home safely.

While on my phone, I discovered a recent message from Max.

Dude. This party is lit. I'm winning big and the food is amazing.

I sent him a fast text back. Happy for you.

Having missed dinner, I was rather hungry myself, but I'd worry about that later. Unpleasant smells were still lingering in my nostrils too much to eat quite yet.

A reply came from Max before I put the phone away. Not too late for you to come. I didn't find a taker for the other invite. You could get in on some later games.

Felix wanted me gone. The easy answer would be to leave and check back with him later, but even if I was tempted, no way could I focus on poker knowing what Felix was dealing with here.

Another text came in from Max before I could reply. Come have some fun. Some great prizes to play for.

Voices from upstairs echoed down the nearby vent, Felix's soothing tones carrying even if I couldn't make out specific words. *Fun.* I sure said that word often enough. And this certainly wasn't a fun evening. But perhaps not everything came down to maximizing enjoyment. I'd been so lonely at the cabin without Felix and the girls there even while objectively having fun.

Max could play for prizes. I had one already and I wasn't letting it go. *Sorry. I'm needed here.*

That's what had been missing from my life. The being needed. I'd thought at first that it was Felix and the way he took care of me. And that was nice, something I hadn't let myself have before. But there was also this, the getting to take care of him in return.

And yes, Felix was capable of saving the day all on his own, but a part of me *needed* to help. It was the mission-critical feel that every action had on deployment, all hands on deck to keep the sub running and every task vital to someone else and the group as a whole.

When I was around Felix and the girls, I felt like part of a team. I'd been so focused on other parts of my life for so long I'd forgotten how a family could be a team, and I hadn't let myself want one for myself because not wanting was way simpler than wanting and never getting. However, now I wanted and I was determined to make it happen.

Phone still in my hand, I headed to the kitchen. Sick people needed hydration. I knew that much, but as I took stock of the pantry and fridge, I wasn't sure what else would be needed. But I knew someone who would have the answers. I dialed before I could talk myself out of the idea.

"Hey, Mom?" I asked when she picked up on the first ring.

"Calder! To what do I owe the pleasure?" She sounded delighted but also more than a little scolding.

I did some fast math in my head as to when I'd called last. She was justified. "Sorry. Guess I haven't called in a while."

"You haven't," she agreed before softening her tone. "But that's okay. I know you get busy."

Typical Mom, making excuses for my shortcomings. I needed to set a damn alarm on my phone or something to check in with her more, even if her questions did grate. She was still my mom, and watching Felix with the girls the past several weeks had underscored how lucky I was to have her.

"Yeah, I've been busy, but I'll try to do better. Promise."

"Good. But what do you need now?"

Ouch. I rubbed the back of my neck. That she immediately knew I was calling with a purpose made my idea of a phone alarm that much more necessary. "I've got a…friend with some sick kids. Like stomach sick. I know you've been there."

"And how." She groaned and there was a rustling sound like she was rearranging something. Like me, she always needed to keep busy, even while on the phone. "Lord, one time it was all four of you during one of Dad's longest deployments."

"I remember. You were a trouper. Anyway, I'm looking at my friend's pantry now, and trying to think what they might need for the next few days." The pantry was now nicely organized, but it was rather sparse now that we'd removed so much, and I wasn't sure what all sick kids needed.

"Got something to write with?" she asked, all serious mom business now.

"Yep." I grabbed a notebook from the drawer where Felix kept his pharmaceutical company samples. "I'm ready."

My mom rattled off a lengthy list of soup types, broth, electrolyte drinks, ice pops, and more.

"You're helping your friend?" she asked after I took notes of what to order. She sounded rather incredulous.

"Yeah." As with Max earlier, I wasn't sure why everyone found it so hard to believe I might choose to stay in on a Friday night or might choose to do something for someone else. If I'd really been that self-centered for years, maybe that was yet another reason to try to change. "My friend is a single dad. Uncle raising his nieces. I like helping him out."

"Single, you say?" She suddenly sounded way more interested in my mission to help Felix with a grocery order.

"Mom."

"Sorry. Anyway, if it's your friend on his own—"

"And me."

"And you. Make sure he stays hydrated and gets rest himself. I slept an ungodly number of hours after being up three days when that virus hit all four of you at once. It's easy to forget to eat and drink when the little ones need you."

"I'm sure. I'll make sure he rests." I nodded to the empty room, glad for another reason to stay even after the groceries came.

"He's lucky to have your help." She praised me like I was twelve and needed a reward for making a good choice.

"It goes both ways," I said absently, leaning against the counter, forgetting what the Mom-radar would likely read into such a statement.

"Oh?" Something else rattled on her end. Even as I groaned, I still loved her predictability.

"Mom. I promise a longer conversation where I tell you everything."

"Does everything mean a potential date to Arthur's wedding?" She sounded so eager that I knew she was leaning forward even without being able to see her.

"We'll see." I wasn't telling her that I'd already asked or I'd be in for another twenty-minute conversation right there. "I'll let you know."

"I'm crossing everything. And call anytime. I'll keep the phone with me tonight in case you or your friend have more questions."

"Thanks. You're the best. I'll keep you posted about how it goes." After I ended the call, I made a large grocery order for delivery using an app on my phone. Then the load of laundry was ready for the dryer, so I went and handled that while waiting for the delivery. Another message came in from Max while I was switching out the laundry.

Dude. I was going to fold in this last game, but decided to play like I was you. Went for it. Scored big.

That's awesome. I sent the reply even as my brain churned on the notion of winning big and thoughts of Felix, not poker. What would it mean to be all-in with Felix? I'd told him I wanted to date for real. Was that enough? I had no clue what Felix's answer was going to be when we finally got to finish our talk, and Max's message underscored how out of my depth I really was here.

I might be a hell of a poker player, but none of those skills seemed applicable now. With poker, no matter how high the stakes, I never bet more than I could stand to lose. This thing with Felix might be a little different though. Maybe I had to take a lesson from Max, be more willing to play outside my comfort zone. Be willing to lose. And that really was the question. Was I prepared to lose this round or was I playing it safe, taking only risks I knew I could win?

Chapter Thirty-Four

Felix

Calder stayed. I shouldn't have been surprised. Anyone who could make it through sub school was totally stubborn enough to ignore my protests that I would be fine if he left.

And I would. *Fine* was subjective anyway. At that moment, late on Friday evening, *fine* was no one needing urgent care. Every sign pointed to a simple stomach virus and neither girl was dangerously dehydrated. I did need to get fluids into them though, which was how I encountered Calder in the kitchen.

"I thought I said—"

"I heard," he said mildly, not reacting to my crankiness and setting a basket of clean and folded clothes on the counter. "This load is done. How's the laundry situation upstairs? Bedding okay?"

"Even with the bowls, at least one set of sheets is toast," I admitted, searching the fridge for a drink the girls might keep down. "Damn it. I thought I had some electrolyte drink in the back here."

"It's on the way." He kept the unflappable tone as he fixed a glass of water and handed it to me.

Huh. Apparently I was thirsty. I took a long swallow as I tried to make sense of his words. "What is on the way?"

"Electrolyte drinks. Juice. Ginger ale. Broth. Mom gave me

a list. I added a delivery app to my phone and made an order for you since I don't have a car here to go to the store myself."

"You ordered groceries?"

"Yep. I nabbed the last order window for the night, so it should be here any minute. Until then, Mom said to try super-weak herbal tea. I brewed some to cool." Moving around the kitchen, he retrieved two plastic cups and filled them from a pitcher near the stove.

I blinked, then shook my head to clear it. "You made tea?"

"No big deal." He shrugged and stuck straws in the cups. "You had peppermint tea bags."

"Well, I appreciate it." I wasn't sure how to even begin to say thank you for all he'd done. Gabrielle's car. Laundry. Groceries. Tea. Being here. Mainly that last one. He kept showing up, even when I tried to send him away. I still wasn't convinced that I was what he needed or wanted long-term, but short-term I had to admire his tenacity. "I'll pay you back for the groceries."

"Felix. It's some drinks and cans of soup." He made a dismissive gesture. "Now, about that laundry. Why don't I come upstairs with you, help you change the bedding?"

"Okay." I gave up pretending he wasn't a huge help and drank the rest of my water. "I have a feeling both beds could use it at this point."

"They'll sleep better with fresh sheets." He handed me the two cups of tea. "You dispense the drinks and check their temps, and I'll swap the sheets. Mom said fever and dehydration are the big worries."

"Smart mom. So far only Madeline has a fever and it's not too high." I was impressed that he'd thought to call his mom for me. I knew that their relationship could be somewhat strained, so him going to her for advice felt significant.

Leading the way up the stairs, I showed Calder the linen

closet in the hall before taking the tea to the girls, moving them to chairs so Calder could change the bedding. I helped him with the far corners on Madeline's canopy bed as he snapped the sheets into place.

"The navy sure taught you well."

"Navy? Ha. My dad hated us making extra work for Mom. When he was home, every Saturday was cleaning, and pity the poor kid who didn't pay attention to the lessons and do their share."

"You had a schedule?" Madeline asked from her perch on the padded armchair in the corner of her room. "I like schedules. Like what you made for the cabin. That was cool."

"Yup. I've got organizer genes." Calder laughed. "If Uncle Felix wants, I could make a chore chart for you like what we had growing up."

"That sounds cool." Madeline burrowed into the blanket I'd draped around her.

"I should have thought of that before." I was always trying to do everything myself, involving the girls on the fly. My cheeks heated. I should have known Madeline wanted a chart.

"Don't be hard on yourself." Calder put a steadying hand on my shoulder. "You're still figuring out what works. Cut yourself some slack."

What worked was him helping and giving suggestions, but my spine still stiffened at the thought of relying on him. He said I could trust him to stay around, but I wasn't so sure. And no matter what he said, I wasn't at all comfortable with him making big career moves with this relationship in mind. That was a recipe for disaster.

Maybe we can be scared together. His words had rung in my ears all evening, even while dealing with the girls. I couldn't give him the answer he wanted. And yet my stomach twisted at the thought of sending him away for good. I didn't want to need him, yet I was increasingly terrified I already did.

"Charlotte's room next?" Calder asked after I helped Madeline back to bed and tucked her in with a book.

"I'm waiting," the small dictator called. Despite the upset stomach, Charlotte was still Charlotte and was far perkier than Madeline. We found her in the rocking chair in her room, feet swinging back and forth. "I want the pink sheets."

"Coming right up." Calder smiled at her before ducking out of the room to get the right sheets. I might have made her deal with the blue-and-white ones he'd been holding, but Calder seemed to have endless reserves of patience.

"I want a story." Charlotte had already drunk over half of her tea. God, I hoped it stayed down.

"All right." I pulled a random book from her cramped shelves only to have her thrust a different one in my face.

"This one." She handed me a worn favorite about a family in need of a vacation.

I was too tired to remind her about manners and at least it wasn't an anatomy text, so instead I settled down on the rug next to her to read while Calder tackled the bed.

"'Once upon a time…'" I started and she yawned big. I knew this book largely by heart, having read it first to Madeline even before the girls came to live with me, and later wearing this copy out with Charlotte's endless requests for it. She loved the bossy little kid who knew best for his family.

"That's not your usual voice for the kid," she interrupted, right as the kid was explaining his big plan. "He's not that grumpy."

"My apologies." She wasn't wrong. The main character of the book was a lot like Calder, actually. Taking charge without being rude, and having bottomless enthusiasm for the prospect of fun and adventure, however small. Unlike the kid in the book, who was mollified with some in-town outings, though, I wasn't sure that I had enough to offer someone with Calder's high need for fun.

"I like all Uncle Felix's voices," Calder said, ever loyal. Sure, he'd given up his Friday night to help us out, but how many times could he do that before other options started looking far more appealing?

"The kid's voice is important." Charlotte made the rocking chair squeak. "It's because he's happy that the family gets happy in the end."

Deep thoughts from the second grader. The kid being happy to start with did make a difference to the story because he provided a good example for the harried parents, who needed to slow down and…

Have fun. Lord, what if Calder was right? Did I need to let more fun into my life?

"And in a family is it important that each person is happy?" I asked carefully, trying to reason out the answer in my own head too. Was my own happiness important enough to risk having another breakup that might impact the kids?

"Of course." Charlotte nodded decisively. "One sad person and everyone is sad."

Oh. I was undoubtedly going to be sad whenever Calder stopped coming around, whether it was this week or next month or ten years from now. The kids would be sad for me because that's what kids and families did. They'd be there to provide sympathy no matter what the cause was, and me quietly longing for a relationship wasn't necessarily any more healthy than actually attempting one.

"You're right," I managed to murmur. And somehow I returned to the story, Charlotte yawning more and more as we approached the end.

"Okay, Miss Charlotte," Calder said softly, coming to

crouch in front of the rocker. "Your bed is ready. Want a lift to it?"

With a gentleness that stole my breath, Calder carried her and her blanket nest back to bed and tucked her in like he'd done it a thousand times before.

I opened my mouth, needing to say something, but I wasn't even sure what. But I couldn't stay silent. I needed—

Bong. Bong. The front door chimed with the sort of perfect timing this whole damn night had had.

"That's the groceries." Calder bent down to rub my shoulder on his way out of the room. "I'll go put them away. Don't fall asleep on the floor."

"I'll try not to."

"I want a stay-cation like the book." Charlotte's voice was all dreamy as I moved closer to the bed and smoothed her covers.

"They did do a good job of making the best of a hard situation, didn't they?"

"It wasn't hard." Her face screwed up.

"It wasn't?"

"No one died," she said flatly.

Gulp. Damn. My voice was rough when I finally managed to speak. "This is true."

She and Madeline had certainly seen enough of real loss in their little lives, from the dad who skipped town to grandparents they had only fuzzy memories of to their mother. It made sense that the book with its two harried parents seemed relatively idealistic from Charlotte's perspective. *No one died.* So many people were gone from my life too—my mom so long ago, but never forgotten, my dad, my grandparents, Courtney, and others. Life's other challenges paled in comparison to surviving those losses.

And I was still here, plodding along. Was I making the

best of my time when I was letting fear paralyze me? *Move on.* The realization I'd had in the kitchen the other day about the need to get my life back returned to echo in my brain. Maybe I was dwelling on the wrong things, losing perspective about what was truly important. What Charlotte loved about the book was the way the family embraced fun in the end, shifted their priorities.

"Perhaps…" I trailed off as I realized Charlotte was already sleeping. I let out a huge yawn of my own. I needed to get off this floor, but my limbs seemed to have turned into iron bars. Instead, my head continued to churn. In many ways, my life was defined by who wasn't here anymore. All the deaths, but also Tim and the loss of that dream when he'd moved on.

I didn't know how much hope I had left in me or what my capacity for fun was. My exhaustion was making it hard to reason, but if Calder truly wanted to stay, maybe I needed to let him.

Chapter Thirty-Five

Calder

Felix was asleep again on the floor. I'd found him earlier dozing off on the floor in Charlotte's room and been about to shuttle him off to his own bed, but then Madeline had needed him. And then Charlotte had puked up the tea. And then Madeline had needed some fever medicine and a story to go back to sleep.

But now it was truly the middle of the night and both girls were sound asleep at last and here Felix was crashed out on the floor of Madeline's room, stuffed animal for a pillow and not even a cover.

If I thought he'd let me get away with it, I'd carry him to his bed. I'd carried heavier crewmates longer distances, but the chances of Felix waking up and loudly protesting were high. Rather than risk him waking up the girls, I knelt next to him and gently shook his shoulder.

"Come on, off to bed with you," I whispered.

"Mmph. I'm fine," he mumbled and clutched the stuffed animal closer.

"You are not. You're freezing and that rabbit is no pillow." I helped him sit up, then gave him a hand up to stand. "You'll sleep better in your own bed, I promise."

"God, I'm a mess." Following me into the hall, Felix

glanced down at his clothing. He'd lost his dress shirt at some point, and his white T-shirt wasn't so white anymore and his pants were hopelessly wrinkled.

"You are." I couldn't disagree. "You want to try a shower first?"

He glanced toward his room, then shook his head. "I shouldn't. One of them might need me, and I can't hear in the shower."

"I'm right here." Opening the linen closet, I found him two clean towels. "I can hold down the fort long enough for you to shower. Trust me."

"If they wake up..."

"I'm planting myself on the couch here." I pointed to the small couch tucked into the loft reading area near the top of the stairs. "I'll hear them. And if they need you, I'll come for you."

However, I planned to try my darnedest to solve whatever came up so he could get some consecutive hours of sleep. I'd already snatched a few naps myself on the couch, but I was used to irregular sleep patterns from my time on the sub. And of the two of us, Felix had had the far rougher night, doing the lion's share of the comforting. Cleaning was easy. The sort of emotional support he'd provided for the girls was the real feat.

"A shower does sound good." He took a few steps toward his room, then stopped to look between the two girls' rooms.

"Go on. I've got this." I used my chief voice even though inside I was hoping the kids stayed asleep. Comfort was far outside my wheelhouse, and I didn't want to have to wake Felix up to admit that.

Finally, Felix grudgingly trotted off to his shower, and since I wanted to stay awake to hear the girls before he did, I busied myself cleaning their bathroom. This would be a fun room to remodel. More involved than the pantry and closet projects, but it would be neat picking out paint and tile with them. If Felix kept me around.

And that was the big *if* hanging over the whole night. He'd decided to let me stay, but I didn't delude myself into thinking our earlier conversation was resolved. He'd appreciated the extra set of hands, but I had no clue as to whether he'd changed his thinking about us at all. At least I'd made sure he wasn't alone, and gotten him some rest. That was something.

Back on the couch on the landing, I checked my phone. Max had won big. I still wasn't jealous. A few hours earlier Gabrielle had thanked me for the updates and reported that she was off to bed. A more recent text from my mom revealed she was up to her old insomniac ways.

How are the kids? she asked. I did a quick reply.

Sleeping. Was a long night. Your grocery ideas helped.

She texted back quickly, exactly as I'd predicted. Good. Hang in there. I bet they wake up far improved.

I hoped she was right. A quick check revealed both of them to be fast asleep, and Madeline was far less flushed. I peeked in Felix's room to discover him sprawled out on the bed, still in a towel, sleeping the sleep of the utterly exhausted. My heart did a weird squeeze I wasn't sure I'd ever felt before. And I'd never had a person where I both wanted to take care of them and wanted them to care for me in return. Perhaps that was what all good relationships were—taking turns caretaking—but I'd never wanted that on such a visceral level before.

I drew the covers up around him and was more than half tempted to lie down next to him if only for a minute, but I wanted to be able to head the girls off before they woke him. After a last long look at him, I returned to the couch with a blanket I'd raided from the linen closet. The couch was nowhere near long enough for my height, but I'd slept worse places.

I let myself doze, but I roused at the first sound of awake noises coming from Charlotte's room. Morning light streamed through her windows, and true to Mom's prediction, she had a big smile, no more groaning.

"I'm hungry," she announced in a voice worthy of a stadium announcer.

"You sure?" I whispered, trying to get her to dial back the volume.

"Yes." My trick worked because she lowered her voice at least somewhat. "My tummy doesn't hurt."

I didn't share her certainty that breakfast would stay down, but I also knew that powerful morning-after-being-ill hunger. "I'll see what I can find and bring you up something small."

"Where's Uncle Felix?" Curls all rumpled, she tilted her head, considering my presence for the first time.

"Asleep. He was really tired."

"Is he sick?" She sounded so worried that I put a hand on her shoulder before she could race down the hall.

"I don't think so, but the rest will help him." I tried to pitch my voice as reassuring as I could. "Let me bring you breakfast in bed while he sleeps longer?"

"That sounds good." She sounded like a businesswoman striking a deal, but then her voice went back to little-kid worried. "I don't want Uncle Felix sick."

"Me either." My voice came out scratchy. I'd known since our first meeting that Felix was the girls' guardian, but I hadn't truly understood until that moment, that fear in Charlotte's eyes, what it truly meant that he was all they had.

If he got sick, they didn't have a fallback plan. They were counting on him to make good choices and to put them first.

His objections to dating made more sense now. It wasn't simply about what Felix wanted for himself and what he should let himself have, but about the best interests of the girls.

And a relationship with me might not be it, and that was deeply humbling. I'd structured my life to be worthy of praise and advancement. To be a winner, no matter what. But Felix's life wasn't a game, wasn't a rank to achieve. My stomach churned the whole time I made Charlotte a breakfast tray.

Taking my mom's advice from the night before, I made her a couple of small things to try—some dry toast, a cup of electrolyte drink, a little applesauce. I returned to find her in Madeline's room, cozied up in her canopy bed, both of them under the covers.

"How are you feeling?" I asked Madeline as I took a fast picture of their adorableness for Felix for later.

"Better." Her eyes turned sly. "Charlotte said we get to eat in bed if we let Uncle Felix sleep?"

"Absolutely." I nodded. Bribery was totally acceptable if it bought Felix another chunk of sleep. "I'll bring you a tray too."

"Can we watch a movie?" Madeline asked. They were undoubtedly taking advantage of me not knowing the weekend rules for screen time, but I'd beg forgiveness from Felix later.

"Sure. I saw your tablet downstairs. I'll bring that up with your breakfast."

Quickly I fixed a second tray and brought up Madeline's tablet. Moving her charger closer to the bed, I then propped it up with some books so they could use it as a TV in bed. And they managed to talk me into using my account to rent them a musical with a soundtrack I recognized even if I hadn't seen the movie yet.

"You stay for the movie," Charlotte ordered sternly. I started to object then remembered how much I wanted Felix to keep sleeping. As I dragged the chair closer to the bed, I also tried to channel the way Felix always indulged their requests like this. He was such a damn good parent, showing up for them over and over in big and small ways.

In many ways, making the girls happy was as easy as pressing play on the movie, but in other ways, complex calculations were needed to determine what their long-term best interests were. Felix was right. They didn't deserve more upheaval in their lives. If I was going to be there for Felix, I needed to be there for all of them.

Partway through the musical, a song came on that I had on a workout playlist of mine and I found myself humming along.

"You know this song?" Eyes wide, Charlotte looked like she'd discovered I had a set of fairy wings.

"Uh. Yeah." My cheeks heated even though she seemed more impressed than ready to tease me.

"That's so cool." She bounced against the mountain of pillows and stuffed animals behind her. "Let's sing along."

"Uh..." The old me would have objected rather strenuously to the suggestion. But why? It was another easy way to make her happy, and with my brain still buzzing with all the way harder choices, I was all about seizing the easy win. "Quietly. Uncle Felix needs the rest."

And so we rewound and watched the number again, singing along this time. I wanted a snapshot of this moment as well, a chance to freeze time with the three of us exactly like this, happy and singing softly, real world pressures far away.

"There's a sequel." Madeline's cheeks were pink with excitement, not fever, and no way could I turn down that enthusiasm.

"We can watch that next."

The question of what was in their best long-term interest continued to loom large, but as we watched and sang, I wanted to be right there. Showing up for them was a grave responsibility, but also a privilege. And not one I could win or charm my way into but rather something to earn. If I was going to make this thing with Felix succeed, I needed to be ready to do that work. And even then, it might not be enough.

Chapter Thirty-Six

Felix

The soft sound of off-key singing woke me gently from the deepest sleep I could remember. My mouth was all cottony and my brain fuzzy like I'd wallowed in dreamland longer than was prudent. Because the noises sounded happy, I took a fast minute to brush my teeth and pull on some clothes.

Damn. Had I really fallen asleep in my towel? I really had been out of it when I'd stumbled out of the bathroom and landed on the bed. Thank God for Calder. He'd been right about me needing the shower and sleep even if I didn't want to admit it.

The sound of his baritone mingling with the girls' voices continued to carry as I headed down the hall. He'd stayed. I'd tried to send him away, and he'd stayed. That mattered.

I passed the hall bathroom, which was sparkling despite the abuse it had taken the night before. If I hadn't already been softening toward Calder, that might have done the trick. He'd literally cleaned up our mess and was still here. Singing even.

I paused in the doorway to Madeline's room. Calder's back was to me. He'd dragged the chair next to the bed and the three of them were watching some show with a lot of people dancing on tables on the tablet, giggling and singing along.

Calder was sprawled in the chair as if he were battling some exhaustion himself, but his laughter was strong and genuine.

He wasn't faking it for my benefit either. None of them had spotted me yet, but they appeared to be having a great time. Two trays with empty dishes indicated he'd even fed them. My chest…

I couldn't even describe the feeling inside me. The first time I'd held Madeline as a baby, it was like my heart found an extra chamber, one that had only expanded when Charlotte came along, and the last few years were full of dozens of little moments when that extra space reserved for them became my whole entire heart.

Watching Calder with the girls was one of those indescribable moments where I wasn't sure my heart was up to the task, let alone my vocabulary. I was still struggling to find my voice when Charlotte turned to Calder.

"I'm hungry again. I want soup."

He sat up a little straighter like he was searching for a new reserve of energy. I knew that feeling well. "I ordered some cans of chicken and rice."

"Ew." Charlotte made a sour face. "I want tomato."

"That sounds like a recipe for disaster." Calder's voice was teasing, not calling her on her rudeness.

"He means you might hurl again," Madeline added, elbowing Charlotte. "I'll have more toast. I'm never puking again."

"Never say never." Calder laughed heartily. Stretching, he caught my eye and smiled wider. "But not today would be helpful."

"Not today would definitely be helpful." I stepped more fully into the room. "You both look well. And cozy."

"We got breakfast in bed," Charlotte announced. They both looked like little queens propped up in the bed on pillows and floating in a sea of blankets and quilts. "And a movie. Calder paid."

"And he sang along," I couldn't help but tease.

"Guilty." Oh, his blush was so damn sweet. I had to work hard to resist kissing him.

"Don't be embarrassed." I settled for touching his shoulder. "You're a lifesaver. Thank you for the sleep."

"No problem. You probably need coffee and food now." He stood up and retrieved the two trays. "There's some I made earlier, but I could do a fresh pot."

"What's there is fine. I can help you with the soup while I find some cereal for me." We were both being too formal with our speech, overly cautious. While the girls had been so sick, we'd been a team, but now that they were better, his question and our prior conversation seemed to hang in the air, impossible to ignore much longer.

"You all set with the sequel?" Calder asked the girls, who nodded.

"Maybe you feel up to lunch at the table?" I suggested, but Charlotte wrinkled up her nose.

"Where's the fun in that?"

"Indeed. And we could all use a little more fun." I shot a meaningful look at Calder, but he was busy collecting dirty dishes and avoiding my eyes.

"We'll be back," he said on our way out the door. The *we* sounded right. A team for more than the dire emergency of the night before. But first we needed to get past this awkward too-polite thing.

"You did a good thing." I followed him down the stairs.

Pausing near the bottom, he shrugged. "You needed the sleep."

"I did. I could have managed—"

"Of course you could have." He laughed but there was a tinge of frustration there too, and that was on me.

"But I didn't have to." I touched his arm as if I could rub away the effect of my stubbornness. "Thank you for being here. I'm sorry I gave you such a hard time about staying."

"It's okay. It was sort of awkward timing." He made a vague gesture that undoubtedly encompassed the unfinished conversation. "And you like to handle things yourself. I get it."

"Yes, but maybe I could dial back the self-sufficiency." Admitting that was hard. My fingers dug into the stair railing. "I think I got so wrapped up in proving that I could do it all for the girls that I forgot how good it feels to not have to."

"I understand." He put a hand over mine before I could gouge the rail. "I really do. I spent so many years trying to prove something as well. I wanted to show the world I was a winner. Over and over. You made me realize that maybe I don't have to always go hard-charging through life."

"You don't." My heart twisted that he couldn't easily see his own innate worth. "You're already a great guy. You don't need to do anything other than be yourself to prove that."

"Thanks." His cheeks turned a faint shade of pink as he trudged the rest of the way to the kitchen. I wasn't sure he believed me, but his voice was fond. "That's what I like most about you. Here I can truly take a load off. And that's why it feels so good to be able to do the same for you. If I can make it so you don't have to always work overtime, then that feels like a different sort of win."

"It's a big win." I swallowed hard. Perhaps he *needed* to take care of me. I'd been so busy trying not to be a burden that I hadn't thought about what he might get out of helping. "And you do take good care of me. Even when I don't want to let you."

He retrieved a can of soup and pot before turning back

to me with a smile. "Hey, I wasn't going to let you sleep all night on that poor rabbit."

"Thanks, Calder." Unable to wait another moment, I gave him a soft kiss before he could set the pot down. He made a soft, almost wistful sound as I released him. "Was that okay? Sorry. I know things are weird..."

His smile turned wry. "They are. But I'm never going to turn down a kiss."

"I want more." Somehow, it was easier to talk to his back while he opened the can of soup and dumped it in the pot.

"Good." He leered over his shoulder at me.

"I don't mean just kissing."

That got him serious again in a hurry. "Yeah?"

"I'm still worried though." Now that he was looking right at me, it was hard again to get the words out. I didn't have a plan for this conversation and that was almost as scary as the emotions involved.

"Me too." He nodded solemnly. "Definitely worried. More so now."

"Oh." My shoulders deflated and I occupied myself by retrieving the coffee I so desperately needed. I should have known. It was too late. He'd likely had second thoughts himself. "It's all right. I understand. It was a hard night."

"Hard doesn't scare me." Setting the soup to simmer, he turned me so I had to look at him. "You're not going to chase me off with a little puke and some lost sleep. I meant more that I get it now. You have to put the girls first and not in some vague idealistic sense. Putting them first means sometimes giving up what might be best for you. It's a lot of responsibility."

"It is." Him coming to understand my point was huge and made it easier to see a path forward. If we both wanted the same things, including what was best for the girls, maybe reaching for each other wasn't such a terrible idea. "I also think the kids thrive when I thrive. Me being happy isn't a trivial thing."

"You being happy is everything." His eyes crinkled before he dropped a kiss to my forehead. "But I'm willing to admit I might not be the right thing for all three of you being happy. I want to be. So badly. But it's not as simple as you and I deciding to give it go."

Cocky and confident Calder turning all humble made my resolve that much stronger. He wasn't trying to charm his way into my heart, and he was truly putting my needs before his own. I trailed my fingers down his jaw.

"Perhaps it could be. I'm not saying we ignore the kids. But if we're cautious, dating doesn't have to be off the table."

"I'm good with cautious. Slow." His smile was still rather tight. "And you need to go slow for more than simply the girls. You're still recovering from the divorce. I want to be more than your rebound."

"You are." I brushed a fast kiss across his lips before sighing. The mention of the divorce reminded me I had baggage beyond the kids to contend with. "I do wish my life were simpler for you."

Calder gripped my shoulders firmly. "I told you. Your mess doesn't scare me. And I trust you to handle it. I only want to be that landing spot for you, something to make a hard day better."

"You do." I gazed up at him, unsure where we went from here, but certain that I wanted to at least try. Because he did make tough things easier. "I want to be scared together. Let's try being the kind of friends who date too."

"I'd like that." He lowered his head to kiss me right as feet sounded on the stairs and we jumped apart.

"Can we watch the third movie when you come back?" Charlotte asked. "And that soup is bubbling."

"Oops." Calder went to rescue the pot, cheeks adorably rosy. "Sure thing on the movie. I don't have anywhere else to be. It's a good day for a movie marathon while you recover."

Nowhere else to be. I continued to work on trusting him that he wanted to be here. He certainly seemed content enough to watch bad musicals and eat slightly burned soup, and maybe that was enough for now. We'd figure out a plan eventually.

Chapter Thirty-Seven

Calder

"Is Calder spending the night again?" Charlotte asked, coming into the kitchen in clean pajamas with freshly washed hair. Felix had sent her and Madeline to shower after dinner, and apparently Charlotte was done first. And full of hard questions.

I gulped because Felix and I hadn't made it that far in our plans. We'd watched movies most of the afternoon, cooked an easy dinner that hopefully stayed down for the girls, and now we were cleaning up and the pint-sized detective was totally calling me on the fact that I'd been stalling on leaving.

"He might," Felix said mildly, casting me a look I couldn't quite read. "I haven't asked him when he has to be back at base."

"Late Sunday afternoon. But it's okay, I can go if you need me to." I didn't want to presume an invite. I had a strong feeling that Felix didn't want to fool around with the girls here, and explaining my presence during a crisis was undoubtedly easier for him than a premeditated sleepover.

"I want pancakes tomorrow morning." Charlotte started rummaging in the drawer with the various pens, sticky notes, and other doctor swag. "With bear faces."

"Maybe I want pancakes too," Felix said slyly, giving me a fast kiss while she was occupied.

"That can probably be arranged." Maybe I'd been wrong in my assumption. If he wanted me here, I was totally staying as long as he'd have me. "How are you feeling? Maybe I should stay in case you get sick next."

I didn't mind giving him an excuse if he needed one to tell the girls, but he simply laughed. Charlotte had wandered away, pen and pad of paper in hand, so I rubbed his arm.

"So far so good. I washed my hands about a hundred times last night and kept disinfecting." His voice turned more serious as he met my eyes. "But I still want you to stay."

"I can do that." I gave him another quick peck, hoping we might get a chance for some longer kisses later even if he didn't want sex.

"Charlotte says Calder's spending the night." Madeline came down the stairs right as I was contemplating another kiss.

"Yes." Felix straightened and stepped closer to Madeline. "Is that all right with you?"

"I guess." Mouth twisting, she shrugged. She didn't look all that happy, but she also didn't outright nix the idea, which I took as a win. "We get pancakes tomorrow?"

"Yep. And bacon." I wasn't above a little bribery to get her on my side.

She tilted her aristocratic nose skyward as she gave me a disdainful once-over. "I like sausage patties more. You better be a good boyfriend."

Ouch. She was more direct than Charlotte and far more suspicious. And a good reminder that dating Felix wasn't all fun and games. This was serious business for all of us, and more than simply our two hearts were on the line. I didn't want to let her down either.

"If Uncle Felix lets me, I'll try." My voice was solemn and I held her gaze, trying to tell her that I'd be careful with all of their feelings.

"Good." She nodded like a princess exacting a promise from a wayward knight. "I still want a story tonight."

"Of course." Felix put an arm around her. "Now that you're better, we can start something new—"

"With bones." Charlotte was back, pad of paper covered with her blocky handwriting.

Felix laughed and folded her into the hug too. "I was thinking we could start this new book I picked up the other week. It has a dragon and a big adventure. Maybe even an injury or two."

"If you want to start the book early, I'll finish up in here," I offered, wanting to give him some alone time with the girls.

"Thanks." He gave me a grateful look before heading up the stairs after the girls. I made fast work of the remaining kitchen tasks and checked to make sure there were pancake supplies for the morning. And sausages. Keeping on Madeline's good side might be a challenge, but I'd meant it when I said I'd try to take good care of Felix.

Creeping upstairs, I lurked in the loft area as Felix finished the story in Madeline's room and escorted Charlotte to her own bed. He'd done a fabulous voice for the dragon main character, and even I had been sad when the chapter ended.

"You're really good at that," I said as he exited Charlotte's room. He'd mentioned to the girls that we were going to watch a movie, so I wasn't surprised when he motioned for me to follow him to his room.

"I try." Laughing, he shut the door behind us. He flipped the TV on low, but I was far more interested in listening to him than in finding something to watch. "I did drama club in high school. And with the girls, I have to work hard to be more entertaining than one of their shows."

He perched on the edge of the bed, still dressed. I followed suit and sat next to him.

"I didn't only mean the story. You're a really good parent. You remind me of my mom."

"Without the meddling?" He bumped shoulders with me.

"Eh. Even with the meddling, she's still pretty great. She stayed up late to check on me last night. You could meet her, you know." Putting an arm around Felix, I drew him closer, but he stiffened at the mention of meeting the family.

"You're still rather set on bringing us to the wedding?"

"I'll go alone if I have to." I kept my tone pragmatic. He didn't need me all sad and begging and laying on the guilt. "I don't want a date just to have a date. But it would be cool for you to get the whole Euler family experience early, make sure they don't scare you away before family camp this summer."

Felix's eyes went adorably wide. "I take it that's not an optional event?"

"Nope." I was absolutely planning on Felix still being around come summer, and he needed to know that while I was good with going slow, this also wasn't a spring fling for me. "Derrick and Arthur are going to try to come back for it, and Eulers from all over will be there. And no way on earth am I missing my first chance ever to have zero mom questions about when I'm going to finally find someone."

"Happy to help you get your mom off your back," Felix said dryly.

"Hey, that's not why I want to date you," I protested, squeezing him closer. The way I saw it, my folks being glad for me was a nice side benefit, but I wasn't about to have a relationship simply to avoid my mom's questions. "Or why I want you to come to Chicago. But you *do* make me happy.

And they like to see me happy, and as much as they drive me up a wall, they are my family. I want to show you off."

"I'll think more about it."

"Good." It was a start, so I nodded enthusiastically.

"I'll want to talk to the girls first," he mused, eyes narrowing like he was already rehearsing the conversation. "Charlotte will be a yes, but Madeline isn't the most on flying. I might be able to sweeten the deal with an art museum or theater."

"I bet such a thing is already on the itinerary, but even if it's not, I'll make it happen for you." I'd enjoyed the movies with the girls far more than I would have predicted. I could sit through a play if it came to that. "I'll likely have training shortly after the trip, so it would be nice to spend the time with all three of you for that reason too."

Mouth pursing, Felix slid out of my grasp. "About that training…"

"I'm not doing it for you." I needed to be clear about this, especially since Felix wrinkled his nose, disbelief clear in his eyes.

"No?"

"That wouldn't be fair to either of us, that sort of pressure. I decided last night that I'd take the training option regardless of what your answer was as to dating."

"Why?" Leaning forward, he balanced his elbows on his knees.

"I want a more balanced life." Somewhere in the middle of all the chaos and Max's messages, I'd come to see that I'd done both of us a disservice by trying to link my decision to a relationship with him. It was time for me to own the direction I wanted for my life, let myself want things like a family, and be willing to risk not getting those things. "Seeing what I truly want out of life *did* have something to do with spending time with you, being happy around you and the kids."

"But you love being on the sub," he protested. "I'm still having a hard time picturing you giving it up."

"Career-wise, the pressure to make this sort of move has been building since before you. I resisted because, like you, I couldn't see myself enjoying the shift."

"And now you can?"

"Yeah. Being on the sub was an awesome phase of my life, but now I see that I can have other phases. And the work itself would be the sort of challenge I thrive on—increased supervisory responsibility. More spreadsheets." I added that last bit to get a laugh from him. All this heaviness was making my chest hurt. I felt raw, like speaking this many hard truths was scraping off all the armor I'd carried around for years now.

And perhaps he realized that because he did chuckle and squeeze my knee. "You are good at those."

"Thanks. And I mean it. I'm doing this for me. I do want to make it work with you. So much." My voice wavered and I had to swallow hard. "But this choice is for me."

"I want to make it work too." He scooted back closer to me.

I exhaled hard, his nearness making it easier to admit where I'd gone wrong. "You were right to be concerned about my motives. I shouldn't have framed this as a win-win. Life isn't a game. You're not my prize for making this choice, and I don't want you to feel like that."

"I believe you." He wrapped an arm around me, smiling ruefully. "Besides, I'm not sure I'm a very fun prize."

"Oh, you still make me feel like I won the lottery." I let my eyes rove over him more deliberately before sobering again. "Watching you with the girls, I realized that life is about more than fun. More than winning. I want a life that matters."

"You already have that." He tipped my face toward him so that I couldn't look away.

"Yeah, I do. But now I can see it and can let myself want more than simply the next win."

"You are more than your win record." Continuing to hold my gaze, he gave me a swift kiss. I wanted to believe him. I didn't entirely, not yet. But for the first time, I wanted to try to work on a version of myself that didn't need the winner label.

"Thanks. And you get a choice here too. I was serious earlier. If I'm not the best thing for you and the girls, I understand." I grimaced, clenching my jaw to get the rest of what I had to say out. "Maybe you don't want to be involved with someone with a few more years of military service to go. And I'm a single dude with no clue about kids."

"I think you sell yourself way short," he said firmly. "You're fabulous with the girls. And you were right about one thing last night. You're not Tim. You're not going to run. And I'm not either. I want to give us a chance."

"Good." Relief flooding my senses, I kissed him hard enough to send us both tumbling backward onto the bed. It wasn't a hot and heavy, going-to-get-lucky sort of kiss, but rather the best way I had to express my gratitude and all the other things I lacked words for. Our mouths were gentle, as if this thing between us was that fragile and new. Tenderness even more than desire seemed to tinge every kiss and touch. Rolling slightly, I peered down at him. "I give us pretty good odds."

"Me too."

As I kissed him again, I hoped with my whole soul that we were right. I didn't know the future with any degree of certainty, but I was more than willing to gamble on him.

Chapter Thirty-Eight

Felix

Calder had warned me that the Euler family was an experience. But I wasn't sure anyone could truly be prepared for this level of family togetherness. They'd taken over a block of rooms at a modest place north of downtown Chicago notable for its large indoor pool and kid-friendly accommodations. The pool had been a deciding factor for Madeline. That and Calder had idly admitted one evening that he too didn't much like flying.

"Oh, well, maybe *I* do," Miss Contrary had declared, and that was that and here we were in Chicago having dinner with the Euler family experience, which really needed to be trademarked. Multiple tables in the hotel restaurant were occupied by relatives who kept stopping to hug new arrivals. Calder had started out with us, but been pulled away by cousins needing details for that evening's card game-slash-bachelor party.

At our table, Madeline was rather down and that was occupying my attention more than the chatty relatives.

"Why so sad?" Calder's mom, Jane, came to sit with us.

"I forgot my dress," Madeline reported glumly. She'd insisted on packing herself but forgotten the dress she'd planned for the theater the next afternoon. "Not the wedding one. The one for the play."

"Ah. That is a problem." Raising a hand, Jane summoned another female, a friend of Arthur's who'd been on our flight from Seattle. She'd been seated a few rows ahead of us and made the girls lifetime fans with cherry-flavored gum and video suggestions.

"Sabrina, we need your talents. There's a dress emergency." Jane explained the details. She was a frighteningly efficient woman, full of itineraries and introductions and solutions, and it was easy to see where Calder got the organizational gene.

"I'm on it." Sabrina cast an appraising eye on Madeline. "Size 10/12? Are we talking super-fancy princess or more grown-up Hollywood or casual fun?"

"We're going to a play. Calder got us tickets. I want to look thirteen," Madeline said as I groaned.

"How about you be ten awhile longer?" I suggested to much laughter from the table.

"Elegant it is." Sabrina clicked around on her phone. "There's an outlet store not far from here. I can order a car with my app. Who's up for a field trip?"

"Oh, me," Jane volunteered.

"You don't have to come." I was sure that with less than forty-eight hours until the wedding, she was needed for far more important things.

"But I want to." She blinked like she wasn't used to being contradicted. "We don't have enough little girls in the family to spoil. And that Calder obtained tickets to a musical is an event worthy of celebration."

"Amen," Sabrina agreed. "Great guy, but dragging him away from the card table prior to the ceremony is a feat. Must be true love."

Her joke earned another huge round of laughter, while making a prickle race up my spine. Was it love? The whole boyfriend label was new enough. Madeline had pinned it on us, and Calder had quickly adopted the term like that might make me less likely to bolt back to friends-only land. Traveling together to the wedding was a big step as was letting Calder introduce me as more than a friend.

The Eulers were a delightfully welcoming bunch, but ever since our afternoon arrival, there had been subtle references to our future. The last couple of weeks, I'd been carefully avoiding dwelling on anything other than the present moment. Calder, on the other hand, liked making casual mention of summer plans and upcoming birthdays, assuming a certain level of togetherness. But even he never used the *L*-word.

The question continued to tumble around in my head as plans were quickly made for an impromptu shopping trip. Assorted Euler women and Sabrina invited themselves along. I insisted Calder go off with the cousins and his brothers. He needed the bonding time more than he needed to tag along with us.

Madeline and Charlotte preened like visiting celebrities under all the female attention. A single dress turned into multiple items carted off to the dressing room.

"Oh, look at you." Jane did the whole hand-on-her-chest fake-swoon thing as Madeline emerged in a navy blue dress, long shimmery satin with a lacy top part. She twirled and my own breath caught. The light danced off her curls, and her angelic expression shook loose a cascade of old memories.

"You look like..." *Courtney.* A sharp pang of loss hit me. She should be here, admiring the dress and joking about how Madeline did indeed look like a teenager. She turned again, and in her smile, I saw a glimpse of the person she'd become. Eyes stinging, I sent a brief thank-you heavenward for trusting me with this responsibility. "Beautiful. You look beautiful."

"Thank you." She gave me a beatific grin, and I hoped somewhere Courtney was proud of both of us, hoped I didn't let her down. Calder often made offhand comments about me as a parent, but as Madeline spun, I truly felt parental, down to the soles of my shoes, and all I could think was *That's my girl.*

"I don't want to take it off." Madeline made the skirt swish again.

"You can't sleep in it, silly." Charlotte opened the adjacent changing cubicle door, revealing the biggest, pinkest, fluffiest dress I'd ever seen paired with a black Halloween-themed shrug she'd found on the clearance rank with skeletons dancing up the sleeves. "Do you like mine?"

"I love it." My voice came out all scratchy. "Very you."

I managed to push back the waterfall of emotions and let the girls enjoy all the fashion tips and accessory suggestions from the women with us. Eventually we made our way to the registers, and Sabrina used her app to order cars back to the hotel.

"Now who's up for movie night!" Jane asked as we exited the cars and collected our many shopping bags.

"That's next on the agenda?" I braced myself for a late night of loud kids and undoubtedly one of the live-action musicals I already knew by heart.

"Not for you." She laughed and touched my sleeve. "We're having a bunch of the grandkids over to our suite for movies and popcorn and a sleepover."

"God bless Grandma," one of the sisters-in-law added reverently.

"Please." Charlotte didn't waste any time in getting her request in, and even Madeline looked eager to go.

"Don't worry. I make sure everyone actually sleeps at some point, and I'll have them at breakfast looking sharp."

I didn't doubt that. This was a woman who could run a whole battle regiment on her own, but she shouldn't have to. I took a breath and reminded myself how much fun the girls would have.

"I can't let you take on all that work yourself. I can be an extra set of adult hands for you."

My back would hate me later for agreeing to sleep on the floor and passing up the chance to sneak a cuddle with Calder, but it was the right thing to do.

"Nope." Calder's mom shook her head. "That's what the older cousins are for. I'll have help, promise."

"You certainly seem to have an answer for everything." For so long I'd done it all on my own, and not having to was still a novel sensation, one my body couldn't seem to decide whether it liked.

"Enjoy one of the best benefits of a big family—built-in babysitters." She steered me toward the bank of elevators. "Go find your man. Play cards. Drink a beer. Go wild. You deserve a night for you."

"I guess I could play a few hands." My pulse galloped. Parts of me were already on board, and I nodded. Maybe I did deserve a night off. I was working on believing that I deserved someone like Calder, deserved a happiness that was all my own. But was it really only for me? One look at the girls' beaming faces revealed that me seizing a little slice of bliss for myself meant more enjoyment for them.

I would go find my man, make sure he knew how damn much I appreciated all he brought to our lives.

Chapter Thirty-Nine

Calder

"Ha. You might be getting lucky this weekend, but your card-playing skills are rusty as hell." Laughing, I shook a finger at Derrick after he folded. We were having a great time in the suite a couple of the single cousins were sharing, drinking beer, playing cards, and catching up.

"Guilty." Derrick rolled his eyes at me. "I've had better uses for my time."

"Yeah, you have." I nodded, a certain understanding passing between us that couldn't have a few months ago. I got it now. I was here and having fun, but I was also missing Felix and counting down until I could sneak into bed with him and quietly snuggle and hear all about the shopping trip. "I'm happy for you. Both of you."

"Oh, please don't go getting sappy before I win," Arthur scoffed. He'd unexpectedly decided to join us, and I was glad. I wanted to say something more, even if it was sappy, about how I could have done a better job of being happy for them earlier on, and how I was happy, truly happy, that they had each other now. But both of them were laughing and it wasn't the right moment. I'd save it for my toast at the reception if I could find the words then.

"Speaking of sappy, your wedding present arrived before

we left," Derrick added, leaning back in his chair. "It's perfect."

"Good." It was pretty awesome, a custom House Rules sign with all sorts of geeky references the two of them would appreciate, and their names and wedding date in big font at the top.

"But fess up. You had help picking it out." Arthur gave a smug smile.

"Yup. I did." I wasn't too proud to admit when I needed a little help, especially not lately. Looking at presents together had been fun, way more fun than bumbling through on my own. "Felix is pretty good at that sort of stuff."

"Bet that's not all he's good at." Waggling his eyebrows at me, Derrick did an excellent job of reminding me exactly how long it had been since I'd had Felix naked. Not that I was complaining. I had my duty schedule and he had the girls, and if that meant that most sleepovers were quiet affairs, I'd take the togetherness anytime.

"Now, are you raising or what?" Arthur demanded. Unlike Derrick, he was still in, and evidently itching to get a win. Too bad for him that I was holding a sweet hand. I might have a personal resolution to be a better brother, but I still played to win.

"Calder?" called one of the cousins, who had been drinking a beer and watching us play. "Your boyfriend's here."

"Hey, you." I couldn't help my wide smile as Felix entered the suite. Arthur could wait a minute. "You going to join us next round?"

"I can, yes." He'd said he might try to stop by this very low-key bachelor party, but I hadn't expected him to actually get free. I'd had every intention of giving him a break in the morning, though, taking the girls to breakfast while he slept in.

"How'd you escape kid duty?" Arthur asked.

"Your mom. I think she's working on her application for sainthood." Felix shook his head, wonder in his tone. "She's hosting a movie and sleepover night in their suite. The girls were excited to go, and now I'm yours all evening."

"All night you say?" Perking way the hell up, I set my cards down.

"Yes, they changed into pajamas and took bedding with them. I'm under strict orders to enjoy the kid-free time." Laughing, he moved toward one of the empty chairs, but before he could sit, I pushed away from the table and stood.

"I fold." Didn't matter that I'd been holding the winning hand. Like Derrick said earlier, I had better uses of my time, and I wasn't about to squander this opportunity.

"Seriously? You're out?" Arthur faked being all wounded as he revealed he'd been holding a full house. I'd been holding a straight flush, but I didn't flip over my cards.

"You win." Chuckling, I pointed between him and Derrick. They'd been making eyes at each other all damn evening. It was rather clear that they weren't doing the whole wait-for-the-wedding-night thing, which I could now find cute rather than irritating. "Don't even pretend you're not relieved by the early night."

"Oh, I'll take the early bedtime." Predictably, Arthur gave Derrick a heated look. "Trust me. No problem there. But I never thought I'd see the day when you turned down the chance to win."

"Sorry." I didn't mean about ending the game early. I wanted to apologize for all the stupid bets I'd goaded him into over the years, and I tried to convey that with my eyes, waiting for Arthur to nod before I continued, "And hey, I already won this trip."

I glanced over at Felix, who blushed rather adorably. I couldn't wait to make him blush more.

"Look at you, having priorities and shit. I'm impressed." Derrick's smile had a different sort of warmth to it, almost like he was genuinely proud of me. And maybe he was. I was proud of me too.

"Thanks. 'Night." After saying our goodbyes, I all but raced Felix back to our room. The space was a small suite—teeny living area where the girls had been planning to sleep and small bedroom with bathroom.

"All alone." I grinned at Felix as he shut the door to the bedroom.

"Yup." He beamed back at me, and my gut fluttered like we were two teens left unsupervised for the first time. "You want to watch a movie? Something with an R rating?"

I liked how Felix never presumed when it came to sex, but right then I knew exactly what I wanted. "I want to watch you. Adults-only rating."

"Yeah?" Felix started in on my shirt buttons, stopping to kiss me every other one. I returned the favor with his clothes, stealing kisses and appreciating each bit of revealed skin until we were both naked and sprawled on the bed.

Stretching, I arranged myself on my side so that the maximum amount of my body was touching him, tapping his foot with mine before kissing him long and slow. "Damn. I missed this."

"Me too." He looked as bemused as I felt, dazed but twinkling eyes and soft mouth just calling out for more kisses. "Phone calls aren't the same as you sleeping over."

"Agreed." Even when all we did was sleep, I still loved being next to him. In the lead-up to the trip, I'd pulled some long hours and so had he and even shared dinners had been sparse. "I'm gonna sleep terrible the whole time I'm at training."

I had dates for the training, which was in Groton and meant getting to see Derrick and Arthur again, but I was going to miss Felix and the girls something awful.

"It'll go fast. I'm proud of you." Felix stroked my shoulder. His faith in me and trust that I was doing the right thing for myself went a long way to reassuring my nerves. I was looking forward to work after the training, the new role I'd assume, and the more I prepped for it, the less I minded not being on a sub. This was going to be good.

"Gonna give me a reward when I get back?" I pulled him closer against me.

"I'm sure I can think of something." Giving a sly smile, he nipped at my jaw before kissing me again. Exhaling, I let any last tension go and went with the kiss, letting it wash over all my senses and carry me along. Felix's familiar scent and taste were both soothing and arousing as fuck.

"Fuck. That's good," I groaned when we finally came up for air, even more dazed now.

"Yeah, it is." He stretched dreamily, which put his chest on display. I playfully rubbed my face against it before kissing my way from his sensitive neck to his flat pink nipples. He shuddered as I licked one. "Oh. Wow."

"You're fun." Laughing, I tickled him lightly before flicking at his nipple again. "On buttons everywhere."

"Feel free to keep— *Oh.*" He ended on a low, lusty moan as I slithered lower on the bed. Kissing his soft and fuzzy abs, I waited until his cock was straining before licking it too. I had to be in the right mood for this, but right then, he smelled and tasted so damn good that there was nowhere else I'd rather be. I didn't like going too deep, preferring to lick and kiss and tease, but Felix didn't seem to mind my lack of deep throating skills.

"Ah. That's…yes. Fuck." Eyes tightly shut, he grasped at the sheets.

"Always a good day when I can make you curse." I licked the underside of his cock until he was writhing on the bed, body tensing like he was already fighting to hold back climax. Fuck but I loved how damn easy he was.

"Fuck. Oh. Hell." A steady stream of soft curses escaped Felix's parted lips. That and the friction of rubbing against the crisp sheets had my own cock throbbing, and I reached down to give it a little relief. Opening his eyes, Felix followed my movements. "I did…ah…pack condoms."

"Mmm. Maybe later." Much as I liked him fucking me, I wanted this easy quiet sexiness more right then. However, when he reached for his cock, a hot image marched through my head. "I've got another idea though."

Moving to stretch out over him, I lined up both of our cocks, gave an experimental stroke of them together.

"I love your ideas." Felix arched up into the contact. It was far different than stroking myself, the drag of his cock against mine, the wider stretch of my fingers, even the weight of the two cocks together sexy and new. In a way, it was like kissing, the way I could let myself wallow in the sensations, let it build and feel good. Trying different things was fun too because Felix reacted to each flick of my wrist or change in pressure like I was touching him with a live wire.

I buried my face in his neck, wanting even more of him, and as soon as my lips found the patch where his shoulder and neck met, he started panting like he was in the last mile of a marathon.

"That's it. You're close, aren't you?" Watching him experience pleasure was seriously even better than having it myself. I could hold him like this forever, high on his reactions, the way I could light him up.

"Yes. Fuck. Yes." Tipping his head back, he gave me even more neck to explore. I raked my teeth against his shoulder and he shuddered. "Going to come."

He clung to me, and I wasn't sure if anyone had ever trusted me that fucking much. I tightened my grip, and even before I could speed up, he was coming, making my fist all slippery.

"Fuck. You're so sexy." Stroking him through it, I waited until his shudders slowed before I released him, taking a firmer hold of my cock. I wasn't used to it so slick, and looking down at my fist was enough to get me right on the edge too. That and the blissed-out expression on his face, the way he was still breathing hard.

"Come on me." Stretching like he was offering himself up, he put a hand on mine, encouraging. The way he arched his back like he couldn't wait for me to climax made heat spark low in my gut, an erotic charge, little explosions of pleasure until I was coming in earnest.

"Damn." I lacked the vocabulary for how fucking amazing it was that I got to share this with him. Instead, all I could do was pepper his face with kisses and collapse next to him.

"We're going to need a shower." He let out something suspiciously like a giggle.

"In a minute." I pulled him against me, mess be damned. "Let me wallow in the ability to lie here naked risk-free."

"I don't know about risk-free. Lie here naked long enough and I might get ideas for round two." Winking at me, he trailed a hand down my torso.

"Look at you, drunk on date night. We need to do this more often."

"We do." Felix surprised me with his ready agreement. "Maybe I'll go wild, ask Gabrielle to have them the weekend you're back from training."

"She'll say yes. She likes me." I smirked. Gabrielle and I

were text friends, her telling me when Felix seemed stressed, both of us doing our best to help as much as Felix would let us.

"She's not the only one." His gaze was so fond that my skin literally heated from it.

"Yeah?"

"I like you. So much." He stroked my cheek before kissing me softly.

"I more than like you," I said softly. Someday soon I was going to say the real words, the ones that made my pulse beat harder, the ones I felt with every kiss, every long look. But for that moment I let them hang between us, unsaid, so much potential, exactly like us.

He pulled me closer with strong hands, whispering in my ear, "I more than like you too."

My heart swelled, pressure rising in my chest, until I almost couldn't stand the joy. No game, no rank, no win had ever compared to the way he could undo me with a single sentence. I'd give it all up to stay right here forever.

Chapter Forty

Felix

"I love weddings," Charlotte said a little too loudly from her spot at our table near the back of the reception room. But we were surrounded by other families with kids, so no one even looked our direction. The toasts were about to start, and I had one eye on the front table where Calder was sitting with the rest of the wedding party. He and Derrick had gone the tux rather than dress uniform route, and Calder looked even more delicious than the chocolate-chocolate wedding cake.

"They're pretty great when they go well," I had to agree. Derrick and Arthur were hopelessly in love, and their ceremony had been joyous, music-filled, truly memorable. Even with all the family members, it was still a relatively intimate gathering. I still wasn't sure if I'd ever take the plunge again myself, but even a confirmed cynic could see the appeal in a celebration like this.

"Cake and fluffy dresses. It's heaven." Charlotte gave a happy sigh as she took another bite of the chocolate cake. Up front, Calder was looking down at his hands, shuffling a small stack of note cards. I tried to send him calming vibes.

"Can't be heaven. There's not a single spooky story anywhere here," I teased her, scraping half of my own cake onto her plate.

"Uncle Felix, you're silly. Not everything has to be spooky." She gestured with her fork like she was making a proclamation. And she wasn't wrong. It was time to let light and fun back in our lives, and some things that I'd been so sure were big and scary, like a new relationship with Calder, had turned out to be not nearly as spooky as I'd feared. Sometimes we all needed a fairy story, not a cautionary tale.

"Says the girl wearing skeletons." I rubbed her sleeve. She'd been wearing the Halloween-themed shrug everywhere. "You're very wise."

"I know." Hamming it up, she preened before devouring the rest of the cake.

"I like it here too," Madeline added much more quietly from my other side.

"I'm glad. Calder says we're maybe invited to a camping thing this summer with his family." Laying the groundwork for that trip might be a good idea. This trip had made me more fearless about reaching for the future I wanted with Calder. And if that future meant dealing with more of the Euler family experience, I was ready. "A lot of the same kids you met this weekend. You interested?"

"That would be cool." She gave me a tentative smile that made my chest clench. This weekend had been good for all of us. Charlotte was even more confident, and Madeline seemed older by the minute.

"I'm in for camping." Charlotte didn't even hesitate. "Lots of ghost stories happen in the woods."

"I'll keep you safe," I promised to them both.

"Calder will too." Charlotte narrowly missed poking me with her fork. And more wisdom from her. I would give up my very last breath to keep these girls safe, but lately I was coming to see that I didn't have to be the only one on duty. I could share a little of the responsibility. And the rewards.

Up front, the microphone was finally being passed around for a seemingly endless string of toasts to the happy couple.

Arthur's friend Sabrina had been his best person and had one of the funnier speeches, mock scolding the grooms. "I'm supposed to get up here and talk about how ridiculously adorable you both are and how you give me hope that love exists. But actually? I'm mad at you both. You've raised the bar impossibly high for the rest of us."

I knew the feeling, but my eyes were on Calder, not Derrick and Arthur. Calder had set such a high standard that no one who followed him would be able to match it for me. And I didn't want to even think about trying to find it. I only wanted what I had with him. Maybe some people did get forever kind of lucky.

After Sabrina, it was finally Calder's turn. He was adorably nervous, looking down at his note cards before shaking his head and shoving them in his pocket.

"As the big brother and best friend, it's probably my duty to share any number of embarrassing tales about life with these two." That got a big laugh from the audience, but Calder held up a hand. "However, I'm not going to do that."

He sucked in a breath and I tried again to send him some strength for whatever it was he needed to say. "I used to think that the most fun thing ever was winning a bet against one of you. I loved how we pushed each other, how winning against either of you felt like a real accomplishment."

That had been the Calder I'd first met too, driven and goal-oriented, fun-seeking, but always competitive. It wasn't the Calder up there now, shifting his weight from side to side, vulnerable in a way that made me want to go wrap him in a tight hug.

"But somehow along the way I lost sight of what was truly important in life. And like Sabrina said, you've set an example for all of us. You inspire me to be a better brother and friend. Better human, really." He gave a half smile at that, and reassuring murmurs came from the audience. "Watching you together, I see that life's real accomplishment is measured by who you have with you, not by how many points you score."

He locked his eyes on me for that last sentence, and warmth swept over me.

Calder raised his glass up before finishing, "You both won big in finding each other. I'm happy for you both. Cheers."

It was probably a good thing that he didn't come right to our table after that. I needed a moment to collect myself. That kind of sincerity was rare, and I hoped Arthur and Derrick knew what a gift his humility was.

Casual like the reception food, the after-party part didn't have a DJ but a custom playlist the grooms had created. Not long after the speeches, the dance floor was filled with kids dancing. A few adult couples ventured to join them as others continued to mingle. Finally, Calder made his way to the table and took the seat Charlotte had vacated to go dance.

"You did a great job." I rubbed his arm. "You need a drink after all that?"

"Had one before." He offered me a wry smile. "Damn. That was more nerve-racking than my chief's exam."

"Well, I thought yours was the best of the bunch." Leaning in, I gave him a swift kiss on the cheek.

"Yeah?" He went charmingly pink.

"Yours was honest. I liked that. And you *have* changed." It didn't matter what others could see. What really mattered was that he knew his truth. "Not everyone can or even wants to try to change, but I believe you when you say you're different now."

Nodding, he took my hand. "I know I gave all the credit to Derrick and Arthur, but it's actually more about you. Meeting you. Getting my priorities straight. Realizing that maybe my approach to life wasn't the healthiest. Falling hard for you."

I squeezed his hand and had to swallow hard. This much honesty coupled with the romance of the day made me braver as well.

"Perhaps my approach wasn't the best either. Going it all on my own, pretending I didn't need or want help. Not being willing to give love another chance." There. I'd said the word and the sky didn't fall, the twinkling lights around the reception room not even flickering. Love didn't have to be scary when it was true.

"I'm glad you took that gamble." His voice had gone all husky.

"Me too." The music shifted to something slower, and more couples headed to dance. Romance was all around us, yet it still felt like we were in our own little bubble. "But I don't think it's that big a risk."

"No?"

"You're a good guy, Calder. I think my heart's safe with you."

"It is." He peered deeply into my eyes. "I love you."

The song playing over the speakers was one I'd never heard before, but I knew I'd remember it the rest of my life. I hadn't expected him to say the words first, but since he had, it made my reply that much easier. "I love you too."

"Good. And damn, I'd thought saying that was going to be harder than that toast, but it turned out to be so simple." Chuckling, he shook his head, beyond cute in his relief. "I really do love you."

"I believe you. Dance with me?" I tugged on his hand. I needed to cement this song in my memory, the rhythm and lyrics, and the way this man made me feel.

"Public speaking and dancing in the same evening?" Calder

faked horror even as he let me tug him into standing. "Yeah, we can dance. I don't promise to be good at it."

"That's okay. We can be bad together."

And as I led him to the dance floor, I knew, deep in my bones, that this wouldn't be the last time we danced together. Wouldn't be the last time I'd see him in a tux. My heart was wide open, a reflection of the future I wanted to reach for. And contrary to my tease, we'd be good together. So good.

Chapter Forty-One

Calder

Fall

"Are we there yet?" Charlotte asked from the back seat. I was stretched out in the passenger seat, trying to snatch a little nap because I'd put in some early hours to ensure I could have the weekend for them and Felix. He and the girls had been listening to the soundtrack for a movie musical we'd all gone to the week prior. Felix sounded good. He sang a lot more these days, his performer side coming out in ways other than the bedtime stories he was so good at.

"You think you'd know this route by heart now." Felix laughed as he navigated the country roads. I knew the route too, and my own pulse sped up as we gained elevation and the trees became thicker.

"Oh, I do." Charlotte shifted in her seat. "I'm just excited to see the cabin."

It had been a busy few weeks, and the cabin had been booked with rentals as well, making it harder to find a time to visit.

"Me too." Slowing for a turn, Felix lowered his voice. "But Calder's trying to rest."

"Calder's awake." I wasn't sure anyone heard me though because Charlotte was already onto her next question.

"Think it will snow?"

"Probably not yet." Felix's patient tone said they'd likely been over this point a number of times before I'd arrived at his place so we could all ride together. "The sledding area won't be open until closer to Christmas."

"I can hope." Charlotte's bouncing around resulted in her kicking my seat. If I hadn't been already awake, I would be now.

"You do that." Madeline had been reading a thick fantasy novel, but wasn't going to miss a chance to try out her newfound tween sarcasm. "Besides, we don't need sledding. We have a hot tub now. I can't wait to see."

"The maintenance company sent pictures after the install, but I can't wait to test it out." Felix sounded as excited as the kids. Which was good because I had all sorts of plans for that tub after the girls were asleep. Felix. Moonlight. Hot tub. Yeah, it was good I'd napped. I was going to need my strength.

"I told Rose about the new hot tub." Charlotte mentioned a new friend from her class. This school year was going smoother for her. Fewer complaints. More friends like this Rose. "Can we bring a friend next time?"

"We'll see. There is an extra bed. But I should probably meet her mom first."

"I already told her about how we have two dads."

I made a choking noise and sat up straighter.

"You told her that?" Madeline asked before either Felix or I could speak.

"Well, Uncle Felix is our dad. We don't have to call him that for him to be the dad."

"He is. And a good one at that." I still wasn't sure anyone was hearing me, but it needed saying. Felix was their dad. There was nothing he wouldn't do for them, and I remained in awe of his devotion to them. Every kid needed a parent like him.

"And now we have like an extra bonus dad." Charlotte sounded almost bored, like this was simply another fact alongside everything she knew about bones and anatomy.

"You think so?" Felix's voice was all mild in contrast to my coughing and sputtering.

"Uh-huh. After all, Christmas—"

"Charlotte. Some things are surprises." Felix turned stern. I turned to try to study his expression more. His eyes were on the road, but his cheeks were pink.

"Christmas, huh?" I had a surprise of my own, but I'd been thinking New Year's Eve. My mom was having a kids-only New Year's sleepover, and I'd been researching various dinner options. But if Felix had a surprise brewing, I was most definitely intrigued.

"We're going to Anacortes." Of all of us, Charlotte was probably most looking forward to the big Christmas celebration at my folks' place. Derrick and Arthur were flying in, and it promised to be a crowded but memorable holiday. More so if Felix had something planned. "See? He already shares his family. And he already has a key."

"There is that." She'd insisted on being around when Felix had given me a key to his house to make it easier for me to come and go as my duty schedule allowed. It wasn't possible to spend every night in Queen Anne, but I tried for as many as I could. And the key thing had been a big deal for me too, another sign that Felix intended to keep me around and that he trusted me.

"And he and Nana watched us when you went to your doctor meeting." That had been a fun weekend. Felix had had a big national geriatric psychiatry conference, and Gabrielle and I had joined forces to take care of the girls so he could go.

And we were doing another tag-team effort so Felix could audition for a community theater thing he'd been eyeing. "That's totally a dad thing. Or extra uncle. Whatever. You said he's family now—"

"Charlotte." Madeline slapped her book shut. "You're gonna ruin Uncle Felix's plans."

"It's okay," I said quickly before this could devolve into a sisterly argument.

Felix made a frustrated noise as he turned into the cabin's drive. "Act somewhat surprised on Christmas? Please?"

"Oh, trust me, I'm surprised." I wasn't lying. If the surprise turned out to be a proposal, I'd been expecting to have to do a fair bit of wheedling and sweet-talking on my end to get him to agree. We discussed the future more readily these days, but I still expected him to go skittish if I brought up a more permanent commitment.

"We're here!" Charlotte crowed as Felix parked. "Hot tub time!"

"Not yet. Why don't you take your things in first?" Felix suggested, then handed Madeline the keys before turning to me as they raced into the cabin. "You okay?"

"Yeah. I'm just...dazed." I struggled for words as I watched the girls' retreating forms. *Two dads.* That even more than the hints about Felix's plans had me shaking my head. "Didn't expect that. Bonus dad. Wow."

"Sorry—" Felix started to apologize, but I held up a hand.

"Don't be sorry." I'd figured I'd have to earn that label with years of hard work, and even then it wasn't a guarantee they'd ever see me as any sort of parental figure. That Charlotte so readily did was humbling. "It's...special. I'm not sure..."

"If it's too soon—"

"It's not," I assured him. Couldn't have him thinking I had cold feet. No way was I missing out on this Christmas surprise of his. My own plans for a New Year's proposal could be a celebration instead. I'd let him and the girls have their fun. "I just wanna be worthy of the title, you know? A *dad*. Wow."

"Calder. You are most definitely worthy of the label. You're putting in the work."

"I try." And not simply with things like watching them for Felix's conference trip or while he did something with the theater group. I knew their teachers' names and which classes were tough this year. I knew their therapist and activity schedules because I'd made the spreadsheet for Felix. And those things mattered to me. Being involved with the whole family, not only my boyfriend.

"I know you do." Felix put his hand over mine on my thigh. "And I love you. They love you too."

"I love you. All of you." My voice came out all crackly. Undoubtedly, I was not going to survive whatever he had planned for the holiday.

"Then that's what matters," Felix said firmly as he leaned across the console to brush a kiss across my mouth. "Is it okay? The girls and I having something planned for Christmas, I mean. Maybe I should have talked to you first..."

Yup, it was totally a proposal and if I beamed any wider my face might split.

"It's more than fine." Not letting him retreat, I captured him for another quick kiss. "I've got plans too."

I did. I planned on being around. That was the only plan that truly mattered. I planned on showing up, sticking it out, loving Felix as long as he'd let me.

"Good." Felix kissed me in earnest, and I'd never felt more like a winner in my life. I loved him so fucking much. It was funny, how long and hard I'd chased that label. I'd wanted so badly to prove I was a success. But it turned out there were other labels I wanted more. *Dad. Partner. Husband.* And hustling for those titles was going to be my biggest score. And Felix was the key, the true prize, not one I could win, but one I could earn if I were truly lucky.

★ ★ ★ ★ ★

Author Note

Every time I undertake a new series, the research is one of my favorite parts. Here and in *Sailor Proof*, I've loved immersing myself in the world of submarines and what it's like to serve on one. Even the titles stem from research into submarine jargon! I spent a lot of time on blogs, message boards, and with other firsthand accounts, but even as I tried for authenticity, certain liberties were taken for the sake of the story and ease of understanding. Notably, each injury is handled differently in the military, and Calder's post-concussion job opportunities are not intended to be representative of how all injuries would be handled or how all lateral career moves would be addressed.

I wrote *Sink or Swim* while the quarantine for COVID-19 continued, and it was so nice to escape to a world without the virus where weddings and dates and travel were still possible. Accordingly, you won't see mention of the virus or masks in the series, and that's an intentional choice to provide readers with the same escape I so badly needed myself.

Acknowledgments

My amazing readers are the reason this series came to be. I asked what they wanted more of from me, and the overwhelming response was more military romance. Readers adored the Out of Uniform SEAL series and wanted more like that. After brainstorming with my team at Carina, I decided to go for a lighter military vibe, one with more time away from base. I also wanted to explore another elite job classification in the navy, and thus my submarine heroes for the Shore Leave series were born. So, thank you, readers, so much for loving my military romances and wanting more! Your support via social media, reviews, notes, shares, likes, and other means makes it possible for me to continue to write stories that mean the world to me, and I don't take that for granted!

As with all my books, I am so grateful for the team supporting me, especially at Carina Press and the Knight Agency. Kerri Buckley at Carina had such early enthusiasm for this series idea and that made a huge difference. My editor, Deb Nemeth, is always the blend of support and critique that I need, and her encouragement means the world to me. My revisions were also assisted by invaluable beta comments from Abbie Nicole, Layla Noureddine, and Edie Danford. My behind-the-scenes team is also the best. My entire Carina Press team does an amazing job, and I am so very lucky to have all of them on board. A special thank-you to the tireless art department and publicity team and to the amazing narrators who bring my books to life for the audio market. A special thank-you to Abbie Nicole, who is the best PA I could ever ask for. I wrote this series during a difficult time for our family, and I am so grateful to my spouse and children for their support. My life is also immeasurably enriched by my friendships, especially those of my writer friends who keep me going with sprints, advice, guidance, and commiseration. I am so grateful for every person in my life who helps me do what I love.

A boss. His employee.

And a scandal that's about to change everything…

Keep reading for an excerpt from Going Public *by Hudson Lin, out from Carina Adores!*

Chapter One

It was a dance Elvin did pretty much every day. A stack of dry cleaning balanced on one arm, a tray of Tim Hortons coffees in the other hand, dodging a stream of office workers speed walking through Toronto's financial district. Elvin jogged across Lakeshore—careful not to spill any precious liquid gold—and slipped down a small side street.

The entrance to Ray's condo building was discreet. Not one of those flashy things popping up all over the city announcing the status of their residents to passersby. No, Ray and his neighbors had no interest in publicizing their wealth. That was how much money they had.

Elvin used his elbow to hit the automatic-door button and slipped inside.

"Mr. Goh, good morning!" The security desk attendant greeted him.

"Good morning, Mohammad!" Elvin set his tray of coffees on the counter and wiggled one cup loose. "Here you go. Large double double."

"Aw, Mr. Goh. You didn't have to do that." Mohammad and his coworkers rotated through the night shift and Elvin had made a point to memorize their schedule. It wouldn't do to bring the wrong coffee order for the hardworking staff who stayed up all night manning the desk.

"Don't worry. I'm charging it to the boss." Elvin winked

before heading to the elevators, Mohammad's laugh ringing behind him.

The elevator doors opened immediately, like it had been waiting there for him. Then it shot up the building so fast Elvin's ears popped on the way.

The condo was mostly quiet when Elvin stepped inside, save for the sound of water running from the primary suite. Good, Ray was up already. Which would make the morning much less awkward for Elvin.

He toed his shoes off and went into the large open-plan living space. Kitchen on the right and living room on the left. A dining table the size of a boat in between. Everything glistened white, from the tiled floors to the walls that reached for the double-height ceilings to the leather-upholstered furnishings.

If something wasn't white, it was made of crystal. Like the multilevel coffee table or the glass-topped dining table or the chandelier that hung from the ceiling, guaranteed to inflict serious damage if it fell on anyone. Also crystal clear was the floor-to-ceiling windows that provided a view of Lake Ontario, glistening green blue in the early morning sun.

Elvin set down the tray of coffees on the large marble island in the kitchen—white, of course—and took the dry cleaning to the primary suite that made up one entire wing of the condo. Everything in here was white too, though punctuated with clothes tossed haphazardly over chairs and couches and the floor. How the hell Ray managed to go through so many clothes over the course of one weekend, Elvin would never know.

Elvin pulled open the sliding doors of the dressing room, which was probably bigger than the whole of his basement apartment, and put away the dry cleaning. Arms free, he made a circuit of the bedroom, picking up discarded clothing and dropping them into the laundry basket for Ray's housekeeper to deal with. With all the clothes cleared off it, the bed sat in pride of place in the room, pristine with hospital corners.

Had Ray not slept in it all weekend? Elvin shook his head as he paused outside the en suite bathroom. The door was ajar and steam billowed from the crack.

"Hey! I'm here!" he called out.

"I'll be out in a minute!" Ray answered from inside, the sound muffled by the rushing water.

Elvin let himself out of Ray's bedroom with a smile on his face. It was silly and stupid, but he couldn't help it. The casualness of their standard weekday morning exchange was often the highlight of Elvin's day. But then, he often felt that way whenever he worked with Ray. The ease of their relationship was unlike anything Elvin had experienced before—with friends, with family, and with the odd ex-boyfriend.

His smile disappeared as he stopped by the kitchen island to grab a coffee on his way to the other wing of the condo, made up of guest bedrooms. He had to pop his head into two empty rooms before finding what he was looking for. A rumpled bed with a distinctly human-shaped lump still wrapped up in the duvet. What kind of one-night stand would Elvin find this morning? He'd seen it all—men, women, nonbinary folks; light-skinned, dark-skinned, and every shade in between; big folks, petite folks, hair color more varied than the colors of the rainbow. Ray wasn't particular when it came to who he took to bed. He could find something attractive in just about anyone he came across.

Today, as he set the coffee on the nightstand, Elvin found himself staring down at a tussled head of short blond hair. The guy had a baby face, accentuated by the duvet pulled all the way up to his chin. Cozy.

"Hey." He leaned over, grabbed the guy by the shoulder, and gave him a firm shake. "Wake up."

The blond groaned and tried to hide under the duvet, which only reminded Elvin of his siblings when he tried to get them up in time for school.

"Hey, kid." He tried again. This time he grabbed the edge of the duvet and pulled it off the bed. "Time to get up and go. Don't you have school or something?"

Exposed to the cool air-conditioned air, the blond curled into the fetal position—completely naked. He presented a long expanse of pale-skinned back and a round ass that could be considered a bubble butt. Elvin examined the sight before him, tilting his head in case it would look more appealing from a different angle. Nope—it didn't work for him. Not that he'd expected it to. Most nudity didn't and he would never fully understand how people got so caught up in images of others undressed.

Whatever. He'd come to terms with his own demisexuality a while ago and Monday morning was not the time to be rehashing it. He picked up the coffee, walked around the bed, and shoved the hot cup into the hands of the naked blond. "Take this. Drink."

He thankfully took the cup and sat up. "Who *are* you?" he asked as he rubbed his eyes.

"It doesn't matter." Elvin pointed to the en suite bathroom. "Wash up and then you can leave."

"Where's Ray?"

Elvin sighed with a pinch of sympathy for the guy. He really had no clue, had he? "Sorry, buddy. He's moved on."

Elvin left him looking morose in the middle of the bed and went back to the kitchen. He wiggled the last coffee cup free from its tray and took a sip of the steaming brew, more sugar than coffee. Then he set it aside to start on Ray's standard morning drink—a handmade cappuccino, fresh from the industrial espresso machine imported from Italy. Elvin ran an affectionate hand along its glossy surface before embarking on the ritual of grinding coffee beans and steaming milk. According to Ray, Elvin made the best cappuccino in the city, a title that Elvin did not take lightly.

By the time he'd poured the palm leaf design onto the top of the brimming cappuccino mug, Ray was sauntering into the main room. His feet were bare, his black hair was still wet, his tie was draped around the back of his neck, and he held his suit jacket in one hand.

"Mmm." He moaned as he took a seat at the kitchen island. Elvin placed the cappuccino in front of him and Ray lifted it to his nose. He took a deep breath with his eyes closed and Elvin grinned at Ray's obvious appreciation.

This was why he woke up extra early in the mornings and trekked all the way to Ray's condo, even when it wasn't a part of his job description. He couldn't quite remember how it'd all started, but he'd come to cherish this time when it was just him and Ray in the intimacy of the kitchen, getting ready for a day of work. There was no one else there to interrupt them and he had Ray all to himself.

Well, no one except the leftover hookups from the night before. Appearing right on cue, the skinny blond materialized at the end of the kitchen island and looked uncertainly between Elvin and Ray. "Uh, hi."

Ray's expression lit up like he was pleasantly surprised to find the blond still around. "Hey." He set his cup down and slipped from his stool. "Good morning. Did you sleep well?" Ray's smile oozed charm, enough to soften the blow and make the guy feel special before kicking him out.

Elvin didn't bother following them to the door, but rather pulled out his laptop and set up a makeshift desk on the kitchen island. He'd already checked both his and Ray's inboxes that morning, sorting through items that needed immediate responses and ones that could wait. He navigated to a folder he kept updated with all the emails that Ray would have to address personally—everything else Elvin would take care of for him.

When Ray came back alone, Elvin pointed to the laptop. "You've got emails to review."

Ray pouted. Full on pouted. And Elvin had to dig deep for his stern big brother expression. "Don't give me that. Do your emails or you're not getting any breakfast sausage."

Ray gave him a mock gasp. "No! Don't take away my breakfast sausage!"

Elvin pinned him with a knowing look, then shifted it to the laptop. "Emails. Then breakfast sausage."

That brought out a chuckle from Ray, who obediently took his seat behind the laptop while sipping his cappuccino. Elvin turned to the giant fridge to pull out the necessary ingredients. Eggs, hash browns, tomatoes, sausage—the appliance was kept fully stocked with every conceivable breakfast food item by Ray's personal cook. On the lower shelves and in the freezer were prepared meals that could be heated in the oven or by a quick *ding* in the microwave.

"Why is this in here?"

Elvin glanced over his shoulder to find Ray frowning at the computer screen. "Why is what in where?"

"A meeting with Ming in my schedule."

He'd been expecting this. "You can't avoid him forever."

Ray turned his frown toward Elvin. "Why not?"

"Oh come on." Elvin went back to tending the eggs in the skillet. "A meeting with Ming isn't the worst thing in the world. Besides, remember Joanna's directive for all senior partners to take a more active role in courting investors?"

It was always safe to invoke Joanna's name. As founder and CEO of Jade Harbour, Joanna was someone no one messed with—not even Ray. She could turn the largest, most brutal man into a simpering fool with one glare. Packed conference rooms fell deadly silent whenever she walked in. She ruled with an iron fist that both terrified and garnered worship from her employees.

Ray dropped his head backward in defeat. "Ugh."

"I don't know why you always get so worked up about this. You're great with investors. They can't resist your charm."

"I don't get worked up." Ray crossed his arms defensively, which was a telltale sign that he was lying through his teeth.

The truth was, Ray was a natural at investor relations. He knew it, Joanna knew it, and unfortunately for Ray, Ming knew it too. As the head of Investor Relations, Ming was responsible for getting the rich and wealthy to invest in Jade Harbour's portfolio companies. It involved a lot of schmoozing with influential people and flattering those with already inflated egos. It was something Ming was good at, and something that annoyed almost everyone else at Jade Harbour. Ray especially.

"Besides," Ray continued, "I already know what Ming wants to talk about."

"Which is?" Elvin pulled a plate from the cabinet and carefully arranged the food on it.

"Phoenix Family Trust. What else?" From the tone of Ray's voice, one would have thought that he'd been asked to dive into the nearest dumpster for pennies.

In reality, Phoenix Family Trust was a conglomerate of the wealthiest families in Hong Kong, who pooled their assets to create greater returns on their investments. It also happened to be managed by Ray's father.

Elvin ran a clean towel around the edges of the plate before setting it carefully in front of Ray with a full set of utensils. "You don't know that. Maybe Ming wants to talk about something else."

"How much do you want to bet on that?" Ray unfurled his napkin and laid it across his lap.

"Nothing." Elvin grabbed another plate for himself and piled the remaining food on it. "Gambling's more your thing than mine."

"Hmm." Ray lifted the fork and knife and cut into the perfectly fried over easy eggs with an elegance that felt overblown for something as simple as breakfast. He created a perfect bite-size morsel of food before lifting it to his mouth.

Elvin watched from the other side of the island with his hip braced against the counter and his own plate in hand. With the edge of his fork, he wiggled it through the egg, stabbed at as many things as he could get onto the tines, and shoveled the whole lot between his lips.

Ray met his gaze as they both chewed. There was a tiny crinkle at the edges of Ray's eyes, hinting at his amusement, and Elvin felt little compunction in returning it. Ray was an only child raised in prep schools. Elvin was the eldest of six and had acted like a third parent to his younger siblings from the time he could hold a baby bottle by himself. For Ray, meal times were an affair to be enjoyed. For Elvin, they were war zones defined by scarcity—if you didn't fight for your share, you went hungry.

They'd had heated discussions about this particular difference numerous times in the past. Ray nagging Elvin to take a seat and slow down for fear of choking on his food. Elvin showing Ray his already empty plate with a shrug; no need to sit down when there was nothing left to eat.

He loaded the dirty dishes into the dishwasher as Ray continued eating. By the time Ray was finished, the kitchen was spotless and Elvin had stashed his laptop away.

"Ready to go?" he asked, giving the kitchen a once-over for anything he might have missed.

Ray stood and stretched. "Ready when you are."

Ray's version of ready meant another twenty minutes of gathering his things from rooms across the condo. His socks and shoes were in the bedroom. His laptop was on the coffee table. His sunglasses were… It had taken a full ten minutes to find them under the bed of the guest bedroom.

By the time they made it to Jade Harbour, the weekly Monday morning investment meeting was about to start. The largest conference room in the office was filled to overflowing. Around the large conference table were all the senior investment and operational professionals. Behind them were their junior staff, sitting in office chairs that had been rolled in from elsewhere. The perimeter of the room was lined with cushioned benches, where all other support staff sat. The unlucky late ones took up standing positions by the doors.

At least Ray and Elvin were the lucky late ones.

Ray strolled in and claimed the last empty chair at the table. Elvin slipped into a narrow spot on the bench next to Mike, Jade Harbour's legal counsel.

"Nice of you to grace us with your presence," Mike whispered to him.

Elvin rolled his eyes. "Monday morning."

"Now that we're all here…" Joanna looked pointedly at Ray. "Let's get started."

She spoke from the front of the room, where she sat with her long legs crossed, hands steepled by her chin. She sat a little back from the conference table, where she'd placed a giant binder. It contained the most up-to-date information on all

Jade Harbour investments and potential investments, everything from monthly financial statements, budget-to-actual reporting, key performance indicators, supply and demand analyses, down to the most recent hiring decisions at each portfolio company. Elvin had no doubt that she had every word on every page memorized. She was one of those people.

A couple junior investment professionals stood and opened a presentation on the TV that spanned nearly one entire wall. They launched into a progress report on a portfolio company that Elvin wasn't familiar with. All he knew was that Ray wasn't working on that company, which meant it wasn't relevant to him.

As he zoned out, Elvin's gaze wandered the room, taking in his coworkers. Some of them were listening intently. Others looked about as engaged as he was. Everyone was dressed immaculately in well-tailored suits or dresses, not one hair out of place. After years at the company, Elvin had mostly gotten used to this world where a single watch could cost twice as much as his parents' car, where thousand-dollar handbags were never more than a season old. But there were times when he marveled at it all. So different from his working-class upbringing where hand-me-downs were considered new.

His gaze landed on Ray, the epitome of this world. Elvin wasn't exactly sure how wealthy Ray's family was. He'd looked it up at one point and the Chao family's net worth had been so high that the number had meant nothing to Elvin. It was well known in the company that Ray didn't *need* this job at Jade Harbour. His family had more money than he could realistically spend in one lifetime. But he still worked—and worked fairly hard—like it was some sort of pet project, something to occupy his time. This was usually spoken of with more than a hint of derision, but Elvin was quick to squelch it whenever he could. So what if Ray didn't need to work? He was here and Jade Harbour was lucky to have him. Ray had saved Jade Harbour from unexpected losses, public humiliation, and generally cleaned up other people's messes more times than Elvin could count. Rather than scolding him for being late, they should be thanking him for showing up at all.

"Ray?"

All heads turned to him and Elvin scrambled to figure out what they were talking about. On the TV screen was a chart labeled with the name of a portfolio company that Ray had helped out with a while ago.

"I've got it handled." Ray sat low in his chair, leaning to one side with an elbow propped on the armrest like it was the only thing keeping him upright. "They've got more than enough dirty laundry that I'm sure they don't want aired. A couple phone calls should be enough to get them on board with our plan."

"Good." Joanna turned to the young woman standing at the front of the room. "Anything else?"

"Nothing else." The young woman took her seat.

"What's next?"

"Caron Paper." A young man took control of the TV screen and brought up the next set of slides. "As you can see from this graph here, we're in a good place to take the company public. It is ahead of our original investment schedule, but with the current market conditions, an initial public offering would give us a generous return on investment."

The young man clutched the remote control in his hands and stared wide-eyed at Joanna. Despite how full the room was, it was eerily silent. An occasional flutter of paper, or squeak of an office chair, but otherwise, the loudest sound was the hum of the building's air-conditioning system.

Joanna studied the TV screen, her expression inscrutable. Listing a company on the stock market was a massive undertaking and usually took months and months of preparation. To make such a recommendation ahead of the anticipated schedule was ballsy. If they pulled it off, it could be the most profitable deal in Jade Harbour's history. But if they didn't, bankruptcy wouldn't be out of the question.

Without turning, Joanna spoke. "Ray, I want a top to bottom audit. Leave no stone unturned. If there's even one dust bunny in Caron's closet, I want it dissected. If they get a clean bill from you, then we can talk about an IPO."

"You got it," Ray responded immediately before shooting a quick look at Elvin.

Elvin gave him a slight nod in response. They were on the job.

Chapter Two

"Ray, my man!" Ming stood in the middle of Ray's office with his arms held out like he was presenting himself for Ray's inspection.

From behind his desk, Ray sighed. "Hello, Ming."

Ray liked to think he got along with everyone, or at least most people. But there was something about Ming that annoyed the hell out of him. He was too friendly, too familiar. Like he wanted to be best friends just a little too desperately.

"I finally managed to get on your calendar!" Ming grinned like he'd won the lottery as he helped himself to one of the guest chairs.

Ray gave him a tight smile and nodded. "Yep."

"You're a busy guy!"

Not nearly as busy as he should be, given Ming was in his office. "Yep."

"Whew." Ming shook his head like landing a meeting with Ray had taken a physical toll on him. "I really had to work that assistant of yours. He's a tough cookie to get through." He pointed over his shoulder with his thumb in the direction of Elvin's desk outside Ray's office.

"You mean Elvin? He has a name."

"Yeah, yeah, Elvin. I know his name." Ming chuckled as if Ray's comment was ridiculous. "Of course I know Elvin. He's got good taste."

Ray's eyebrows shot up. What the hell did Ming know about Elvin's tastes? "Excuse me?"

"You know, musical theater!" Ming wiggled his fingers in a poor imitation of jazz hands. "We've been chatting about the shows coming through Toronto this season!"

Musical theater. Right. It was one of Elvin's rare hobbies, about the only thing he talked about aside from work and family. Ray hadn't realized Ming was a fan as well. How often had they been chatting exactly and why hadn't Elvin mentioned anything about it to him? Hrm.

Ming was still talking. Something about some show Ray had never heard of. He raised a hand to stop Ming. "What did you want to talk about?"

Ming sat there with his mouth gaping like he'd stalled his engine. Ray forced himself to take a slow breath so he wouldn't reach across his desk and shake the life out of Ming.

"Yes, right!" Ming shifted forward in his seat. "I wanted to touch base about Phoenix Family Trust."

He *knew* it! Elvin owed him. Ray ran a hand over his face to stifle a groan. "No."

Ming opened his mouth and closed it again with a confused look. "What?"

"No," Ray said louder in case Ming hadn't heard him the first time. "We've tried this before and it didn't work. Why do you think it will this time?"

"Because it's been years since we've pitched them! The market has changed! We've got a stronger track record!" Ming's hands got more animated with every sentence.

"So set up the meeting yourself." Ray pushed back his chair to stand. "You have their contact information. What do you need me for?"

"Oh come on, Ray. They're much more likely to respond to you than they are to me."

Ray paced around the room, stretching his arms over his

head. Talking about PFT always made him antsy and restless. "I don't know why you think that. I'm not exactly a welcomed entity over there."

"Why not?"

Ray rolled his eyes. He wasn't about to detail his complicated family history to Ming of all people. "I'm just not."

"But why?"

Ray spun toward Ming, not entirely sure he was hearing right. Was Ming seriously pressing this point? "Because!"

"Okay! Okay!" Ming settled back into the chair like he planned to be there for a while.

Ray planted his hands on his hips. "Anything else I can help you with?"

"Are you sure there's no one there you can ask for a meeting? As a favor? For me?"

As if Ming was anyone Ray wanted to do favors for. The dude didn't understand the word no. But, if it would get him off Ray's back… Ray sighed. "I can try to make a couple calls."

Ming jumped up and slapped his hands together. "Great! I knew I could count on you!" He came over and clapped a hand on Ray's shoulder before shaking it a little too forcefully. "We're going to make a great team, buddy. Just you wait and see."

Ming headed toward the door, spinning halfway so he was walking backward. "You and me, Ray!" He shot finger guns at Ray. "Joanna's going to be stoked."

Ray let out an audible groan as Ming let himself out. What the hell had he gotten himself into?

Elvin poked his head in. "You still alive?"

"Barely." Ray flopped onto the long couch on the far side of his office. He stuck out an arm and pointed in Elvin's general direction. "I win our bet. Ming wouldn't stop going on about PFT."

"Would it really be so bad to reach out? It's not like you have to talk to your father."

His father. Ugh. That was the real problem. Once upon a time, Ray had been groomed to take over management of the trust. But he'd ruined all his father's plans when he insisted on joining Jade Harbour instead. It was still a sore spot for the family and Ray had been all but disowned for wanting to work for someone else.

A number of Ray's relatives held senior positions within the trust. All good people who knew what they were doing, but every single one of them had gotten to where they were because of their last name. Nepotism wasn't only alive and well, it was considered a fucking virtue, and Ray didn't want anything to do with it.

"I know." He ran through the short list of cousins and uncles he could call. Who wouldn't give him too hard of a time for missing the family reunion the year before? Or try to ask for an IOU in return? There was no way he'd be able to avoid a lecture on filial piety, giving back to the family, and carrying on their good name. He let out a frustrated groan and shot to his feet so fast that his head spun a little.

"You okay?"

"Yeah. I'm great."

"You don't look great." Elvin looked like he was trying really hard to hold back a laugh.

Ray shot him a glare. "I need to get out of here." He shook out his limbs, trying to throw off the feeling of insects crawling across his skin. "I need a swim."

Elvin nodded. "I'll cover for you if anyone asks where you are."

"Thanks." Trust Elvin to always know exactly what to say at exactly the right time.

Ray grabbed his suit jacket from the coat hanger and

slipped it on. "Stop by later and catch me up on anything I missed, okay?"

"Sure."

"Great." Ray stopped at the door. "And for the love of god, don't put Ming on my calendar again."

Elvin chuckled and shrugged. "I'll do my best."

Ray headed for the elevator. Few people, including Elvin, understood the weird dynamic between Ray and his family. Hell, he didn't fully understand it himself. His parents hadn't been around for most of his childhood, happy to shuffle him from boarding school to vacation resort and back again depending on the time of year. They'd paid for him to have music lessons and language classes. His closet was always full of the latest high-end fashions; his garage with luxury cars. There wasn't a single thing he'd wanted that they didn't buy for him, so they were baffled when he refused to join the family trust like all his relatives had.

He stepped out onto the sidewalk outside Jade Harbour's office building and found his driver waiting for him by the curb. Elvin must have given him a heads-up that Ray was on his way down.

"Home, Mr. Chao?" The driver opened the car door as Ray approached.

"Yes, thank you."

What do you mean you want to join a private equity company no one has ever heard of? Ray could still hear the incredulity in his father's voice when he'd broken the news. It wasn't like Ray wanted to become a monk in some remote monastery. Hell, his father might actually prefer that over the prospect of Ray working anywhere other than PFT.

He'd met Joanna while completing his MBA. His family had sent him as a representative to some fundraising event and over the course of the evening, Joanna had enthralled him with her take-no-prisoners attitude. Then a few months later, he ran into her at a restaurant where she was meeting an executive of a struggling portfolio company. She'd invited Ray to sit down with them and by the time he'd finished his drink, he'd managed to come up with three viable solutions to their problems.

She'd called him with a job offer the next day. Nothing fancy. No corner office or unlimited expense account. Jade Harbour had been in the early stages of its growth at the time. But the chance to build something from nothing was too enticing to give up. PFT was established, well-known, stable. He'd be taking over an organization that already ran on autopilot. Where was the fun in that? Jade Harbour was an opportunity to see what he could do without the safety net of his family's wealth and status.

The car pulled up in front of Ray's building and stopped. "Thanks," Ray called to the driver before letting himself out.

What was so wrong with wanting to do his own thing? To see if he had the chops to make it on the basis of his abilities rather than what name he'd been born with? He'd never gotten a satisfactory answer from his father and after a while they'd settled into an uncomfortable stalemate on the subject. The less they interacted, the better.

Ray scrolled through his phone as the elevator spat him out into his condo. He found the number he was looking for and hit dial. After a couple rings, it went to voice mail. Thank the fucking lord.

"Hey, Ginny. It's Ray. I need to talk to you about something. Call me back."

Don't miss Going Public *by Hudson Lin, out from Carina Adores!*